The Red Knight stopped Manuel and demanded who was his lady-love.

"I have no living love, except the woman whom I am leaving without ceremony, to save argument."

"You are a rascally betrayer of women, then, and an unmanly scoundrel."

"Yes, I suppose so," said Manuel.

The vermilion-armoured knight came on him like a whirlwind, and Manuel, having no choice, fought, and presently killed him. It was noticeable that from the death-wound came no blood, but only a flowing of fine black sand, out of which scampered a small, vermilion-colored mouse.

Manuel had been directed to seek a peculiarly irrational part of the forest; it was clear that he had found it.

THE SAGA OF POICTESME
By JAMES BRANCH CABELL

* Now available from Del Rey Books
** Coming Soon

Figures of Earth

James Branch Cabell

A Comedy of Appearances

Introduction by Lin Carter
Illustrated by Frank C. Papé

"Cascun se mir el jove Manuel,
Qu'era del mon lo plus valens dels pros."

A Del Rey Book

BALLANTINE BOOKS • NEW YORK

A Del Rey Book
Published by Ballantine Books

Copyright 1921, 1927, by James Branch Cabell
Copyright renewed, 1948, by James Branch Cabell
Introduction © 1969 by Lin Carter

This edition printed from the *Storisende Edition*.

All rights reserved under International and Pan-American
Copyright Conventions. Published in the United States by
Ballantine Books, a division of Random House, Inc., New
York, and simultaneously in Canada by Random House of
Canada, Limited, Toronto, Canada.

ISBN 0-345-28170-5

Manufactured in the United States of America

First Ballantine Books Edition: November 1969
Second Printing: May 1979

First Canadian Printing: April 1970

Cover art by Howard Koslow

Contents

❁❁❁❁❁❁❁❁❁❁❁❁❁

PART FOUR
THE BOOK OF SURCHARGE

PART FIVE
THE BOOK OF SETTLEMENT

About Figures of Earth
and James Branch Cabell

The Geste of Manuel Pig-Tender

James Branch Cabell is the single greatest fantasy novelist America has ever produced.

Let me immediately explain what I mean by this outrageous and inflammatory statement, to nip in the bud a torrent of letters from enraged devotees of A. Merritt, H.P. Lovecraft, Robert E. Howard, Clark Ashton Smith. And the one or two lonely letters from college professors who will plaintively remind me of the existence of Edgar Allan Poe.

There is no really precise and unequivocal way to define that much-overworked term, *greatness.* It does not, of necessity, imply "best" or "most successful and popular" or "most literary and artistic" or even "most permanent." I suppose Merritt is the most widely published of the above rather small American pantheon of fantasy authors, and few would question his right to bestseller status (in slightly more than twenty years, Avon Books sold *five million* copies of his novels). And Lovecraft is perhaps the writer with the most fanatic, devoted following, and may very well endure as a permanent classic of sorts, second only to Poe. As for Howard, the creator of Conan the Cimmerian seems destined for ever-widening popularity. Indeed, the character has long outlasted his creator, who lived to see Conan enshrined only in the pages of the late, lamented magazine, *Weird Tales*, and could not possibly have foreseen hardcover publication twenty years after his death, the enormously successful paperback revival in the 1960's, or the species of immortality Hollywood may shortly confer on his grim-jawed barbarian hero.

But Cabell is something else again. For one thing, unlike these others, Cabell did not write for the pulp magazine markets. His early stories and verses appeared in slick-paper literary periodicals and important mass market magazines. He graduated swiftly to book publication, and was soon writing exclusively for hardcover. In other words, whereas Merritt, Lovecraft, Howard and Smith had to do their best in the hope that their finer work would someday be retrieved from crumbling pulp for preservation in clothbound books, Cabell was one up on them from the start. For another, Cabell was basically a different kind of writer. He was essentially a sophisticated and intelligent artist, writing not for kids or common folk, but for mature and cosmopolitan people of taste and discernment.

This meant he had to forego mass popularity, to appeal instead to the natural aristocracy of good taste.

And that is a risky business. Cabell began writing —or reached his early success at any rate—during the teens and twenties of this century, smack in the middle of the first great American literary revolution. All about him, giants were burgeoning: Dreiser, Hemingway, Wolfe, Pound, Faulkner, Sinclair Lewis, Eliot, Scott Fitzgerald, Cummings. Cabell had to try to find a place for himself among some of the most powerful literary figures this country had yet produced. And he picked the worst possible era for a writer of his particular genius. For Faulkner, Hemingway, Dreiser *et al* were conducting a revolution in reading taste—the triumph of earthy, modern realism over the decayed and languid splendors of late-Victorian neo-classicism and romantic literature. The trouble was that Cabell himself was a product of a classical and Continental education. The writers he admired and learned from were courtly, aristocratic, erudite and leisurely stylists of an earlier century. Like—but listen to Cabell on the subject, from his autobiography, *As I Remember It* (1955):

> "I pause here to meditate a trifle forlornly upon the writers a fair quota of whose work my judgment still admires. I recall, at almost complete random, Lucian and Horace, Villon and Montaigne and Marlowe, Sir Thomas Browne and Molière, Wycherley and Congreve and Sheridan . . . Arthur Machen and Walter Pater and Oscar Wilde."

Nor is he deliberately bragging. His graceful, ironic, subtle, witty and disillusioned prose stems directly from these writers, to say nothing of Voltaire and Aristophanes and Pope and Anatole France. Not only his prose, but his fanciful and mythological allusions, his flavor of romance and mystery, his innate sense of "other days gone by."

Of course he was a flop. When everybody is doing titanic industrial post-office murals, the limner of delicate Persian miniatures is doomed to starve in the nearest garret. He never made much of an impact on the general trend of the mainstream. But a handful of kindred spirits warmed to his superb craftsmanship. And the curious chance of the seizure and trial of *Jurgen* on charges of obscenity brought him a brief yet decisive popularity, calling the attention of millions to his work.

Out of all this came a lasting measure of fame. Cabell came to the attention of the educated and perceptive readers of the more literary forms of imaginative literature, and he moved into what one might call the underground or anti-establishment pantheon of greats, rather as Henry Miller did long before his own *Tropic of Cancer* trial—a curious parallel to *Jurgen* —raised him to bestsellerdom.

An entire generation of fantasy writers who came after, display their indebtedness to Cabell. Paul Jordan-Smith frankly imitates him in *Nomad* (1925), which is dedicated to Cabell, by the way; I doubt if John Erskine would have written *The Private Life of Helen of Troy* (1925), or *Adam and Eve* (1927), had there been no Cabell. Theodora Du Bois did the best imitation of Cabell I have ever seen with her novel, *The Devil's Spoon* (1930), which is charming in its own right. Claire Myers Spotswood's *The Improbable Adventure* (1935), is thoroughly Cabellian, as is John Myers Myers' *Silverlock* (1949). And a great number of fantasy and science-fiction writers would seem to have learned something from Cabell: David H. Keller, M.D., Nelson S. Bond, Poul Anderson, L. Sprague de Camp, and Fritz Leiber (who appears, in part, to have based his character, the Gray Mouser, on Cabell's Horvendile), to name only the most prominent.

Cabell's best work lies in the group of three novels, *Figures of Earth* (1921), *Jurgen* (1919), and *The Silver Stallion* (1926). These three books are not strictly a trilogy, but they stand together nicely, describing the rise of Dom Manuel from the lowly status of a pig-keeper, through his heroic quests and wars, to his mysterious and very debatable death; the rise thereafter of a cult which worships him as a coming Redeemer, to the decline and dispersal of the little group of warrior lords who knew and loved him in his lifetime. This group of novels fits very well into the sort of heroic, other-world adventure fantasy we have in mind when we think of writers like Eddison, Dunsany, Pratt and Tolkien.

The most perfect heroic fantasy of the three is *Figures of Earth*. It follows beautifully the general pattern of the great heroic myths—Achilles, Theseus, Jason, Roland, Arthur. Quiet, solemn, lonely and secretive, young Manuel is drawn into exalted deeds when the young daughter of the Count of Arnaye is carried off by a dread and mysterious wizard. This personage, Miramon Lluagor—"lord of the nine kinds of sleep and prince of the seven madnesses"—lives in mythic splendor atop the mountain of Vraidex, where he contrives illusions to trouble the dreams of men. Somewhat against his will, Manuel finds himself on a quest to rescue the fair maiden by means of the enchanted sword Flamberge.

We follow Manuel through a series of fantastic and highly colored adventures. We encounter the famous Zhar-Ptitza bird, the secret magic of the Apsarasas, the enchanted ring Schamir, a horde of savage Northmen, the magic kingdom of Audela, and a rare and delightful group of nine rogues and adventurers who gather before the banners of Manuel and become the Fellowship of the Silver Stallion. Through it all runs the scarlet thread of Cabell's mocking wit, the rich detail of his mythological allusions, and the gaudy filigree of his word games, puns, anagrams (the childhood sweetheart, "Suskind," whom Manuel regretfully leaves behind as he marches off to perform great deeds, is an anagram for "Unkiss'd"), hidden meanings and in-jokes.

Books as good as this cannot be allowed to lapse into limbo, so the best of Cabell has lasted, even while the giants who rose beyond him have fallen—for who today reads Theodore Dreiser or Sherwood Anderson or even Sinclair Lewis? Hemingway himself is beginning to fade and tarnish; Cabell's wry, ironic wit shines brighter than ever.

A James Branch Cabell Society has recently been founded to help encourage the resurgeence of interest in his work. The Society publishes an elegant, handsome, very enjoyable magazine devoted to Cabell and kindred matters. It is called *Kalki* and the editor is science-fiction writer James Blish. If you are interested in either this book or in *The Silver Stallion* (also available in the Ballantine Adult Fantasy Series), let me suggest that you write to Paul Spencer, 665 Lotus Avenue, Oradell, New Jersey, 07649, for membership in the Society.

LIN CARTER
Editorial Consultant:
The Ballantine Adult Fantasy Series

Hollis, Long Island, New York.

To

SIX MOST GALLANT CHAMPIONS

Is dedicated this history of a champion: less to repay than to acknowledge large debts to each of them, collectively at outset, as hereafter seriatim

POIC T

SGARRIGUES
CARIG AMON
the Doubtful Palace
CAIWEN
Vraidex
Eyre
Church of
Holy Hoprig
Naimes
Aigremont
NAIMOUSIN
Lower
Morven
AMNERAN
Lusern's Home
Forest of
Amneran
Bellegarde
Beauvillage
St. Didol
FOREST of BEAIR
Montpellier
BELPAYSAGE
Château des Roches
Golfe de l'âne
SINT
GOLFE du LION
Manville

Author's Note
❦❦❦❦❦❦❦❦❦❦❦❦❦

FIGURES OF EARTH is, with some superficial air of paradox, the one volume in the long Biography of Dom Manuel's life which deals with Dom Manuel himself. Most of the matter strictly appropriate to a Preface you may find, if you so elect, in the Foreword addressed to Sinclair Lewis. And, in fact, after writing two prefaces to this "Figures of Earth"—first, in this epistle to Lewis, and, secondly, in the remarks* affixed to the illustrated edition,—I had thought this volume could very well continue to survive as long as its deficiencies permit, without the confection of a third preface, until I began a little more carefully to consider this romance, in the seventh year of its existence.

But now, now, the deficiency which I note in chief (like the superior officer of a disastrously wrecked crew) lies in the fact that what I had meant to be the main "point" of "Figures of Earth," while explicitly enough stated in the book, remains for every practical end indiscernible. . . . For I have written many books during the last quarter of a century. Yet this is the only one of them which began at one plainly recognizable instant with one plainly recognizable imagining. It is the only book by me which ever, virtually, came into being, with its goal set, and with its theme and its contents more or less pre-determined throughout, between two ticks of the clock.

*Omitted in this edition since it was not possible to include all of Frank C. Papé's magnificent illustrations.—THE PUBLISHER

Egotism here becomes rather unavoidable. At Dumbarton Grange the library in which I wrote for some twelve years was lighted by three windows set side by side and opening outward. It was in the instant of unclosing one of these windows, on a fine afternoon in the spring of 1919, to speak with a woman and a child who were then returning to the house (with the day's batch of mail from the post office), that, for no reason at all, I reflected it would be, upon every personal ground, regrettable if, as the moving window unclosed, that especial woman and that particular child proved to be figures in the glass, and the window opened upon nothingness. For that, I believed, was about to happen. There would be, I knew, revealed beyond that moving window, when it had opened all the way, not absolute darkness, but a gray nothingness, rather sweetly scented. . . . Well! there was not. I once more enjoyed the quite familiar experience of being mistaken. It is gratifying to record that nothing whatever came of that panic surmise, of that second-long nightmare—of that brief but over-tropical flowering, for all I know, of indigestion,—save, ultimately, the 80,000 words or so of this book.

For I was already planning, vaguely, to begin on, later in that year, "the book about Manuel." And now I had the germ of it,—in the instant when Dom Manuel opens the over-familiar window, in his own home, to see his wife and child, his lands, and all the Poictesme of which he was at once the master and the main glory, presented as bright, shallow, very fondly loved illusions in the protective glass of Ageus. I knew that the fantastic thing which had not happened to me,—nor, I hope, to anybody,—was precisely the thing, and the most important thing, which had happened to the gray Count of Poictesme.

So I made that evening a memorandum of that historical circumstance; and for some months this book existed only in the form of that memorandum. Then, through, as it were, this wholly isolated window, I began to grope at "the book about Manuel,"—of whom I had hitherto learned only, from my other romances, who were his children, and who had been the sole witness of Dom Manuel's death, inasmuch as I had read about that also, with some interest, in the fourth chapter of "Jurgen"; and from the unclosing of this window I developed "Figures of Earth," for the most part toward, necessarily, anterior events. For it seemed to me—as it still seems,—that the opening of this particular magic casement, upon an outlook rather more perilous than the bright foam of fairy seas, was alike the climax and the main "point" of my book.

Yet this fact, I am resignedly sure, as I nowadays appraise this seven-year-old romance, could not ever be detected by any reader of "Figures of Earth." In consequence, it has seemed well here to confess at some length the original conception of this volume, without at all going into the value of that conception, nor into, heaven knows, how this conception came so successfully to be obscured.

So I began "the book about Manuel" that summer, —in 1919, upon the back porch of our cottage at the Rockbridge Alum Springs, whence, as I recall it, one could always, just as Manuel did upon Upper Morven, regard the changing green and purple of the mountains and the tall clouds trailing northward, and could observe that the things one viewed were all gigantic and lovely and seemed not to be very greatly bothering about humankind. I suppose, though, that, in point of fact, it occasionally rained. In any case, upon that same porch, as it happened, this book was finished in the summer of 1920.

And the notes made at this time as to "Figures of Earth" show much that nowadays is wholly incomprehensible. There was once an Olrun in the book; and I can recall clearly enough how her part in the story was absorbed by two of the other characters,— by Suskind and by Alianora. Freydis, it appears, was originally called Hlif. Miramon at one stage of the book's being, I find with real surprise, was married *en secondes noces* to Math. Othmar has lost that prominence which once was his. And it seems, too, there once figured in Manuel's heart affairs a Bel-Imperia, who, so near as I can deduce from my notes, was a lady in a tapestry. Someone unstitched her, to, I imagine, her destruction, although I suspect that a few skeins of this quite forgotten Bel-Imperia endure in the Radegonde of another tale.

Nor can I make anything whatever of my notes about Guivret (who seems to have been in no way connected with Guivric the Sage), nor about Biduz, nor about the Anti-Pope,—even though, to be sure, one mention of this heresiarch yet survives in the present book. I am wholly baffled to read, in my own penciling, such proposed chapter headings as "The Jealousy of Niafer" and "How Sclaug Loosed the Dead,"—which latter is with added incomprehensibility annotated "(?Phorgemon)." And "The Spirit Who Had Half of Everything" seems to have been exorcised pretty thoroughly. . . . No; I find the most of my old notes as to this book merely bewildering; and I find, too, something of pathos in these embryons of unborn dreams which, for one cause or another, were obliterated and have been utterly forgotten by their creator, very much as in this book vexed Miramon

Lluagor twists off the head of a not quite satisfactory, whimpering design, and drops the valueless fragments into his waste-basket. . . . But I do know that the entire book developed, howsoever helterskelter, and after fumbling in no matter how many blind alleys, from that first memorandum about the troubling window of Ageus. All leads toward—and through—that window.

THE book, then, was published in the February of 1921. I need not here deal with its semi-serial appearance in the guise of short stories: these details are recorded elsewhere. But I confess with appropriate humility that the reception of "Figures of Earth" by the public was, as I have written in another place, a depressing business. This romance, at that time, through one extraneous reason and another, disappointed well-nigh everybody, for all that it has since become, so near as I can judge, the best liked of my books, especially among women. It seems, indeed, a fact sufficiently edifying that, in appraising the two legendary heroes of Poictesme, the sex of whom Jurgen esteemed himself a connoisseur, should, almost unanimously, prefer Manuel.

For the rest,—since, as you may remember, this is the third preface which I have written for this book, —I can but repeat more or less what I have conceded elsewhere. This "Figures of Earth" appeared immediately following, and during the temporary sequestration of, "Jurgen." The fact was forthwith, quite unreticently, discovered that in "Figures of Earth" I had not succeeded in my attempt to rewrite its predecessor: and this crass failure, so open, so flagrant, and so undeniable, caused what I can only describe as the instant and overwhelming and universal triumph of "Figures of Earth" to be precisely what did not occur. In 1921 Comstockery still surged, of course, in full cry against the imprisoned pawnbroker and the crimes of his author, both literary and personal; and the, after all, tolerably large portion of the reading public who were not disgusted by Jurgen's lechery were now, so near as I could gather, enraged by Manuel's lack of it.

It followed that—among the futile persons who use serious, long words in talking about mere books,—aggrieved reproof of my auctorial malversations, upon the one ground or the other, became in 1921 biloquial and pandemic. Not many other volumes, I believe, have been burlesqued and cried down in the public prints by their own dedicatees. . . . But from the cicatrix of that healed wound I turn away. I preserve a forgiving silence, comparable to that of Hermione in the fifth act of "A Winter's Tale": I resolve that whenever I mention the names of Louis Untermeyer and H. L. Mencken it shall be in some connection more pleasant, and that here I will not mention them at all.

Meanwhile the fifteen or so experiments in contrapuntal prose were, in particular, uncharted passages from which I stayed unique in deriving pleasure where others found bewilderment and no tongue-tied irritation: but, in general, and above every misdemeanor else, the book exasperated everybody by not being a more successfully managed re-hashing of the then notorious "Jurgen."

Since 1921, and since the rehabilitation of "Jurgen," the notion has uprisen, gradually, among the more bold and speculative thinkers, that perhaps I was not, after all, in this "Figures of Earth" attempting to rewrite "Jurgen": and Manuel has made his own friend.

Richmond-in-Virginia   James Branch Cabell
30 April 1927

A FOREWORD
"Amoto quæramus seria ludo

To

SINCLAIR LEWIS

A Foreword

MY DEAR LEWIS:

To you (whom I take to be as familiar with the Manuelian cycle of romance as is any person now alive) it has for some while appeared, I know, a not uncurious circumstance that in the *Key to the Popular Tales of Poictesme* there should have been included so little directly relative to Manuel himself. No reader of the *Popular Tales* (as I recall your saying at the Alum when we talked over, among so many other matters, this monumental book) can fail to note that always Dom Manuel looms obscurely in the background, somewhat as do King Arthur and white-bearded Charlemagne in their several cycles, dispensing justice and bestowing rewards, and generally arranging the future, for the survivors of the outcome of stories which more intimately concern themselves with Anavalt and Coth and Holden, and with Kerin and Ninzian and Gonfal and Donander, and with Miramon (in his rôle of Manuel's seneschal), or even with Sclaug and Thragnar, than with the liege-lord of Poictesme. Except in the old sixteenth-century chap-book (unknown to you, I believe, and never reprinted since 1822, and not ever modernized into any cognizable spelling), there seems to have been nowhere an English rendering of the legends in which Dom Manuel is really the main figure.

Well, this book attempts to supply that desideratum, and is, so far as the writer is aware, the one fairly complete epitome in modern English of the Manuelian historiography not included by Lewistam which has yet been prepared.

It is obvious, of course, that in a single volume of this bulk there could not be included more than a selection from the great body of myths which, we may assume, have accumulated gradually round the mighty though shadowy figure of Manuel the Redeemer. Instead, my aim has been to make choice of such stories and traditions as seemed most fit to be cast into the shape of a connected narrative and regular sequence of events; to lend to all that wholesome, edifying and optimistic tone which in reading-matter is so generally preferable to mere intelligence; and meanwhile to preserve as much of the quaint style of the gestes as is consistent with clearness. Then, too, in the original mediæval romances, both in their prose and metrical form, there are occasional allusions to natural processes which make these stories unfit to be placed in the hands of American readers, who, as a body, attest their respectability by insisting that their parents were guilty of unmentionable conduct; and such passages of course necessitate considerable editing.

II

No schoolboy (and far less the scholastic chronicler of those last final upshots for whose furtherance "Hannibal invaded Rome and Erasmus wrote in Oxford cloisters") needs nowadays to be told that the Manuel of these legends is to all intents a fictitious person. That in the earlier half of the thirteenth century there was ruling over the Poictoumois a powerful chieftain named Manuel, nobody has of late disputed seriously. But the events of the actual human existence of this Lord of Poictesme—very much as the Emperor Frederick Barbarossa has been identified with the wood-demon Barbatos, and the prophet Elijah, "caught up into the chariot of the Vedic Vayu," has become one with the Slavonic Perun,—have been inextricably blended with the legends of the Dirghic Manu-Elul, Lord of August.

Thus, even the irregularity in Manuel's eyes is taken by Vanderhoffen, in his *Tudor Tales*, to be a myth connecting Manuel with the Vedic Rudra and the Russian Magarko and the Servian Vii,—"and every beneficent storm-god represented with his eye perpetually winking (like sheet lightning), lest his concentrated look (the thunderbolt) should reduce the universe to ashes. . . . His watery parentage, and the storm-god's relationship with a swan-maiden of the Apsarasas (typifying the mists and clouds), and with Freydis the fire queen, are equally obvious: whereas Niafer is plainly a variant of Nephthys, Lady of the House, whose personality Dr. Budge sums up as 'the goddess of the death which is not eternal,' or Nerthus, the Subterranean Earth, which the warm rainstorm quickens to life and fertility."

All this seems dull enough to be plausible. Yet no less an authority than Charles Garnier has replied, in rather indignant rebuttal: "Qu'ont été en réalité Manuel et Siegfried, Achille et Rustem? Par quels exploits ont-ils mérité l'éternelle admiration que leur ont vouée les hommes de leur race? Nul ne répondra jamais à ces questions. . . . Mais Poictesme croit à la réalité de cette figure que ses romans ont faite si belle, car le pays n'a pas d'autre histoire. Cette figure du Comte Manuel est réelle d'ailleurs, car elle est l'image purifiée de la race qui l'a produite, et, si on peut s'exprimer ainsi, l'incarnation de son génie."

—Which is quite just, and, when you come to think it over, proves Dom Manuel to be nowadays, for practical purposes, at least as real as Dr. Paul Vanderhoffen.

III

Between the two main epic cycles of Poictesme, as embodied in *Les Gestes de Manuel* and *La Haulte Histoire de Jurgen*, more or less comparison is inevitable. And Codman, I believe, has put the gist of the matter succinctly enough.

Says Codman: "The Gestes are mundane stories, the History is a cosmic affair, in that, where Manuel faces the world, Jurgen considers the universe. . . . Dom Manuel is the Achilles of Poictesme, as Jurgen is its Ulysses."

And, roughly, the distinction serves. Yet minute consideration discovers, I think, in these two sets of legends a more profound, if subtler, difference, in the handling of the protagonist: with Jurgen all of the physical and mental man is rendered as a matter of course; whereas in dealing with Manuel there is, always, I believe, a certain perceptible and strange, if not inexplicable, aloofness. Manuel did thus and thus, Manuel said so and so, these legends recount: yes, but never anywhere have I detected any firm assertion as to Manuel's thoughts and emotions, nor any peep into the workings of this hero's mind. He is "done" from the outside, always at arm's length. It is not merely that Manuel's nature is tinctured with the cool unhumanness of his father the water-demon: rather, these old poets of Poictesme would seem, whether of intention or no, to have dealt with their national hero as a person, howsoever admirable in many of his exploits, whom they have never been able altogether to love, or entirely to sympathize with, or to view quite without distrust.

There are several ways of accounting for this fact, —ranging from the hurtful as well as beneficent aspect of the storm-god, to the natural inability of a poet to understand a man who succeeds in everything: but the fact is, after all, of no present importance save that it may well have prompted Lewistam to scamp his dealings with this always somewhat ambiguous Manuel, and so to omit the hereinafter included legends, as unsuited to the clearer and sunnier atmosphere of the *Popular Tales*.

For my part, I am quite content, in this Comedy of Appearances, to follow the old romancers' lead. "Such and such things were said and done by our great Manuel," they say to us, in effect: "such and such were the appearances, and do you make what you can of them."

I say that, too, with the addition that in real life, also, such is the fashion in which we are compelled to deal with all happenings and with all our fellows, whether they wear or lack the gaudy name of heroism.

Dumbarton Grange
October, 1920

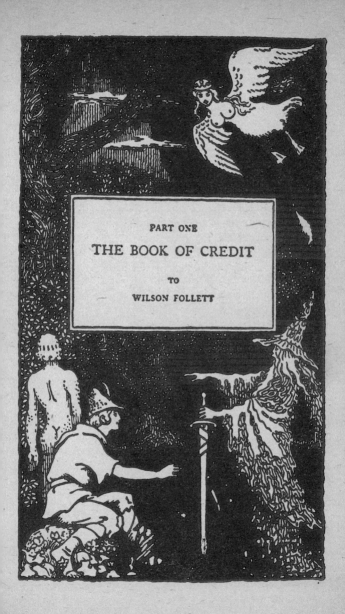

PART ONE

THE BOOK OF CREDIT

TO

WILSON FOLLETT

Then *answered the Magician dredefully: Manuel, Manuel, now I shall shewe unto thee many bokes* of Nygromancy, *and howe thou shalt cum by it lyghtly and knowe the practyse therein. And, more-ouer, I shall shewe and informe you so that thou shall have thy Desyre, whereby my thynke it is a great Gyfte for so lytyll a doynge.*

I

How Manuel Left the Mire
✦✦✦✦✦✦✦✦✦✦✦✦✦

THEY of Poictesme narrate that in the old days when miracles were as common as fruit pies, young Manuel was a swineherd, living modestly in attendance upon the miller's pigs. They tell also that Manuel was content enough: he knew not of the fate which was reserved for him.

Meanwhile in all the environs of Rathgor, and in the thatched villages of Lower Targamon, he was well liked: and when the young people gathered in the evening to drink brandy and eat nuts and gingerbread, nobody danced more merrily than Squinting Manuel. He had a quiet way with the girls, and with the men a way of solemn, blinking simplicity which caused the more hasty in judgment to consider him a fool. Then, too, young Manuel was very often detected smiling sleepily over nothing, and his gravest care in life appeared to be that figure which Manuel had made out of marsh clay from the pool of Haranton.

This figure he was continually reshaping and realtering. The figure stood upon the margin of the pool; and near by were two stones overgrown with moss, and supporting a cross of old worm-eaten wood, which commemorated what had been done there.

3

One day, toward autumn, as Manuel was sitting in this place, and looking into the deep still water, a stranger came, and he wore a fierce long sword that interfered deplorably with his walking.

"Now I wonder what it is you find in that dark pool to keep you staring so?" the stranger asked, first of all.

"I do not very certainly know," replied Manuel, "but mistily I seem to see drowned there the loves and the desires and the adventures I had when I wore another body than this. For the water of Haranton, I must tell you, is not like the water of other fountains, and curious dreams engender in this pool."

"I speak no ill against oneirology, although broad noon is hardly the best time for its practise," declared the snub-nosed stranger. "But what is that thing?" he asked, pointing.

"It is the figure of a man, which I have modeled and re-modeled, sir, but cannot seem to get exactly to my liking. So it is necessary that I keep laboring at it until the figure is to my thinking and my desire."

"But, Manuel, what need is there for you to model it at all?"

"Because my mother, sir, was always very anxious for me to make a figure in the world, and when she lay a-dying I promised her that I would do so, and then she put a geas upon me to do it."

"Ah, to be sure! but are you certain it was this kind of figure she meant?"

"Yes, for I have often heard her say that, when I grew up, she wanted me to make myself a splendid and admirable young man in every respect. So it is necessary that I make the figure of a young man, for my mother was not of these parts, but a woman of Ath Cliath, and so she put a geas upon me—"

4

"Yes, yes, you had mentioned this geas, and I am wondering what sort of a something is this geas."

"It is what you might call a bond or an obligation, sir, only it is of the particularly strong and unreasonable and affirmative and secret sort which the Virbolg use."

The stranger now looked from the figure to Manuel, and the stranger deliberated the question (which later was to puzzle so many people) if any human being could be as simple as Manuel appeared. Manuel at twenty was not yet the burly giant he became. But already he was a gigantic and florid person, so tall that the heads of few men reached to his shoulder; a person of handsome exterior, high featured and blond, having a narrow small head, and vivid light blue eyes, and the chest of a stallion; a person whose left eyebrow had an odd oblique droop, so that the stupendous boy at his simplest appeared to be winking the information that he was in jest.

All in all, the stranger found this young swineherd ambiguous; and there was another curious thing too which the stranger noticed about Manuel.

"Is it on account of this geas," asked the stranger, "that a great lock has been sheared away from your yellow hair?"

In an instant Manuel's face became dark and wary. "No," he said, "that has nothing to do with my geas, and we must not talk about that."

"Now you are a queer lad to be having such an obligation upon your head, and to be having well-nigh half the hair cut away from your head, and to be having inside your head such notions. And while small harm has ever come from humoring one's mother, yet I wonder at you, Manuel, that you should sit here sleeping in the sunlight among your pigs, and be giving your young time to improbable sculpture and stagnant water, when there is such a fine adventure awaiting you, and when the Norns are foretelling such high things about you as they spin the thread of your living."

"Hah, glory be to God, friend, but what is this adventure?"

"The adventure is that the Count of Arnaye's daughter yonder has been carried off by a magician, and that the high Count Demetrios offers much wealth and broad lands, and his daughter's hand in marriage, too, to the lad that will fetch back this lovely girl."

"I have heard talk of this in the kitchen of Arnaye, where I sometimes sell them a pig. But what are such matters to a swineherd?"

"My lad, you are to-day a swineherd drowsing in the sun, as yesterday you were a baby squalling in the cradle, but to-morrow you will be neither of these if there by any truth whatever in the talking of the Norns as they gossip at the foot of their ash-tree beside the door of the Sylan's House."

Manuel appeared to accept the inevitable. He bowed his brightly colored high head, saying gravely: "All honor be to Urdhr and Verdandi and Skuld! If I am decreed to be the champion that is to rescue the Count of Arnaye's daughter, it is ill arguing with the Norns. Come, tell me now, how do you call this doomed magician, and how does one get to him to sever his wicked head from his foul body?"

"Men speak of him as Miramon Lluagor, lord of the nine kinds of sleep and prince of the seven madnesses. He lives in mythic splendor at the top of the gray mountain called Vraidex, where he contrives all manner of illusions, and, in particular, designs the dreams of men."

"Yes, in the kitchen of Arnaye, also, such was the report concerning this Miramon: and not a person in the kitchen denied that this Miramon is an ugly customer."

"He is the most subtle of magicians. None can withstand him, and nobody can pass the terrible serpentine designs which Miramon has set to guard the gray scarps of Vraidex, unless one carries the more terrible sword Flamberge, which I have here in its blue scabbard."

"Why, then, it is you who must rescue the Count's daughter."

"No, that would not do at all: for there is in the life of a champion too much of turmoil and of buffetings and murderings to suit me, who am a peace-loving person. Besides, to the champion who rescues the Lady Gisèle will be given her hand in marriage, and as I have a wife, I know that to have two wives would lead to twice too much dissension to suit me, who am a peace-loving person. So I think it is you who had better take the sword and the adventure."

"Well," Manuel said, "much wealth and broad lands and a lovely wife are finer things to ward than a parcel of pigs."

So Manuel girded on the charmed scabbard, and with the charmed sword he sadly demolished the clay figure he could not get quite right. Then Manuel sheathed Flamberge, and Manuel cried farewell to the pigs.

"I shall not ever return to you, my pigs, because, at worst, to die valorously is better than to sleep out one's youth in the sun. A man has but one life. It is his all. Therefore I now depart from you, my pigs, to

7

win me a fine wife and much wealth and leisure wherein to discharge my geas. And when my geas is lifted I
shall not come back to you, my pigs, but I shall travel
everywhither, and into the last limits of earth, so that I
may see the ends of this world and may judge them
while my life endures. For after that, they say, I judge
not, but am judged: and a man whose life has gone out
of him, my pigs, is not even good bacon."

"So much rhetoric for the pigs," says the stranger,
"is well enough, and likely to please them. But come,
is there not some girl or another to whom you should
be saying good-bye with other things than words?"

"No, at first I thought I would also bid farewell to
Suskind, who is sometimes friendly with me in the
twilight wood, but upon reflection it seems better not
to. For Suskind would probably weep, and exact
promises of eternal fidelity, and otherwise dampen the
ardor with which I look toward to-morrow and the
winning of the wealthy Count of Arnaye's lovely
daughter."

"Now, to be sure, you are a queer cool candid fellow, you young Manuel, who will go far, whether for
good or evil!"

"I do not know about good or evil. But I am Manuel, and I shall follow after my own thinking and my
own desires."

"And certainly it is no less queer you should be
saying that: for, as everybody knows, that used to be
the favorite byword of your namesake the famous
Count Manuel who is so newly dead in Poictesme
yonder."

At that the young swineherd nodded gravely. "I
must accept the omen, sir. For, as I interpret it, my
great namesake has courteously made way for me, in
order that I may go far beyond him."

Then Manuel cried farewell and thanks to the mild-mannered, snub-nosed stranger, and Manuel left the miller's pigs to their own devices by the pool of Haranton, and Manuel marched away in his rags to meet a fate that was long talked about.

II

Niafer
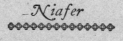

THE first thing of all that Manuel did, was to fill a knapsack with simple and nutritious food, and then he went to the gray mountain called Vraidex, upon the remote and cloud-wrapped summit of which dread Miramon Lluagor dwelt, in a doubtful palace wherein the lord of the nine sleeps contrived illusions and designed the dreams of men. When Manuel had passed under some very old maple-trees, and was beginning the ascent, he found a smallish, flat-faced, dark-haired boy going up before him.

"Hail, snip," says Manuel, "and whatever are you doing in this perilous place?"

"Why, I am going," the dark-haired boy replied, "to find out how the Lady Gisèle d'Arnaye is faring on the tall top of this mountain."

"Oho, then we will undertake this adventure together, for that is my errand too. And when the adventure is fulfilled, we will fight together, and the survivor will have the wealth and broad lands and the Count's daughter to sit on his knee. What do they call you, friend?"

"I am called Niafer. But I believe that the Lady Gisèle is already married, to Miramon Lluagor. At least, I sincerely hope she is married to this great magician, for otherwise it would not be respectable for her to be living with him at the top of this gray mountain."

"Fluff and puff! what does that matter?" says Manuel. "There is no law against a widow's remarrying forthwith: and widows are quickly made by any champion about whom the wise Norns are already talking. But I must not tell you about that, Niafer, because I do not wish to appear boastful. So I must simply say to you, Niafer, that I am called Manuel, and have no other title as yet, being not yet even a baron."

"Come now," says Niafer, "but you are rather sure of yourself for a young boy!"

"Why, of what may I be sure in this shifting world if not of myself?"

"Our elders, Manuel, declare that such self-conceit is a fault, and our elders, they say, are wiser than we."

"Our elders, Niafer, have long had the management of this world's affairs, and you can see for yourself what they have made of these affairs. What sort of a world is it, I ask you, in which time peculates the gold from hair and the crimson from all lips, and the north wind carries away the glow and glory and contentment of October, and a driveling old magician steals a lovely girl? Why, such maraudings are out of reason, and show plainly that our elders have no notion how to manage things."

"Eh, Manuel, and will you re-model the world?"

"Who knows?" says Manuel, in the high pride of his youth. "At all events, I do not mean to leave it unaltered."

Then Niafer, a more prosaic person, gave him a long look compounded equally of admiration and pity, but Niafer did not dispute the matter. Instead, these two pledged constant fealty until they should have rescued Madame Gisèle.

"Then we will fight for her," says Manuel, again.

"First, Manuel, let me see her face, and then let me see her state of mind, and afterward I will see about fighting you. Meanwhile, this is a very tall mountain, and the climbing of it will require all the breath which we are wasting here."

So the two began the ascent of Vraidex, by the winding road upon which the dreams traveled when they were sent down to men by the lord of the seven madnesses. All gray rock was the way at first. But they soon reached the gnawed bones of those who had ascended before them, scattered about a small plain that was overgrown with ironweed: and through and over the tall purple blossoms came to destroy the boys the Serpent of the East, a very dreadful design with which Miramon afflicted the sleep of Lithuanians and Tartars. The snake rode on a black horse, a black falcon perched on his head, and a black hound followed him. The horse stumbled, the falcon clamored, the hound howled.

Then said the snake: "My steed, why do you stumble? my hound, why do you howl? and, my falcon, why do you clamor? For these three doings foresay some ill to me."

"Oh, a great ill!" replies Manuel, with his charmed sword already half out of the scabbard.

But Niafer cried: "An endless ill is foresaid by these doings. For I have been to the Island of the Oaks: and under the twelfth oak was a copper casket, and in the casket was a purple duck, and in the duck was an egg: and in the egg, O Norka, was and is your death."

"It is true that my death is in such an egg," said the

Serpent of the East, "but nobody will ever find that egg, and therefore I am resistless and immortal."

"To the contrary, the egg, as you can perceive, is in my hand; and when I break this egg you will die, and it is smaller worms than you that will be thanking me for their supper this night."

The serpent looked at the poised egg, and he trembled and writhed so that his black scales scattered everywhither scintillations of reflected sunlight. He cried, "Give me the egg, and I will permit you two to ascend unmolested, to a more terrible destruction."

Niafer was not eager to do this, but Manuel thought it best, and so at last Niafer consented to the bargain, for the sake of the serpent's children. Then the two lads went upward, while the serpent bandaged the eyes of his horse and of his hound, and hooded his falcon, and crept gingerly away to hide the egg in an unmentionable place.

"But how in the devil," says Manuel, "did you manage to come by that invaluable egg?"

"It is a quite ordinary duck egg, Manuel. But the Serpent of the East has no way of discovering the fact unless he breaks the egg: and that is the one thing the serpent will never do, because he thinks it is the magic egg which contains his death."

"Come, Niafer, you are not handsome to look at, but you are far cleverer than I thought you!"

Now, as Manuel clapped Niafer on the shoulder, the forest beside the roadway was agitated, and the underbrush crackled, and the tall beech-trees crashed and snapped and tumbled helter-skelter. The crust of the earth was thus broken through by the Serpent of the North. Only the head and throat of this design of Miramon's was lifted from the jumbled trees, for it was requisite of course that the serpent's lower coils should never loose their grip upon the foundations of Norroway. All of the design that showed was overgrown with seaweed and barnacles.

"It is the will of Miramon Lluagor that I forthwith demolish you both," says this serpent, yawning with a mouth like a fanged cave.

Once more young Manuel had reached for his charmed sword Flamberge, but it was Niafer who spoke.

"No, for before you can destroy me," says Niafer, "I shall have cast this bridle over your head."

"What sort of bridle is that?" inquired the great snake scornfully.

"And are those goggling flaming eyes not big enough and bright enough to see that this is the soft bridle called Gleipnir, which is made of the breath of fish and of the spittle of birds and of the footfall of a cat?"

"Now, although certainly such a bridle was foretold," the snake conceded, a little uneasily, "how can I make sure that you speak the truth when you say this particular bridle is Gleipnir?"

"Why, in this way: I will cast the bridle over your head, and then you will see for yourself that the old prophecy will be fulfilled, and that all power and all life will go out of you, and that the Northmen will dream no more."

"No, do you keep that thing away from me, you little fool! No, no: we will not test your truthfulness in that way. Instead, do you two continue your ascent, to a more terrible destruction, and to face barbaric dooms coming from the West. And do you give me the bridle to demolish in place of you. And then, if I live forever I shall know that this is indeed Gleipnir, and that you have spoken the truth."

So Niafer consented to this testing of his veracity, rather than permit this snake to die, and the foundations of Norroway (in which kingdom, Niafer confessed, he had an aunt then living) thus to be dissolved by the loosening of the dying serpent's grip upon Middlegarth. The bridle was yielded, and Niafer and Manuel went upward.

Manuel asked, "Snip, was that in truth the bridle called Gleipnir?"

"No, Manuel, it is an ordinary bridle. But this Serpent of the North has no way of discovering this fact except by fitting the bridle over his head: and this one thing the serpent will never do, because he knows that then, if my bridle proved to be Gleipnir, all power and all life would go out of him."

"O subtle, ugly little snip!" says Manuel: and again he patted Niafer on the shoulder. Then Manuel spoke very highly in praise of cleverness, and said that, for one, he had never objected to it in its place.

III

Ascent of Vraidex
❋❋❋❋❋❋❋❋❋❋❋

Now it was evening, and the two sought shelter in a queer windmill by the roadside, finding there a small wrinkled old man in a patched coat. He gave them lodgings for the night, and honest bread and cheese, but for his own supper he took frogs out of his bosom, and roasted these in the coals.

Then the two boys sat in the doorway, and watched that night's dreams going down from Vraidex to their allotted work in the world of visionary men, to whom these dreams were passing in the form of incredible white vapors. Sitting thus, the lads fell to talking of this and the other, and Manuel found that Niafer was a pagan of the old faith: and this, said Manuel, was an excellent thing.

"For, when we have achieved our adventure," says Manuel, "and must fight against each other for the Count's daughter, I shall certainly kill you, dear Niafer. Now if you were a Christian, and died thus unholily in trying to murder me, you would have to go thereafter to the unquenchable flames of purgatory or to even hotter flames: but among the pagans all that die valiantly in battle go straight to the pagan paradise. Yes, yes, your abominable religion is a great comfort to me."

"It is a comfort to me also, Manuel. But, as a Christian, you ought not ever to have any kind words for heathenry."

"Ah, but," says Manuel, "while my mother Dorothy of the White Arms was the most zealous sort of Christian, my father, you must know, was not a communicant."

"Who was your father, Manuel?"

"No less a person than the Swimmer, Oriander, who is in turn the son of Mimir."

"Ah, to be sure! and who is Mimir?"

"Well, Niafer, that is a thing not very generally known, but he is famed for his wise head."

"And, Manuel, who, while we speak of it, is Oriander?"

Said Manuel:

"Oh, out of the void and the darkness that is peopled by Mimir's brood, from the ultimate silent fastness of the desolate deep-sea gloom, and the peace of that ageless gloom, blind Oriander came, from Mimir, to be at war with the sea and to jeer at the sea's desire. When tempests are seething and roaring from the Æsir's inverted bowl all seamen have heard his shouting and the cry that his mirth sends up: when the rim of the sea tilts up, and the world's roof wavers down, his face gleams white where distraught waves smite the Swimmer they may not tire. No eyes were allotted this Swimmer, but in blindness, with ceaseless jeers, he battles till time be done with, and the love-songs of earth be sung, and the very last dirge be sung, and a baffled and outworn sea begrudgingly own Oriander alone may mock at the might of its ire."

"Truly, Manuel, that sounds like a parent to be proud of, and not at all like a church-going parent, and of course his blindness would account for that squint of yours. Yes, certainly it would. So do you tell me about this blind Oriander, and how he came to meet your mother Dorothy of the White Arms, as I suppose he did somewhere or other."

"Oh, no," says Manuel, "for Oriander never leaves off swimming, and so he must stay always in the water. So he never actually met my mother, and she married Emmerick, who was my nominal father. But such and such things happened."

Then Manuel told Niafer all about the circumstances of Manuel's birth in a cave, and about the circumstances of Manuel's upbringing in and near Rathgor: and the two boys talked on and on, while the unborn dreams went drifting by outside; and within, the small wrinkled old man sat listening with a very doubtful smile, and saying never a word.

"And why is your hair cut so queerly, Manuel?"

"That, Niafer, we need not talk about, in part because it is not going to be cut that way any longer, and in part because it is time for bed."

The next morning Manuel and Niafer paid the ancient price which their host required. They left him cobbling shoes, and, still ascending, encountered no more bones, for nobody else had climbed so high. They presently came to a bridge whereon were eight spears, and the bridge was guarded by the Serpent of the West. This snake was striped with blue and gold, and wore on his head a great cap of humming-birds' feathers.

Manuel half drew his sword to attack this serpentine design, with which Miramon Lluagor made sleeping terrible for the red tribes that hunt and fish behind the Hesperides. But Manuel looked at Niafer.

And Niafer displayed a drolly marked small turtle, saying, "Maskanako, do you not recognize Tulapin, the turtle that never lies?"

The serpent howled, as though a thousand dogs had been kicked simultaneously, and the serpent fled.

"Why, snip, did he do that?" asked Manuel, smiling sleepily and gravely, as for the third time he found that his charmed sword Flamberge was unneeded.

"Truly, Manuel, nobody knows why this serpent dreads the turtle: but our concern is less with the cause than with the effect. Meanwhile, those eight spears are not to be touched on any account."

"Is what you have a quite ordinary turtle?" asked Manuel, meekly.

Niafer said: "Of course it is. Where would I be getting extraordinary turtles?"

"I had not previously considered that problem," replied Manuel, "but the question is certainly unanswerable."

They then sat down to lunch, and found the bread and cheese they had purchased from the little old man that morning was turned to lumps of silver and virgin gold in Manuel's knapsack. "This is very disgusting," said Manuel, "and I do not wonder my back was near breaking." He flung away the treasure, and they lunched frugally on blackberries.

From among the entangled blackberry bushes came the glowing Serpent of the South, who was the smallest and loveliest and most poisonous of Miramon's designs. With this snake Niafer dealt curiously. Niafer employed three articles in the transaction: two of these things are not to be talked about, but the third was a little figure carved in hazel-wood.

"Certainly you are very clever," said Manuel, when they had passed this serpent. "Still, your employment of those first two articles was unprecedented, and your disposal of the carved figure absolutely embarrassed me."

"Before such danger as confronted us, Manuel, it does not pay to be squeamish," replied Niafer, "and my exorcism was good Dirgham."

And many other adventures and perils they encountered, such as if all were told would make a long and most improbable history. But they had clear favorable weather, and they won through each pinch, by one or another fraud which Niafer evolved the instant that gullery was needed. Manuel was loud in his praises of the surprising cleverness of his flat-faced dark comrade, and protested that hourly he loved Niafer more and more: and Manuel said too that he was beginning to think more and more distastefully of the time when Niafer and Manuel would have to fight for the Count of Arnaye's daughter until one of them had killed the other.

Meanwhile the sword Flamberge stayed in its curious blue scabbard.

IV

In the Doubtful Palace
❖❖❖❖❖❖❖❖❖❖❖

So Manuel and Niafer came unhurt to the top of the
gray mountain called Vraidex, and to the doubtful
palace of Miramon Lluagor. Gongs, slowly struck,
were sounding as if in languid dispute among themselves, when the two lads came across a small level
plain where grass was interspersed with white clover.
Here and there stood wicked looking dwarf trees
with violet and yellow foliage. The doubtful palace
before the circumspectly advancing boys appeared to
be constructed of black and gold lacquer, and it was
decorated with the figures of butterflies and tortoises
and swans.

This day being a Thursday, Manuel and Niafer entered unchallenged through gates of horn and ivory;
and came into a red corridor in which five gray
beasts, like large hairless cats, were casting dice. These
animals grinned, and licked their lips, as the boys
passed deeper into the doubtful palace.

In the centre of the palace Miramon had set like a
tower one of the tusks of Behemoth: the tusk was
hollowed out into five large rooms, and in the inmost
room, under a canopy with green tassels, they found
the magician.

21

"Come forth, and die now, Miramon Lluagor!" shouts Manuel, brandishing his sword, for which, at last, employment was promised here.

The magician drew closer about him his old threadbare dressing-gown, and he desisted from his enchantments, and he put aside a small unfinished design, which scuttled into the fireplace, whimpering. And Manuel perceived that the dreadful prince of the seven madnesses had the appearance of the mild-mannered stranger who had given Manuel the charmed sword.

"Ah, yes, it was good of you to come so soon," says Miramon Lluagor, rearing back his head, and narrowing his gentle and sombre eyes, as the magician looked at them down the sides of what little nose he had. "Yes, and your young friend, too, is very welcome. But you boys must be quite worn out, after toiling up this mountain, so do you sit down and have a cup of wine before I surrender my dear wife."

Says Manuel, sternly, "But what is the meaning of all this?"

"The meaning and the upshot, clearly," replied the magician, "is that, since you have the charmed sword Flamberge, and since the wearer of Flamberge is irresistible, it would be nonsense for me to oppose you."

"But, Miramon, it was you who gave me the sword!"

Miramon rubbed his droll little nose for a while, before speaking. "And how else was I to get conquered? For, I must tell you, Manuel, it is a law of the Léshy that a magician cannot surrender his prey unless the magician be conquered. I must tell you, too, that when I carried off Gisèle I acted, as I by and by discovered, rather injudiciously."

"Now, by holy Paul and Pollux! I do not understand this at all, Miramon."

22

"Why, Manuel, you must know she was a very charming girl, and in appearance just the type that I had always fancied for a wife. But perhaps it is not wise to be guided entirely by appearances. For I find now that she has a strong will in her white bosom, and a tireless tongue in her glittering head, and I do not equally admire all four of these possessions."

"Still, Miramon, if only a few months back your love was so great as to lead you into abducting her—"

The prince of the seven madnesses said gravely:

"Love, as I think, is an instant's fusing of shadow and substance. They that aspire to possess love utterly, fall into folly. This is forbidden: you cannot. The lover, beholding that fusing move as a golden-hued goddess, accessible, kindly and priceless, wooes and ill-fatedly wins all the substance. The golden-hued shadow dims in the dawn of his married life, dulled with content, and the shadow vanishes. So there remains, for the puzzled husband's embracing, flesh which is fair and dear, no doubt, yet is flesh such as his; and talking and talking and talking; and kisses in all ways desirable. Love, of a sort, too remains, but hardly the love that was yesterday's."

Now the unfinished design came out of the fireplace, and climbed up Miramon's leg, still faintly whimpering. He looked at it meditatively, then twisted off the creature's head and dropped the fragments into his waste-basket.

Miramon sighed. He said:

"This is the cry of all husbands that now are or may be hereafter,—'What has become of the girl that I married? and how should I rightly deal with this woman whom somehow time has involved in my doings? Love, of a sort, now I have for her, but not the love that was yesterday's—'"

23

While Miramon spoke thus, the two lads were looking at each other blankly: for they were young, and their understanding of this matter was as yet withheld.

Then said Miramon:

"Yes, he is wiser that shelters his longing from any such surfeit. Yes, he is wiser that knows the shadow makes lovely the substance, wisely regarding the ways of that irresponsible shadow which, if you grasp at it, flees, and, when you avoid it, will follow, gilding all life with its glory, and keeping always one woman young and most fair and most wise, and unwon; and keeping you always never contented, but armed with a self-respect that no husband manages quite to retain in the face of being contented. No, for love is an instant's fusing of shadow and substance, fused for that instant only, whereafter the lover may harvest pleasure from either alone, but hardly from these two united."

"Well," Manuel conceded, "all this may be true; but I never quite understood hexameters, and so I could not ever see the good of talking in them."

"I always do that, Manuel, when I am deeply affected. It is, I suppose, the poetry in my nature welling to the surface the moment that inhibitions are removed, for when I think about the impending severance from my dear wife I more or less lose control of myself—You see, she takes an active interest in my work, and that does not do with a creative artist in any line. Oh, dear me, no, not for a moment!" says Miramon, forlornly.

"But how can that be?" Niafer asked him.

"As all persons know, I design the dreams of men. Now Gisèle asserts that people have enough trouble in real life, without having to go to sleep to look for it—"

"Certainly that is true," says Niafer.

"So she permits me only to design bright optimistic dreams and edifying dreams and glad dreams. She says you must give tired persons what they most need; and is emphatic about the importance of everybody's sleeping in a wholesome atmosphere. So I have not been permitted to design a fine nightmare or a creditable terror—nothing morbid or blood-freezing, no sea-serpents or krakens or hippogriffs, nor anything that gives me a really free hand,—for months and months: and my art suffers. Then, as for other dreams, of a more roguish nature—"

"What sort of dreams can you be talking about, I wonder, Miramon?"

The magician described what he meant. "Such dreams also she has quite forbidden," he added, with a sigh.

"I see," said Manuel: "and now I think of it, it is true that I have not had a dream of that sort for quite a while."

"No man anywhere is allowed to have that sort of dream in these degenerate nights, no man anywhere in the whole world. And here again my art suffers, for my designs in this line were always especially vivid and effective, and pleased the most rigid. Then, too, Gisèle is always doing and telling me things for my own good—In fine, my lads, my wife takes such a flattering interest in all my concerns that the one way out for any peace-loving magician was to contrive her rescue from my clutches," said Miramon, fretfully.

"It is difficult to explain to you, Manuel, just now, but after you have been married to Gisèle for a while you will comprehend without any explaining."

"Now, Miramon, I marvel to see a great magician controlled by a woman who is in his power, and who can, after all, do nothing but talk."

25

Miramon for some while considered Manuel, rather helplessly. "Unmarried men do wonder about that," said Miramon. "At all events, I will summon her, and you can explain how you have conquered me, and then you can take her away and marry her yourself, and Heaven help you!"

"But shall I explain that it was you who gave me the resistless sword?"

"No, Manuel: no, you should be candid within more rational limits. For you are now a famous champion, that has crowned with victory a righteous cause for which many stalwart knights and gallant gentlemen have made the supreme sacrifice, because they knew that in the end the right must conquer. Your success thus represents the working out of a great moral principle, and to explain the practical minutiæ of these august processes is not always quite respectable. Besides, if Gisèle thought I wished to get rid of her she would most certainly resort to comments of which I prefer not to think."

But now into the room came the magician's wife, Gisèle.

"She is, certainly, rather pretty," said Niafer, to Manuel.

Said Manuel, rapturously: "She is the finest and loveliest creature that I have ever seen. Beholding her unequalled beauty, I know that here are all the dreams of yesterday fulfilled. I recollect, too, my songs of yesterday, which I was used to sing to my pigs, about my love for a far princess who was 'white as a lily, more red than roses, and resplendent as rubies of the Orient,' for here I find my old songs to be applicable, if rather inadequate. And by this shabby villain's failure to appreciate the unequalled beauty of his victim I am amazed."

"As to that, I have my suspicions," Niafer replied. "And now she is about to speak I believe she will justify these suspicions, for Madame Gisèle is in no placid frame of mind."

"What is this nonsense," says the proud shining lady, to Miramon Lluagor, "that I hear about your having been conquered?"

"Alas, my love, it is perfectly true. This champion has, in some inexplicable way, come by the magic weapon Flamberge which is the one weapon wherewith I can be conquered. So I have yielded to him, and he is about, I think, to sever my head from my body."

The beautiful girl was indignant, because she had recognized that, magician or no, there is small difference in husbands after the first month or two; and with Miramon tolerably well trained, she had no intention of changing him for another husband. Therefore Gisèle inquired, "And what about me?" in a tone that foreboded turmoil.

The magician rubbed his hands, uncomfortably. "My dear, I am of course quite powerless before Flamberge. Inasmuch as your rescue appears to have been effected in accordance with every rule in these matters, and the victorious champion is resolute to requite my evil-doing and to restore you to your grieving parents, I am afraid there is nothing I can well do about it."

"Do you look me in the eye, Miramon Lluagor!" says the Lady Gisèle. The dreadful prince of the seven madnesses obeyed her, with a placating smile. "Yes, you have been up to something," she said, "And Heaven only knows what, though of course it does not really matter."

Madame Gisèle then looked at Manuel. "So you are

27

the champion that has come to rescue me!" she said, unhastily, as her big sapphire eyes appraised him over her great fan of gaily colored feathers, and as Manuel somehow began to fidget.

Gisèle looked last of all at Niafer. "I must say you have been long enough in coming," observed Gisèle.

"It took me two days, madame, to find and catch a turtle," Niafer replied, "and that delayed me."

"Oh, you have always some tale or other, trust you for that, but it is better late than never. Come, Niafer, and do you know anything about this gawky, ragtag, yellow-haired young champion?"

"Yes, madame, he formerly lived in attendance upon the miller's pigs, down Rathgor way, and I have seen him hanging about the kitchen at Arnaye."

Gisèle turned now toward the magician, with her thin gold chains and the innumerable brilliancies of her jewels flashing no more brightly than flashed the sapphire of her eyes. "There!" she said, terribly: "and you were going to surrender me to a swineherd, with half the hair chopped from his head, and with the shirt sticking out of both his ragged elbows!"

"My dearest, irrespective of tonsorial tastes, and disregarding all sartorial niceties, and swineherd or not, he holds the magic sword Flamberge, before which all my powers are nothing."

"But that is easily settled. Have men no sense whatever! Boy, do you give me that sword, before you hurt yourself fiddling with it, and let us have an end of this nonsense."

Thus the proud lady spoke, and for a while the victorious champion regarded her with very youthful looking, hurt eyes. But he was not routed.

"Madame Gisèle," replied Manuel, "gawky and poorly clad and young as I may be, so long as I retain this sword I am master of you all and of the future too. Yielding it, I yield everything my elders have taught me to prize, for my grave elders have taught me that much wealth and broad lands and a lovely wife are finer things to ward than a parcel of pigs. So, if I yield at all, I must first bargain and get my price for yielding."

He turned now from Gisèle to Niafer. "Dear snip," said Manuel, "you too must have your say in my bargaining, because from the first it has been your cleverness that has saved us, and has brought us two so high. For see, at last I have drawn Flamberge, and I stand at last at the doubtful summit of Vraidex, and I am master of the hour and of the future. I have but to sever the wicked head of this doomed magician from his foul body, and that will be the end of him—"

"No, no," says Miramon, soothingly, "I shall merely be turned into something else, which perhaps we had better not discuss. But it will not inconvenience me in the least, so do you not hold back out of mistaken kindness to me, but instead do you smite, and take your well-earned reward."

"Either way," submitted Manuel, "I have but to strike, and I acquire much wealth and sleek farming-lands and a lovely wife, and the swineherd becomes a great nobleman. But it is you, Niafer, who have won all these things for me with your cleverness, and to me it seems that these wonderful rewards are less wonderful than my dear comrade."

"But you too are very wonderful," said Niafer, loyally.

Says Manuel, smiling sadly: "I am not so wonderful but that in the hour of my triumph I am frightened by my own littleness. Look you, Niafer, I had thought I would be changed when I had become a famous champion, but for all that I stand posturing here with this long sword, and am master of the hour and of the future, I remain the boy that last Thursday was tending pigs. I was not afraid of the terrors which beset me on my way to rescue the Count's daughter, but of the Count's daughter herself I am horribly afraid. Not for worlds would I be left alone with her. No, such fine and terrific ladies are not for swineherds, and it is another sort of wife that I desire."

"Whom then do you desire for a wife," says Niafer, "if not the loveliest and the wealthiest lady in all Rathgor and Lower Targamon?"

"Why, I desire the cleverest and dearest and most wonderful creature in all the world," says Manuel,— "whom I recollect seeing some six weeks ago when I was in the kitchen at Arnaye."

"Ah, ah! it might be arranged, then. But who is this marvelous woman?"

Manuel said, "You are that woman, Niafer."

Niafer replied nothing, but Niafer smiled. Niafer raised one shoulder a little, rubbing it against Manuel's broad chest, but Niafer still kept silence. So the two young people regarded each other for a while, not speaking, and to every appearance not valuing Miramon Lluagor and his emcompassing enchantments at a straw's worth, nor valuing anything save each other.

"All things are changed for me," says Manuel, presently, in a hushed voice, "and for the rest of time I live in a world wherein Niafer differs from all other persons."

"My dearest," Niafer replied, "there is no sparkling queen nor polished princess anywhere but the woman's heart in her would be jumping with joy to have you looking at her twice, and I am only a servant girl!"

"But certainly," said the rasping voice of Gisèle, "Niafer is my suitably disguised heathen waiting-woman, to whom my husband sent a dream some while ago, with instructions to join me here, so that I might have somebody to look after my things. So, Niafer, since you were fetched to wait on me, do you stop pawing at that young pig-tender, and tell me what is this I hear about your remarkable cleverness!"

Instead, it was Manuel who proudly told of the shrewd devices through which Niafer had passed the serpents and the other terrors of sleep. And the while that the tall boy was boasting, Miramon Lluagor smiled, and Gisèle looked very hard at Niafer: for Miramon and his wife both knew that the cleverness of Niafer was as far to seek as her good looks, and that the dream which Miramon had sent had carefully instructed Niafer as to these devices.

"Therefore, Madame Gisèle," says Manuel, in conclusion, "I will give you Flamberge, and Miramon and Vraidex, and all the rest of earth to boot, in exchange for the most wonderful and clever woman in the world."

And with a flourish, Manuel handed over the charmed sword Flamberge to the Count's lovely daughter, and he took the hand of the swart, flat-faced servant girl.

"Come now," says Miramon, in a sad flurry, "this is an imposing performance. I need not say it arouses in me the most delightful sort of surprise and all other appropriate emotions. But as touches your own interests, Manuel, do you think your behavior is quite sensible?"

Tall Manuel looked down upon him with a sort of

31

scornful pity. "Yes, Miramon: for I am Manuel, and I follow after my own thinking and my own desire. Of course it is very fine of me to be renouncing so much wealth and power for the sake of my wonderful dear Niafer: but she is worth the sacrifice, and, besides, she is witnessing all this magnanimity, and cannot well fail to be impressed."

Niafer was of course reflecting: "This is very foolish and dear of him, and I shall be compelled, in mere decency, to pretend to corresponding lunacies for the first month or so of our marriage. After that, I hope, we will settle down to some more reasonable way of living."

Meanwhile she regarded Manuel fondly, and quite as though she considered him to be displaying unusual intelligence.

But Gisèle and Miramon were looking at each other, and wondering: "What can the long-legged boy see in this stupid and plain-featured girl who is years older than he? or she in the young swaggering ragged fool? And how much wiser and happier is our marriage than, in any event, the average marriage!"

And Miramon, for one, was so deeply moved by the staggering thought which holds together so many couples in the teeth of human nature that he patted his wife's hand. Then he sighed. "Love has conquered my designs," said Miramon, oracularly, "and the secret of a contented marriage, after all, is to pay particular attention to the wives of everybody else."

Gisèle exhorted him not to be a fool, but she spoke without acerbity, and, speaking, she squeezed his hand. She understood this potent magician better than she intended ever to permit him to suspect.

Whereafter Miramon wiped the heavenly bodies from the firmament, and set a miraculous rainbow

there, and under its arch was enacted for the swineherd and the servant girl such a betrothal masque of
fantasies and illusions as gave full scope to the art of
Miramon, and delighted everybody, but delighted Miramon in particular. The dragon that guards hidden
treasure made sport for them, the naiads danced, and
cherubim fluttered about singing very sweetly and asking droll conundrums. Then they feasted, with
unearthly servitors to attend them, and did all else appropriate to an affiancing of deities. And when these
junketings were over, Manuel said that, since it seemed
he was not to be a wealthy nobleman after all, he and
Niafer must be getting, first to the nearest priest's and
then back to the pigs.

"I am not so sure that you can manage it," said
Miramon, "for, while the ascent of Vraidex is incom-
moded by serpents, the quitting of Vraidex is very apt
to be hindered by death and fate. For I must tell you
I have a rather arbitrary half-brother, who is one of
those dreadful Realists, without a scrap of æsthetic
feeling, and there is no controlling him."

"Well," Manuel considered, "one cannot live forever among dreams, and death and fate must be encountered by all men. So we can but try."

Now for a while the sombre eyes of Miramon Lluagor appraised them. He, who was lord of the nine
sleeps and prince of the seven madnesses, now gave a
little sigh; for he knew that these young people were
enviable and, in the outcome, were unimportant.

So Miramon said, "Then do you go your way, and
if you do not encounter the author and destroyer of
us all it will be well for you, and if you do encounter
him that too will be well in that it is his wish."

"I neither seek nor avoid him," Manuel replied. "I
only know that I must follow after my own thinking,

33

and after a desire which is not to be satisfied with dreams, even though they be"—the boy appeared to search for a comparison, then, smiling, said,—"as resplendent as rubies of the Orient."

Thereafter Manuel bid farewell to Miramon and Miramon's fine wife, and Manuel descended from marvelous Vraidex with his plain-featured Niafer, quite contentedly. For happiness went with them, if for no great way.

V

The Eternal Ambuscade
❖❖❖❖❖❖❖❖❖❖❖❖

MANUEL AND NIAFER came down from Vraidex without hindrance. There was no happier nor more devoted lover anywhere than young Manuel.

"For we will be married out of hand, dear snip," he says, "and you will help me to discharge my geas, and afterward we will travel everywhither and into the last limits of earth, so that we may see the ends of this world and may judge them."

"Perhaps we had better wait until next spring, when the roads will be better, Manuel, but certainly we will be married out of hand."

In earnest of this, Niafer permitted Manuel to kiss her again, and young Manuel said, for the twenty-second time, "There is nowhere any happiness like my happiness, nor any love like my love."

Thus speaking, and thus disporting themselves, they came leisurely to the base of the gray mountain and to the old maple-trees, under which they found two persons waiting. One was a tall man mounted on a white horse, and leading a riderless black horse. His hat was pulled down about his head so that his face could not be clearly seen.

Now the companion that was with him had the appearance of a bare-headed youngster, with dark red hair, and his face too was hidden as he sat by the roadway trimming his long finger-nails with a small green-handled knife.

"Hail, friends," said Manuel, "and for whom are you waiting here?"

"I wait for one to ride on this black horse of mine," replied the mounted stranger. "It was decreed that the first person who passed this way must be his rider, but you two come abreast. So do you choose between you which one rides."

"Well, but it is a fine steed surely," Manuel said, "and a steed fit for Charlemagne or Hector or any of the famous champions of the old time."

"Each one of them has ridden upon this black horse of mine," replied the stranger.

Niafer said, "I am frightened." And above them a furtive wind began to rustle in the torn, discolored maple-leaves.

"—For it is a fine steed and an old steed," the stranger went on, "and a tireless steed that bears all away. It has the fault, some say, that its riders do not return, but there is no pleasing everybody."

"Friend," Manuel said, in a changed voice, "who are you, and what is your name?"

"I am half-brother to Miramon Lluagor, lord of the nine sleeps, but I am lord of another kind of sleeping; and as for my name, it is the name that is in your thoughts and the name which most troubles you, and the name which you think about most often."

There was silence. Manuel worked his lips foolishly. "I wish we had not walked abreast," he said. "I wish we had remained among the bright dreams."

"All persons voice some regret or another at meeting me. And it does not ever matter."

36

"But if there were no choosing in the affair, I could make shift to endure it, either way. Now one of us, you tell me, must depart with you. If I say, 'Let Niafer be that one,' I must always recall that saying with self-loathing."

"But I too say it!" Niafer was petting him and trembling.

"Besides," observed the rider of the white horse, "you have a choice of sayings."

"The other saying," Manuel replied, "I cannot utter. Yet I wish I were not forced to confess this. It sounds badly. At all events, I love Niafer better than I love any other person, but I do not value Niafer's life more highly than I value my own life, and it would be nonsense to say so. No; my life is very necessary to me, and there is a geas upon me to make a figure in this world before I leave it."

"My dearest," says Niafer, "you have chosen wisely."

The veiled horseman said nothing at all. But he took off his hat, and the beholders shuddered. The kinship to Miramon was apparent, you could see the resemblance, but they had never seen in Miramon Lluagor's face what they saw here.

Then Niafer bade farewell to Manuel with pitiable whispered words. They kissed. For an instant Manuel stood motionless. He queerly moved his mouth, as though it were stiff and he were trying to make it more supple. Thereafter Manuel, very sick and desperate looking, did what was requisite. So Niafer went away with Grandfather Death, in Manuel's stead.

"My heart cracks in me now," says Manuel, forlornly considering his hands, "but better she than I. Still, this is a poor beginning in life, for yesterday

37

great wealth and to-day great love was within my reach, and now I have lost both."

"But you did not go the right way about to win success in anything," says the remaining stranger.

And now this other stranger arose from the trimming of his long fingernails; and you could see this was a tall, lean youngster (though not so tall as Manuel, and nothing like so stalwart), with ruddy cheeks, wide-set brown eyes, and crinkling, rather dark red hair.

Then Manuel rubbed his wet hands as clean as might be, and this boy walked on a little way with Manuel, talking of that which had been and of some things which were to be. And Manuel said, "Now assuredly, Horvendile, since that is your name, such talking is insane talking, and no comfort whatever to me in my grief at losing Niafer."

"This is but the beginning of your losses, Manuel, for I think that a little by a little you will lose everything which is desirable, until you shall have remaining at the last only a satiation, and a weariness, and an uneasy loathing of all that the human wisdom of your elders shall have induced you to procure."

"But, Horvendile, can anybody foretell the future? Or can it be that Miramon spoke seriously in saying that fate also was enleagued to forbid the leaving of this mountain?"

"No, Manuel, I do not say that I am fate nor any of the Léshy, but rather it seems to me that I am insane. So perhaps the less attention you pay to my talking, the better. For I must tell you that this wasted country side, this mountain, this road, and these old maples, and that rock yonder, appear to me to be things I have imagined, and that you, and the Niafer whom you have just disposed of so untidily, and Miramon and his fair shrew, and all of you, appear to me to be persons I have imagined; and all the living in this world appears to me to be only a notion of mine."

"Why, then, certainly I would say, or rather, I would think it unnecessary to say, that you are insane."

"You speak without hesitation, and it is through your ability to settle such whimseys out of hand that you will yet win, it may be, to success."

"Yes, but," asked Manuel, slowly, "what is success?"

"In your deep mind, I think, that question is already answered."

"Undoubtedly I have my notion, but it was about your notion I was asking."

Horvendile looked grave, and yet whimsical too. "Why, I have heard somewhere," says he, "that at its uttermost this success is but the strivings of an ape reft of his tail, and grown rusty at climbing, who yet feels himself to be a symbol and the frail representative of Omnipotence in a place that is not home."

Manuel appeared to reserve judgment. "How does the successful ape employ himself, in these not quite friendly places?"

"He strives blunderingly, from mystery to mystery, with pathetic makeshifts, not understanding anything, greedy in all desires, and honeycombed with poltroonery, and yet ready to give all, and to die fighting for the sake of that undemonstrable idea, about his being Heaven's vicar and heir."

Manuel shook his small bright head. "You use too many long words. But so far I can understand you, that is not the sort of success I want. No, I am Manuel, and I must follow after my own thinking and my own desire, without considering other people and their notions of success."

"As for denying yourself consideration for other people, I am of the opinion, after witnessing your recent disposal of your sweetheart, that you are already tolerably expert in that sort of abnegation."

"Hah, but you do not know what is seething here," replied Manuel, smiting his broad chest. "And I shall not tell you of it, Horvendile, since you are not fate nor any of the Léshy, to give me my desire."

"What would be your desire?"

"My wish would be for me always to obtain whatever I may wish for. Yes, Horvendile, I have often wondered why, in the old legends, when three wishes were being offered, nobody ever made that sensible and economical wish the first of all."

"What need is there to trouble the Léshy about that foolish wish when it is always possible, at a paid price, to obtain whatever one desires? You have but to go about it in this way." And Horvendile told Manuel a queer and dangerous thing. Then Horvendile said sadly: "So much knowledge I can deny nobody at Michaelmas. But I must tell you the price also, and it is that with the achieving of each desire you will perceive its worth."

Thus speaking, Horvendile parted the thicket beside the roadway. A beautiful dusk-colored woman waited there, in a green-blue robe, and on her head was a blue coronet surmounted with green feathers: she carried a vase. Horvendile stepped forward, and the thicket closed behind him, concealing Horvendile and this woman.

Manuel, looking puzzled, went on a little way, and when he was assured of being alone he flung himself face downward and wept. The reason of this was, they relate, that young Manuel had loved Niafer as he could love nobody else. Then he arose, and went toward the pool of Haranton, on his way homeward, after having failed in everything.

VI

Economics of Math

❖❖❖❖❖❖❖❖❖❖❖

WHAT FORTHWITH happened at the pool of Haranton is not nicely adapted to exact description, but it was sufficiently curious to give Manuel's thoughts a new turn, although it did not seem, even so, to make them happy thoughts. Certainly it was not with any appearance of merriment that Manuel returned to his half-sister Math, who was the miller's wife.

"And wherever have you been all this week?" says Math, "with the pigs rooting all over creation, and with that man of mine forever flinging your worthlessness in my face, and with that red-haired Suskind coming out of the twilight a-seeking after you every evening and pestering me with her soft lamentations? And for the matter of that, whatever are you glooming over?"

"I have cause, and cause to spare."

Manuel told her of his adventures upon Vraidex, and Math said that showed what came of neglecting his proper business, which was attendance on her husband's pigs. Manuel then told her of what had just befallen by the pool of Haranton.

Math nodded. "Take shame to yourself, young rascal with your Niafer hardly settled down in paradise, and with your Suskind wailing for you in the twilight! But that would be Alianora the Unattainable Princess. Thus she comes across the Bay of Biscay, traveling from the far land of Provence, in, they say, the appearance of a swan: and thus she bathes in the pool wherein strange dreams engender: and thus she slips into the robe of the Apsarasas when it is high time to be leaving such impudent knaves as you have proved yourself to be."

"Yes, yes! a shift made all of shining white feathers, Sister. Here is a feather that was broken from it as I clutched at her."

Math turned the feather in her hand. "Now to be sure! and did you ever see the like of it! Still, a broken feather is no good to anybody, and, as I have told you any number of times, I cannot have trash littering up my kitchen."

So Math dropped this shining white feather into the fire, on which she was warming over a pot of soup for Manuel's dinner, and they watched this feather burn.

Manuel says, sighing, "Even so my days consume, and my youth goes out of me, in a land wherein Suskind whispers of uncomfortable things, and wherein there are no maids so clever and dear as Niafer, nor so lovely as Alianora."

Math said: "I never held with speaking ill of the dead. So may luck and fair words go with your Niafer in her pagan paradise. Of your Suskind too"— Math crossed herself,—"the less said, the better. But as for your Alianora, no really nice girl would be flying in the face of heaven and showing her ankles to five nations, and bathing, on a Monday too, in places where almost anybody might come along. It is not proper, but I wonder at her parents."

"But, Sister, she is a princess!"

"Just so: therefore I burned the feather, because it is not wholesome for persons of our station in life to be robbing princesses of anything, though it be only of a feather."

"Sister, that is the truth! It is not right to rob anybody of anything, and this would appear to make another bond upon me and another obligation to be discharged, because in taking that feather I have taken what did not belong to me."

"Boy, do not think you are fooling me, for when your face gets that look on it, I know you are considering some nonsense over and above the nonsense you are talking. However, from your description of the affair, I do not doubt that gallivanting, stark-naked princess thought you were for taking what did not belong to you. Therefore I burned the feather, lest it be recognized and bring you to the gallows or to a worse place. So why did you not scrape your feet before coming into my clean kitchen? and how many times do you expect me to speak to you about that?"

Manuel said nothing. But he seemed to meditate over something that puzzled him. In the upshot he went into the miller's chicken-yard, and caught a goose, and plucked from its wing a feather.

Then Manuel put on his Sunday clothes.

"Far too good for you to be traveling in," said Math.

Manuel looked down at his half-sister, and once or twice he blinked those shining strange eyes of his. "Sister, if I had been properly dressed when I was master of the doubtful palace, the Lady Gisèle would have taken me quite seriously. I have been thinking about her observations as to my elbows."

"The coat does not make the man," replied Math piously.

"It is your belief in any such saying that has made a miller's wife of you, and will keep you a miller's wife until the end of time. Now I learned better from my misadventures upon Vraidex, and from my talking with that insane Horvendile about the things which have been and some things which are to be."

Math, who was a wise woman, said queerly, "I perceive that you are letting your hair grow."

Manuel said, "Yes."

"Boy, fast and loose is a mischancy game to play."

"And being born, also, is a most hazardous speculation, Sister, yet we perforce risk all upon that cast."

"Now you talk stuff and nonsense—"

"Yes, Sister; but I begin to suspect that the right sort of stuff and nonsense is not unremunerative. I may be wrong, but I shall afford my notion a testing."

"And after what shiftless idiocy will you be chasing now, to neglect your work?"

"Why, as always, Sister, I must follow my own thinking and my own desire," says Manuel, lordlily, "and both of these are for a flight above pigs."

Thereafter Manuel kissed Math, and, again without taking leave of Suskind in the twilight, or of anyone else, he set forth for the far land of Provence.

VII

The Crown of Wisdom

❈❈❈❈❈❈❈❈❈❈❈❈

So DID IT come about that as King Helmas rode a-hunting in Nevet under the Hunter's Moon he came upon a gigantic and florid young fellow, who was very decently clad in black, and had a queer droop to his left eye, and who appeared to be wandering at adventure in the autumn woods: and the King remembered what had been foretold.

Says King Helmas to Manuel the swineherd, "What is that I see in your pocket wrapped in red silk?"

"It is a feather, King, wrapped in a bit of my sister's best petticoat."

"Now, glory be to your dark magics, friend, and at what price will you sell me that feather?"

"But a feather is no use to anybody, King, for, as you see, it is a quite ordinary feather?"

"Come, come!" the King says, shrewdly, "do people anywhere wrap ordinary feathers in red silk? Friend, do not think to deceive King Helmas of Albania, or it will be worse for you. I perfectly recognize that shining white feather as the feather which was moulted in this forest by the Zhar-Ptitza Bird, in the old time before my grandfathers came into this country. For it was foretold that such a young sorcerer as

46

you would bring to me, who have long been the silliest King that ever reigned over the Peohtes, this feather which confers upon its owner perfect wisdom: and for you to dispute the prophecy would be blasphemous."

"I do not dispute your silliness, King Helmas, nor do I dispute anybody's prophecies in a world wherein nothing is certain."

"One thing at least is certain," remarked King Helmas, frowning uglily, "and it is that among the Peohtes all persons who dispute our prophecies are burned at the stake."

Manuel shivered slightly, and said: "It seems to me a quite ordinary feather: but your prophets—most deservedly, no doubt,—are in higher repute for wisdom than I am, and burning is a discomfortable death. So I recall what a madman told me, and, since you are assured that this is the Zhar-Ptitza's feather, I will sell it to you for ten sequins."

King Helmas shook a disapproving face. "That will not do at all, and your price is out of reason, because it was foretold that for this feather you would ask ten thousand sequins."

"Well, I am particularly desirous not to appear irreligious now that I have become a young sorcerer. So you may have the feather at your own price, rather than let the prophecies remain unfulfilled."

Then Manuel rode pillion with a king who was unwilling to let Manuel out of his sight, and they went thus to the castle called Brunbelois. They came to two doors with pointed arches, set side by side, the smaller being for foot passengers, and the other for horsemen. Above was an equestrian statue in a niche, and a great painted window with traceries of hearts and thistles.

47

They entered the larger door, and that afternoon twelve heralds, in bright red tabards that were embroidered with golden thistles, rode out of this door, to proclaim the fulfilment of the prophecy as to the Zhar-Ptitza's feather, and that afternoon the priests of the Peohtes gave thanks in all their curious underground temples. The common people, who had for the last score of years taken shame to themselves for living under such a foolish king, embraced one another, and danced, and sang patriotic songs at every street-corner: the Lower Council met, and voted that, out of deference of his majesty, All Fools' Day should be stricken from the calendar: and Queen Pressina (one of the water folk) declared there were two ways of looking at everything, the while that she burned a quantity of private papers. Then at night were fireworks, the King made a speech, and to Manuel was delivered in wheel-barrows the sum of ten thousand sequins.

Thereafter Manuel abode for a month at the court of King Helmas, noting whatever to this side and to that side seemed most notable. Manuel was well liked by the nobility, and when the barons and the fine ladies assembled in the evening for pavanes and branles and pazzamenos nobody danced more statelily than Messire Manuel. He had a quiet way with the ladies, and with the barons a way of simplicity which was vastly admired in a sorcerer so potent that his magic had secured the long sought Zhar-Ptitza's feather. "But the most learned," as King Helmas justly said, "are always the most modest."

Helmas now wore the feather from the wing of the miller's goose affixed to the front of Helmas' second best crown, because that was the one he used to give judgments in. And when it was noised abroad that

King Helmas had the Zhar-Ptitza's feather, the Peohtes came gladly to be judged, and the neighboring kings began to submit to him their more difficult cases, and all his judgings were received with reverence, because everybody knew that King Helmas' wisdom was now infallible, and that to criticize his verdict as to anything was merely to expose your own stupidity.

And now that doubt of himself had gone out of his mind, Helmas lived untroubled, and his digestion improved, and his loving-kindness was infinite, because he could not be angry with the pitiable creatures haled before him, when he considered how little able they were to distinguish between wisdom and unwisdom where Helmas was omniscient: and all his doings were merciful and just, and his people praised him. Even the Queen conceded that, once you were accustomed to his ways, and exercised some firmness about being made a doormat of, and had it understood once for all that meals could not be kept waiting for him, she supposed there might be women worse off.

And Manuel got clay and modeled the figure of a young man which had the features and the wise look of King Helmas.

"I can see the resemblance," the King said, "but it does not half do me justice, and, besides, why have you made a young whipper-snapper of me, and mixed up my appearance with your appearance?"

"I do not know," said Manuel, "but I suppose it is because of a geas which is upon me to make myself a splendid and admirable young man in every respect, and not an old man."

"And does the sculpture satisfy you?" asks the King, smiling wisely.

"No, I like this figure well enough, now it is done,

but it is not, I somehow know, the figure I desire to make. No, I must follow after my own thinking and my own desire, and wisdom is not requisite to me."

"You artists!" said the King, as people always say that. "Now I would consider that, for all the might of your sorceries, wisdom is rather clamantly requisite to you, Messire Manuel, who inform me you must soon be riding hence to find elsewhere the needful look for your figure. For thus to be riding about this world of men, in search of a shade of expression, and without even being certain of what look you are looking for, does not appear to me to be good sense."

But young Manuel replied sturdily:

"I ride to encounter what life has in store for me, who am made certain of this at least, that all high harvests which life withholds for me spring from a seed which I sow—and reap. For my geas is potent, and, late or soon, I serve my geas, and take my doom as the pay well-earned that is given as pay to me, for the figure I make in this world of men.

"This figure, foreseen and yet hidden away from me, glimpsed from afar in the light of a dream,—will I love it, once more, or will loathing awake in me after its visage is plainlier seen? No matter: as fate says, so say I, who serve my geas, and gain in time such payment, at worst, as is honestly due to me, for the figure I make in this world of men.

"To its shaping I consecrate youth that is strong in me, ardently yielding youth's last least gift, who know that all grace which the gods have allotted me avails me in naught if it fails me in this. For all that a man has, that must I bring to the image I shape, that my making may live when time unmakes me and death dissevers me from the figure I make in this world of men."

To this the King rather drily replied: "There is something in what you say. But that something is, I can assure you, not wisdom."

So everyone was satisfied in Albania except Manuel, who declared that he was pleased but not contented by the image he had made in the likeness of King Helmas.

"Besides," they told him, "you look as though your mind were troubling you about something."

"In fact, I am puzzled to see a foolish person made wise in all his deeds and speeches by this wisdom being expected of him."

"But that is a cause for rejoicing, and for applauding the might of your sorceries, Messire Manuel, whereas you are plainly thinking of vexatious matters."

Manuel replied, "I think that it is not right to rob anybody of anything, and I reflect that wisdom weighs exactly the weight of a feather."

Then Manuel went into King Helmas' chickenyard, and caught a goose, and plucked from its wing a feather. Manuel went glitteringly now, in brocaded hose, and with gold spurs on his heels: the figure which he had made in the likeness of King Helmas was packed in an expensive knapsack of ornamented leather, and tall shining Manuel rode on a tall dappled horse when he departed southward, for Manuel nowadays had money to spare.

VIII

The Halo of Holiness
❖❖❖❖❖❖❖❖❖❖❖❖

NOW MANUEL TAKES SHIP across the fretful Bay of
Biscay, traveling always toward Provence and Alianora, whom people called the Unattainable Princess.
Oriander the Swimmer followed this ship, they say,
but he attempted to do Manuel no hurt, at least not
for that turn.

So Manuel of the high head comes into the country
of wicked King Ferdinand; and, toward All-Hallows,
they bring a stupendous florid young man to the
King in the torture-chamber. King Ferdinand was not
idle at the moment, and he looked up good-tem-
peredly enough from his employment: but almost instantly his merry face was overcast.

"Dear me!" says Ferdinand, as he dropped his white
hot pincers sizzlingly into a jar of water, "and I had
hoped you would not be bothering me for a good ten
years!"

"Now if I bother you at all it is against my will,"
declared Manuel, very politely, "nor do I willingly in-
trude upon you here, for, without criticizing anybody's domestic arrangements, there are one or two
things that I do not fancy the looks of in this torture-chamber."

"That is as it may be. In the mean time, what is that I see in your pocket wrapped in red silk?"

"It is a feather, King, wrapped in a bit of my sister's best petticoat."

Then Ferdinand sighed, and he arose from his interesting experiments with what was left of the Marquess de Henestrosa, to whom the King had taken a sudden dislike that morning.

"Tut, tut!" said Ferdinand: "yet, after all, I have had a brave time of it, with my enormities and my iniquities, and it is not as though there were nothing to look back on! So at what price will you sell me that feather?"

"But surely a feather is no use to anybody, King, for does it not seem to you a quite ordinary feather?"

"Come!" says King Ferdinand, as he washed his hands, "do people anywhere wrap ordinary feathers in red silk? You squinting rascal, do not think to swindle me out of eternal bliss by any such foolish talk! I perfectly recognize that feather as the feather which Milcah plucked from the left pinion of the Archangel Oriphiel when the sons of God were on more intricate and scandalous terms with the daughters of men than are permitted nowadays."

"Well, sir," replied Manuel, "you may be right in a world wherein nothing is certain. At all events, I have deduced, from one to two things in this torture-chamber, that it is better not to argue with King Ferdinand."

"How can I help being right, when it was foretold long ago that such a divine emissary as you would bring this very holy relic to turn me from my sins and make a saint of me?" says Ferdinand, peevishly.

"It appears to me a quite ordinary feather, King: but I recall what a madman told me, and I do not dispute that your prophets are wiser than I, for I have been a divine emissary for only a short while."

"Do you name your price for this feather, then!"

"I think it would be more respectful, sir, to refer you to the prophets, for I find them generous and big-hearted creatures."

Ferdinand nodded his approval. "That is very piously spoken, because it was prophesied that this relic would be given me for no price at all by a great nobleman. So I must forthwith write out for you a count's commission, I suppose, and must write out your grants to fertile lands and a stout castle or two, and must date your title to these things from yesterday."

"Certainly," said Manuel, "it would not look well for you to be neglecting due respect to such a famous prophecy, with that bottle of ink at your elbow."

So King Ferdinand sent for the Count of Poictesme, and explained to him as between old friends how the matter stood, and that afternoon the high Count was confessed and decapitated. Poictesme being now a vacant fief, King Ferdinand ennobled Manuel, and made him Count of Poictesme.

It was true that all Poictesme was then held by the Northmen, under Duke Asmund, who denied King Ferdinand's authority with contempt, and defeated him in battle with annoying persistence: so that Manuel for the present acquired nothing but the sonorous title.

"Some terrible calamity, however," as King Ferdinand pointed out, "is sure to befall Asmund and his iniquitous followers before very long, so we need not bother about them."

"But how may I be certain of that, sir?" Manuel asked.

"Count, I am surprised at such scepticism! Is it not very explicitly stated in Holy Writ that though the wicked may flourish for a while they are presently felled like green bay-trees?"

"Yes, to be sure! So there is no doubt that your soldiers will soon conquer Duke Asmund."

"But I must not send any soldiers to fight against him, now that I am a saint, for that would not look well. It would have an irreligious appearance of prompting Heaven."

"Still, King, you are sending soldiers against the Moors—"

"Ah, but it is not your lands, Count, but my city of Ubeda, which the Moors are attacking, and to attack a saint, as you must undoubtedly understand, is a dangerous heresy which it is my duty to put down."

"Yes, to be sure! Well, well!" says Manuel, "at any rate, to be a count is something, and it is better to ward a fine name than a parcel of pigs, though it appears the pigs are the more nourishing."

In the mean while the King's heralds rode everywhither in fluted armor, to proclaim the fulfilment of the old prophecy as to the Archangel Oriphiel's feather. Never before was there such a hubbub in those parts, for the bells of all the churches sounded all day, and all the people ran about praying at the top of their voices, and forgiving their relatives, and kissing the girls, and blowing whistles and ringing cowbells, because the city now harbored a relic so holy that the vilest sinner had but to touch it to be purified of iniquity.

And that day King Ferdinand dismissed the evil companions with whom he had so long rioted in every manner of wickedness, and Ferdinand lived henceforward as became a saint. He builded two churches a year, and fared edifyingly on roots and herbs; he washed the feet of three indigent persons daily, and went in sackcloth; whenever he burned heretics he fetched and piled up the wood himself, so as to inconvenience nobody; and he made prioresses and abbesses of his more intimate and personal associates of yesterday, because he knew that people are made holy by contact with holiness, and that sainthood is retroactive.

Thereafter Count Manuel abode for a month at the court of King Ferdinand, noting whatever to this side and to that side seemed most notable. Manuel was generally liked by the elect, and in the evening when the court assembled for family-prayers nobody was more devout than the Count of Poictesme. He had a quiet way with the abbesses and prioresses, and with the anchorites and bishops a way of simplicity which was vastly admired in a divine emissary. "But the particular favor of Heaven," as King Ferdinand pointed out, "is always reserved for modest persons."

The feather from the wing of Helmas' goose King Ferdinand had caused to be affixed to the unassuming skullcap with a halo of gold wire which Ferdinand now wore in the place of a vainglorious earthly crown; so that perpetual contiguity with this relic might keep him in augmenting sanctity. And now that doubt of himself had gone out of his mind, Ferdinand lived untroubled, and his digestion improved on his light diet of roots and herbs, and his loving-kindness was infinite, because he could not now be angry with the pitiable creatures haled before him, when he considered what lengthy and ingenious torments awaited every one of them, either in hell or purgatory, while Ferdinand would be playing a gold harp in heaven.

So Ferdinand dealt tenderly and generously with all. Half of his subjects said that simply showed you: and the rest of them assented that indeed you might well say that, and they had often thought of it, and had wished that young people would take profit by considering such things more seriously.

And Manuel got clay and modeled a figure which had the features and the holy look of King Ferdinand.

"Yes, this young fellow you have made of mud is something like me," the King conceded, "although clay of course cannot do justice to the fine red cheeks and nose I used to have in the unregenerate days when I thought about such vanities, and, besides, it is rather more like you. Still, Count, the thing has feeling, it is wholesome, it is refreshingly free from these modern morbid considerations of anatomy, and it does you credit."

"No, King, I like this figure well enough, now that it is done, but it is not, I somehow know, the figure I desire to make. No, I must follow after my own thinking and my own desires, and I do not need holiness."

"You artists!" the King said. "But there is more than mud upon your mind."

"In fact, I am puzzled, King, to see you made a saint of by its being expected of you."

"But, Count, that ought to grieve nobody, so long as I do not complain, and it is of something graver you are thinking."

"I think, sir, that it is not right to rob anybody of anything, and I reflect that absolute righteousness is a fine feather in one's cap."

Then Manuel went into the chicken-yard behind the red-roofed palace of King Ferdinand, and caught a goose, and plucked from its wing a feather. Thereafter the florid young Count of Poictesme rode east, on a tall dappled horse, and a retinue of six lackeys in silver and black liveries came cantering after him, and the two foremost lackeys carried in knapsacks, marked with a gold coronet, the images which Dom Manuel had made. A third lackey carried Dom Manuel's shield, upon which were emblazoned the arms of Poictesme. The black shield displayed a silver stallion which was rampant in every member and was bridled with gold, but the ancient arms had been given a new motto.

"What means this Greek?" Dom Manuel had asked.

"*Mundus decipit*, Count," they told him, "is the old pious motto of Poictesme: it signifies that the affairs of this world are a vain fleeting show, and that terrestrial appearances are nowhere of any particular importance."

"Then your motto is green inexperience," said Manuel, "and for me to bear it would be black ingratitude."

So the writing had been changed in accordance with his instructions, and it now read *Mundus vult decipi.*

IX

The Feather of Love

❖❖❖❖❖❖❖❖❖❖❖❖❖

IN SUCH ESTATE IT was that Count Manuel came, on Christmas morning, just two days after Manuel was twenty-one, into Provence. This land, reputed sorcerous, in no way displayed to him any unusual features, though it was noticeable that the King's marmoreal palace was fenced with silver pikes whereon were set the embalmed heads of young men who had wooed the Princess Alianora unsuccessfully. Manuel's lackeys did not at first like the looks of these heads, and said they were unsuitable for Christmas decorations: but Dom Manuel explained that at this season of general merriment this palisade also was mirth-provoking because (the weather being such as was virtually unprecedented in these parts) a light snow had fallen during the night, so that each head seemed to wear a nightcap.

They bring Manuel to Raymond Bérenger, Count of Provence and King of Arles, who was holding the Christmas feast in his warm hall. Raymond sat on a fine throne of carved white ivory and gold, beneath a purple canopy. And beside him, upon just such another throne, not quite so high, sat Raymond's daughter, Alianora the Unattainable Princess, in a robe of watered silk which was of seven colors and was lined with the dark fur of barbiolets. In her crown were chrysolites and amethysts: it was a wonder to note how brightly they shone, but they were not so bright as Alianora's eyes.

She stared as Manuel of the high head came through the hall, wherein the barons were seated according to their degrees. She had, they say, four reasons for remembering the impudent, huge, squinting, yellow-haired young fellow whom she had encountered at the pool of Haranton. She blushed, and spoke with her father in the whistling and hissing language which the Apsarasas use among themselves: and her father laughed long and loud.

Says Raymond Bérenger: "Things might have fallen out much worse. Come tell me now, Count of Poictesme, what is that I see in your breast pocket wrapped in red silk?"

"It is a feather, King," replied Manuel, a little wearily, "wrapped in a bit of my sister's best petticoat."

"Ay, ay," says Raymond Bérenger, with a grin that was becoming even more benevolent, "and I need not ask what price you come expecting for that feather. None the less, you are an excellently spoken-of young wizard of noble condition, who have slain no doubt a reasonable number of giants and dragons, and who have certainly turned kings from folly and wickedness. For such fine rumors speed before the man who has fine deeds behind him that you do not come into my realm as a stranger: and, I repeat, things might have fallen out much worse."

"Now listen, all ye that hold Christmas here!" cried Manuel. "A while back I robbed this Princess of a feather, and the thought of it lay in my mind more heavy than a feather, because I had taken what did not belong to me. So a bond was on me, and I set out toward Provence to restore to her a feather. And such happenings befell me by the way that at Michaelmas I brought wisdom into one realm, and at All-Hallows I brought piety into another realm. Now what I may be bringing into this realm of yours at Heaven's most holy season, Heaven only knows. To the eye it may seem a quite ordinary feather. Yet life in the wide world, I find, is a queerer thing than ever any swineherd dreamed of in his wattled hut, and people everywhere are nourished by their beliefs, in a way that the meat of pigs can nourish nobody."

Raymond Bérenger said, with a wise nod: "I perceive what is in your heart, and I see likewise what is in your pocket. So why do you tell me what everybody knows? Everybody knows that the robe of the Apsarasas, which is the peculiar treasure of Provence, has been ruined by the loss of a feather, so that my daughter can no longer go abroad in the appearance of a swan, because the robe is not able to work any more wonders until that feather in your pocket has been sewed back into the robe with the old incantation."

"Now, but indeed does everybody know that!" says Manuel.

"—Everybody knows, too, that my daughter has pined away with fretting after her lost ways of outdoor exercise, and the healthful changes of air which she used to be having. And finally, everybody knows that, at my daughter's very sensible suggestion, I have offered my daughter's hand in marriage to him who would restore that feather, and death to every impudent young fellow who dared enter here without it, as my palace fence attests."

"Oh, oh!" says Manuel, smiling, "but seemingly it is

no wholesome adventure which has come to me unsought!"

"—So, as you tell me, you came into Provence: and,
as there is no need to tell me, I hope, who have still
two eyes in my head, you have achieved the adventure.
And why do you keep telling me about matters with
which I am as well acquainted as you are?"

"But, King of Arles, how do you know that this is
not an ordinary feather?"

"Count of Poictesme, do people anywhere—?"

"Oh, spare me that vile bit of worldly logic, sir, and
I will concede whatever you desire!"

"Then do you stop talking such nonsense, and do
you stop telling me about things that everybody
knows, and do you give my daughter her feather!"

Manuel ascends the white throne of Alianora.
"Queer things have befallen me," said Manuel, "but
nothing more strange than this can ever happen, than
that I should be standing here with you, and holding
this small hand in mine. You are not perhaps quite so
beautiful nor so clever as Niafer. Nevertheless, you are
the Unattainable Princess, whose loveliness recalled
me from vain grieving after Niafer, within a half-hour
of Niafer's loss. Yes, you are she whose beauty kindled a dream and a dissatisfaction in the heart of a
swineherd, to lead him forth into the wide world, and
through the puzzling ways of the wide world, and
into its high places: so that at the last the swineherd is
standing—a-glitter in satin and gold and in rich furs,
—here at the summit of a throne; and at the last the
hand of the Unattainable Princess is in his hand, and
in his heart is misery."

The Princess said, "I do not know anything about
this Niafer, who was probably no better than she

should have been, nor do I know of any conceivable reason for your being miserable."

"Why, is it not the truth," asks Manuel of Alianora, speaking not very steadily, "that you are to marry the man who restores the feather of which you were robbed at the pool of Haranton? and can marry none other?"

"It is the truth," she answered, in a small frightened lovely voice, "and I no longer grieve that it is the truth, and I think it a most impolite reason for your being miserable."

Manuel laughed without ardor. "See how we live and learn! I recall now the droll credulity of a lad who watched a shining feather burned, while he sat within arm's reach thinking about cabbage soup, because his grave elders assured him that a feather could never be of any use to anybody. And that, too, after he had seen what uses may be made of an old bridle or of a duck egg or of anything! Well, but all water that is past the dam must go its way, even though it be a flood of tears—"

Here Manuel gently shrugged broad shoulders. He took out of his pocket the feather he had plucked from the wing of Ferdinand's goose.

He said: "A feather I took from you in the red autumn woods, and a feather I now restore to you, my Princess, in this white palace of yours, not asking any reward, and not claiming to be remembered by you in the gray years to come, but striving to leave no obligation undischarged and no debt unpaid. And whether in this world wherein nothing is certain, one feather is better than another feather, I do not know. It well may come about that I must straightway take a foul doom from fair lips, and that presently my head will be drying on a silver pike. Even so, one never knows: and I have learned that it is well to put all doubt of oneself quite out of mind."

He gave her the feather he had plucked from the third goose, and the trumpets sounded as a token that the quest of Alianora's feather had been fulfilled, and all the courtiers shouted in honor of Count Manuel.

Alianora looked at what was in her hand, and saw it was a goose-feather, in nothing resembling the feather which, when she had fled in maidenly embarrassment from Manuel's over-friendly advances, she had plucked from the robe of the Apsarasas, and had dropped at Manuel's feet, in order that her father might be forced to proclaim this quest, and the winning of it might be predetermined.

Then Alianora looked at Manuel. Now before her the queer unequal eyes of this big young man were bright and steadfast as altar candles. His chin was well up, and it seemed to her that this fine young fellow expected her to declare the truth, when the truth would be his death-sentence. She had no patience with his nonsense.

Says Alianora, with that lovely tranquil smile of hers: "Count Manuel has fulfilled the quest. He has restored to me the feather from the robe of the Apsarasas. I recognize it perfectly."

"Why, to be sure," says Raymond Bérenger. "Still, do you get your needle and the recipe for the old incantation, and the robe too, and make it plain to all my barons that the power of the robe is returned to it, by flying about the hall a little in the appearance of a swan. For it is better to conduct these affairs in due order and without any suspicion of irregularity."

Now matters looked ticklish for Dom Manuel, since he and Alianora knew that the robe had been spoiled, and that the addition of any number of goose-feathers was not going to turn Alianora into a swan. Yet the boy's handsome and high-colored face stayed courteously attentive to the wishes of his host, and did not change.

But Alianora said indignantly: "My father, I am surprised at you! Have you no sense of decency at all? You ought to know it is not becoming for an engaged girl to be flying about Provence in the appearance of a swan, far less among a parcel of men who have been drinking all morning. It is the sort of thing that leads to a girl's being talked about."

"Now, that is true, my dear," said Raymond Bérenger, abashed, "and the sentiment does you credit. So perhaps I had better suggest something else—"

"Indeed, my father, I see exactly what you would be suggesting. And I believe you are right."

"I am not infallible, my dear: but still—"

"Yes, you are perfectly right: it is not well for any married woman to be known to possess any such robe. There is no telling, just as you say, what people would be whispering about her, nor what disgraceful tricks she would get the credit of playing on her husband."

"My daughter, I was only about to tell you—"

"Yes, and you put it quite unanswerably. For you, who have the name of being the wisest Count that ever reigned in Provence, and the shrewdest King that Arles has ever had, know perfectly well how people talk, and how eager people are to talk, and to place the very worst construction on everything: and you know, too, that husbands do not like such talk. Certainly I had not thought of these things, my father, but I believe that you are right."

Raymond Bérenger stroked his thick short beard,

and said: "Now truly, my daughter, whether or not I be wise and shrewd—though, as you say, of course there have been persons kind enough to consider—and in petitions too—However, be that as it may, and putting aside the fact that everybody likes to be appreciated, I must confess I can imagine no gift which would at this high season be more acceptable to any husband than the ashes of that robe."

"This is a saying," Alianora here declares, "well worthy of Raymond Bérenger: and I have often wondered at your striking way of putting things."

"That, too, is a gift," the King-Count said, with proper modesty, "which to some persons is given, and to others not: so I deserve no credit for it. But, as I was saying when you interrupted me, my dear, it is well for youth to have its fling, because (as I have often thought) we are young only once: and so I have not ever criticized your jauntings in far lands. But a husband is another pair of sandals. A husband does not like to have his wife flying about the tree tops and the tall lonely mountains and the low long marshes, with nobody to keep an eye on her, and that is the truth of it. So, were I in your place, and wise enough to listen to the old father who loves you, and who is wiser than you, my dear—why, now that you are about to marry, I repeat to you with all possible earnestness, my darling, I would destroy this feather and this robe in one red fire, if only Count Manuel will agree to it. For it is he who now has power over all your possessions, and not I."

"Count Manuel," says Alianora, with that lovely tranquil smile of hers, "you perceive that my father is insistent, and it is my duty to be guided by him. I do not deny that, upon my father's advice, I am asking you to let perish a strong magic which many persons would value above a woman's pleading. But I know now"—her eyes met his, and to any young man anywhere with a heart moving in him, that which Manuel could see in the bright frightened eyes of Alianora could not but be a joy well-nigh intolerable,—"but I know now that you, who are to be my husband, and who have brought wisdom into one kingdom, and piety into another, have brought love into the third kingdom: and I perceive that this third magic is a stronger and a nobler magic than that of the Apsarasas. And it seems to me that you and I would do well to dispense with anything which is second rate."

"I am of the opinion that you are a singularly intelligent young woman," says Manuel, "and I am of the belief that it is far too early for me to be crossing my wife's wishes, in a world wherein all men are nourished by their beliefs."

All being agreed, the Yule-log was stirred up into a blaze, which was duly fed with the goose-feather and the robe of the Apsarasas. Thereafter the trumpets sounded a fanfare, to proclaim that Raymond Bérenger's collops were cooked and peppered, his wine casks broached, and his puddings steaming. Then the former swineherd went in to share his Christmas dinner with the King-Count's daughter, Alianora, whom people everywhere had called the Unattainable Princess.

And they relate that while Alianora and Manuel sat cosily in the hood of the fireplace and cracked walnuts, and in the pauses of their talking noted how the snow was drifting by the windows, the ghost of Niafer went restlessly about green fields beneath an ever radiant sky in the paradise of the pagans. When the kindly great-browed warders asked her what it was she was seeking, the troubled spirit could not tell

them, for Niafer had tasted Lethe, and had forgotten
Dom Manuel. Only her love for him had not been
forgotten, because that love had become a part of her,
and so lived on as a blind longing and as a desire
which did not know its aim. And they relate also that
in Suskind's low red-pillared palace Suskind waited
with an old thought for company.

PART TWO

THE BOOK OF SPENDING

TO

LOUIS UNTERMEYER

Often *tymes herde Manuel tell of the fayrness of this Queene of* Furies *and* Gobblins *and* Hydræs, *insomuch that he was enamoured of hyr, though he neuer sawe hyr: then by this Connynge made he a Hole in the fyer, and went ouer to hyr, and when he had spoke with hyr, he shewed hyr his mynde.*

X

Alianora

✦✦✦✦✦✦✦✦✦✦✦✦✦

THEY of Poictesme narrate that after dinner King
Raymond sent messengers to his wife, who was
spending that Christmas with their daughter, Queen
Meregrett of France, to bid Dame Beatrice return as
soon as might be convenient, so that they might marry
off their daughter Alianora to the famous Count Manuel. They tell also how the holiday season passed with
every manner of festivity, and how Dom Manuel got
on splendidly with his Princess, and how it appeared
to onlookers that for both of them, even for the
vaguely condescending boy, love-making proved a very
marvelous and dear pursuit.

Dom Manuel confessed, in reply to jealous questionings, that he did not think Alianora quite so beautiful
nor so clever as Niafer had been, but this, as Manuel
pointed out, was hardly a matter which could be rem-
edied. At all events, the Princess was a fine-looking
and intelligent girl, as Dom Manuel freely conceded to
her: and the magic of the Apsarasas, in which she was
instructing him, Dom Manuel declared to be very interesting if you cared for that sort of thing.

The Princess humbly admitted, in reply, that of
course her magic did not compare with his, since hers

was powerful only over the bodies of men and beasts, whereas Dom Manuel's magic had so notably controlled the hearts and minds of kings. Still, as Alianora pointed out, she could blight corn and cattle, and raise tempests very handily, and, given time, could smite an enemy with almost any physical malady you selected. She could not kill outright, to be sure, but even so, these lesser mischiefs were not despicable accomplishments in a young girl. Anyhow, she said in peroration, it was atrocious to discourage her by laughing at the best she could do.

"Ah, but come now, my dear," says Manuel, "I was only teasing. I really think your work most promising. You have but to continue. Practise, that is the thing, they say, in all the arts."

"Yes, and with you to help me—"

"No, I have graver matters to attend to than devil-mongering," says Manuel, "and a bond to lift from myself before I can lay miseries on others."

For because of the geas that was on him to make a figure in the world, Dom Manuel had unpacked his two images, and after vexedly considering them, he had fallen again to modeling in clay, and had made a third image. This image also was in the likeness of a young man, but it had the fine proud features and the loving look of Alinora.

Manuel confessed to being fairly well pleased with this figure, but even so, he did not quite recognize in it the figure he desired to make, and therefore, he said, he deduced that love was not the thing which was essential to him.

Alianora did not like the image at all.

"To have made an image of me," she considered, "would have been a very pretty compliment. But when it comes to pulling about my features, as if they did not satisfy you, and mixing them up with your features, until you have made the appearance of a young man that looks like both of us, it is not a compliment. Instead, it is the next thing but one to egotism."

"Perhaps, now I think of it, I am an egotist. At all events, I am Manuel."

"Nor, dearest," says she, "is it quite befitting that you, who are now betrothed to a princess, and who are going to be Lord of Provence and King of Arles, as soon as I can get rid of Father, should be always messing with wet mud."

"I know that very well," Manuel replied, "but, none the less, a geas is on me to honor my mother's wishes, and to make an admirable and significant figure in the world. Apart from that, though, Alianora, I repeat to you, this scheme of yours, about poisoning your father as soon as we are married, appears to me for various reasons ill-advised. I am in no haste to be King of Arles, and, in fact, I am not sure that I wish to be king at all, because my geas is more important."

"Sweetheart, I love you very much, but my love does not blind me to the fact that, no matter what your talents at sorcery, you are in everyday matters a hopelessly unpractical person. Do you leave this affair to me, and I will manage it with every regard to appearances."

"Ah, and does one have to preserve appearances even in such matters as parricide?"

"But certainly it looks much better for Father to be supposed to die of indigestion. People would be suspecting all sorts of evil of the poor dear if it were known that his own daughter could not put up with him. In any event, sweetheart, I am resolved that, since

73

very luckily Father has no sons, you shall be King of Arles before this new year is out."

"No, I am Manuel: and it means more to me to be Manuel than to be King of Arles, and Count of Provence, and seneschal of Aix and Brignoles and Grasse and Massilia and Draguignan and so on."

"Oh, you are breaking my heart with this neglect of your true interests! And it is all the doing of these three vile images, which you value more than the old throne of Boson and Rothbold, and oceans more than you do me!"

"Come, I did not say that."

"Yes, and you think, too, a deal more about that dead heathen servant girl than you do about me, who am a princess and the heir to a kingdom."

Manuel looked at Alianora for a considerable while, before speaking. "My dear, you are, as I have always told you, an unusually fine looking and intelligent girl. And yes, you are a princess, of course, though you are no longer the Unattainable Princess: that makes a difference certainly—But, over and above all this, there was never anybody like Niafer, and it would be nonsense to pretend otherwise."

The Princess said: "I wonder at myself. You are schooled in strange sorceries unknown to the Apsarasas, there is no questioning that, after the miracles you wrought with Helmas and Ferdinand: even so, I too have a neat hand at magic, and it is not right for you to be treating me as though I were the dirt under your feet. And I endure it! It is that which puzzles me, it makes me wonder at myself, and my sole comfort is that, at any rate, this wonderful Niafer of yours is dead and done with."

Manuel sighed. "Yes, Niafer is dead, and these images also are dead things, and both these facts continually trouble me. Nothing can be done about Niafer, I suppose, but if only I could give some animation to these images I think the geas upon me would be satisfied."

"Such a desire is blasphemous, Manuel, for the Eternal Father did no more than that with His primal sculptures in Eden."

Dom Manuel blinked his vivid blue eyes as if in consideration. "Well, but," he said, gravely, "but if I am a child of God it is only natural, I think, that I should inherit the tastes and habits of my Father. No, it is not blasphemous, I think, to desire to make an animated and lively figure, somewhat more admirable and significant than that of the average man. No, I think not. Anyhow, blasphemous or not, that is my need, and I must follow after my own thinking and my own desire."

"If that desire were satisfied," asks Alianora, rather queerly, "would you be content to settle down to some such rational method of living as becomes a reputable sorcerer and king?"

"I think so, for a king has no master, and he is at liberty to travel everywhither, and to see the ends of this world and judge them. Yes, I think so, in a world wherein nothing is certain."

"If I but half way believed that, I would endeavor to obtain Schamir."

"And what in the devil is this Schamir?"

"A slip of the tongue," replied Alianora, smiling. "No, I shall have nothing to do with your idiotic mud figures, and I shall tell you nothing further."

"Come now, pettikins!" says Manuel. And he began coaxing the Princess of Provence with just such cajoleries as the big handsome boy had formerly exercised against the peasant girls of Rathgor.

"Schamir," said Alianora, at last, "is set in a signet-ring which is very well known in the country on the other side of the fire. Schamir has the appearance of a black pebble; and if, after performing the proper ceremonies, you were to touch one of these figures with it the figure would become animated."

"Well, but," says Manuel, "the difficulty is that if I attempt to pass through the fire in order to reach the country behind it, I shall be burned to a cinder, and so I have no way of obtaining this talisman."

"In order to obtain it," Alianora told him, "one must hard-boil an egg from the falcon's nest, then replace it in the nest, and secrete oneself near by with a cross-bow, under a red and white umbrella, until the mother bird, finding one of her eggs resists all her endeavors to infuse warmth into it, flies off, and plunges into the nearest fire, and returns with this ring in her beak. With Schamir she will touch the boiled egg, and so restore the egg to its former condition. At that moment she must be shot, and the ring must be secured, before the falcon can return the talisman to its owner. I mean, to its dreadful owner, who is"—here Alianora made an incomprehensible sign,—"who is Queen Freydis of Audela."

"Come," said Manuel, "what is the good of my knowing this in the dead of winter! It will be months before the falcons are nesting again."

"Manuel, Manuel, there is no understanding you! Do you not see how badly it looks for a grown man, and far more for a famed champion and a potent sorcerer, to be pouting and scowling and kicking your heels about like that, and having no patience at all?"

"Yes, I suppose it does look badly, but I am Manuel, and I follow—"

"Oh, spare me that," cried Alianora, "or else, no

76

matter how much I may love you, dearest, I shall box
your jaws!"

"None the less, what I was going to say is true,"
declared Manuel, "and if only you would believe it,
matters would go more smoothly between us."

XI

Magic of the Apsarasas
❖❖❖❖❖❖❖❖❖❖❖❖❖

Now THE TALE tells how, to humor Alianora, Count
Manuel applied himself to the magic of the Apsarasas.
He went with the Princess to a high secret place, and
Alianora, crying sweetly, in the famous old fashion,
"Torolix, Ciccabau, Tio, Tio, Torolililix!" performed
the proper incantations, and forthwith birds came
multitudinously from all quarters of the sky, in a de-
scending flood of color and flapping and whistling
and screeching.

The peacock screamed, "With what measure thou
judgest others, thou shalt thyself be judged."

Sang the nightingale, "Contentment is the greatest
happiness."

The turtle-dove called, "It were better for some
created things that they had never been created."

The peewit chirped, "He that hath no mercy for
others, shall find none for himself."

The stork said huskily, "The fashion of this world
passeth away."

And the wail of the eagle was, "Howsoever long
life may be, yet its inevitable term is death."

"Now that is virtually what I said," declared the

78

stork, "and you are a bold-faced and bald-headed plagiarist."

"And you," replied the eagle, clutching the stork's throat, "are a dead bird that will deliver no more babies."

But Dom Manuel tugged at the eagle's wing, and asked him if he really meant that to hold good before this Court of the Birds. And when the infuriated eagle opened his cruel beak, and held up one murderous claw, to make solemn oath that indeed he did mean it, and would show them too, the stork very intelligently flew away.

"I shall not ever forget your kindness, Count Manuel," cried the stork, "and do you remember that the customary three wishes are always yours for the asking."

"And I too am grateful," said the abashed eagle,— "yes, upon the whole, I am grateful, for if I had killed that long-legged pest it would have been in contempt of the court, and they would have set me to hatching red cockatrices. Still, his reproach was not unfounded, and I must think up a new cry."

So the eagle perched on a rock, and said tentatively, "There is such a thing as being too proud to fight." He shook his bald head disgustedly, and tried, "The only enduring peace is a peace without victory," but that did not seem to content him either. Afterward he cried out, "All persons who oppose me have pygmy minds," and "If everybody does not do exactly as I order, the heart of the world will be broken": and many other foolish things he repeated, and shook his head over, for none of these axioms pleased the eagle, and he no longer admired the pedagogue who had invented them.

So in his worried quest for a saying sufficiently orotund and meaningless to content his ethics, and to be hailed with convenience as a great moral principle, the eagle forgot all about Count Manuel: but the stork did not forget, because in the eyes of the stork the life of the stork is valuable.

The other birds uttered various such sentiments as have been recorded, and all these, they told Manuel, were accredited sorceries. The big yellow-haired boy did not dispute it, he rarely disputed anything: but the droop to that curious left eye of his was accentuated, and he admitted to Alianora that he wondered if such faint-hearted smug little truths were indeed the height of wisdom, outside of religion and public speaking. Then he asked which was the wisest of the birds, and they told him the Zhar-Ptitza, whom others called the Fire-Bird.

Manuel induced Alianora to summon the Zhar-Ptitza, who is the oldest and the most learned of all living creatures, although he has thus far learned nothing assuredly except that appearances have to be kept up. The Zhar-Ptitza came, crying wearily, "Fine feathers make fine birds." You heard him from afar.

The Zhar-Ptitza himself had every reason to get comfort out of this axiom, for his plumage was everywhere the most brilliant purple, except that his neck feathers were the color of new gold, and his tail was blue with somewhat longer red feathers intermingled. His throat was wattled gorgeously, and his head was tufted, and he seemed a trifle larger than the eagle. The Fire-Bird brought with him his nest of cassia and sprigs of incense, and this he put down upon the lichened rocks, and he sat in it while he talked with Manuel.

The frivolous question that Manuel raised as to his clay figures, the Zhar-Ptitza considered a very human

HE WAS DRYING OUT IN THE SUN

bit of nonsense: and the wise creature said he felt forced to point out that no intelligent bird would ever dream of making images.

"But, sir," said Manuel, "I do not wish to burden this world with any more lifeless images. Instead, I wish to make in this world an animated figure, very much as, they say, a god did once upon a time—"

"Come, you should not try to put too much responsibility upon Jahveh," protested the Zhar-Ptitza, tolerantly, "for Jahveh made only one man, and did not ever do it again. I remember the making of that first man very clearly, for I was created the morning before, with instructions to fly above the earth in the open firmament of heaven, so I saw the whole affair. Yes, Jahveh did create the first man on the sixth day. And I voiced no criticism. For of course after working continuously for nearly a whole week, and making so many really important things, no creative artist should be blamed for not being in his happiest vein on the sixth day."

"And did you happen to notice, sir," asks Manuel, hopefully, "by what method animation was given to Adam?"

"No, he was drying out in the sun when I first saw him, with Gabriel sitting at his feet, playing on a flageolet: and naturally I did not pay any particular attention to such foolishness."

"Well, well, I do not assert that the making of men is the highest form of art, yet, none the less, a geas is upon me to make myself a very splendid and admirable young man."

"But why should you be wasting your small portion of breath and strength? To what permanent use could one put a human being even if the creature were virtuous and handsome to look at? Ah, Manuel, you have not seen them pass, as I have seen them pass in swarms, with their wars and their reforms and their great causes, and leaving nothing but their bones behind them."

"Yes, yes, to you, at your age, who were old when Nineveh was planned, it must seem strange; and I do not know why my mother desired that I should make myself a splendid and admirable young man. But the geas is upon me."

The Zhar-Ptitza sighed. "Certainly these feminine whims are not easily explained. Yet your people have some way of making brand-new men and women of all kinds. I am sure of this, for otherwise the race would have been extinct a great while since at the rate they kill one another. And perhaps they do adhere to Jahveh's method, and make fresh human beings out of earth, for, now I think of it, I have seen the small, recently completed ones, who looked exactly like red clay."

"It is undeniable that babies do have something of that look," assented Manuel. "So then, at least, you think I may be working in the proper medium?"

"It seems plausible, because I am certain your people are not intelligent enough to lay eggs, nor could, of course, such an impatient race succeed in getting eggs hatched. At all events, they have undoubtedly contrived some method or other, and you might find out from the least foolish of them about that method."

"Who, then, is the least foolish of mankind?"

"Probably King Helmas of Albania, for it was prophesied by me a great while ago that he would become the wisest of men if ever he could come by one of my shining white feathers, and I hear it reported he has done so."

"Sir," said Manuel, dubiously, "I must tell you in confidence that the feather King Helmas has is not yours, but was plucked from the wing of an ordinary goose."

"Does that matter?" asked the Zhar-Ptitza. "I never prophesied, of course, that he actually would find one of my shining white feathers, because all my feathers are red and gold and purple."

"But how can there be any magic in a goose-feather?"

"There is this magic, that, possessing it, King Helmas has faith in, and has stopped bothering about, himself."

"Is not to bother about yourself the highest wisdom?"

"Oh, no! Oh, dear me, no! I merely said it is the highest of which man is capable."

"But the sages and philosophers, sir, that had such fame in the old time, and made the maxims for you birds! Why, did King Solomon, for example, rise no higher than that?"

"Yes, yes, to be sure!" said the Zhar-Ptitza, sighing again, "now that was a sad error. The poor fellow was endowed with, just as an experiment, considerable wisdom. And it caused him to perceive that a man attains to actual contentment only when he is drunk or when he is engaged in occupations not very decorously described. So Sulieman-ben-Daoud gave over all the rest of his time to riotous living and to co-educational enterprises. It was logic, but it led to a most expensive seraglio and to a very unbecoming appearance, and virtually wrecked the man's health. Yes, that was the upshot of one of you being endowed with actual wisdom, just as an experiment, to see what would come of it: so the experiment, of course, has never been repeated. But of living persons, I dare assert that you will find King Helmas appreciably freed from a thousand general delusions by his one delusion about himself."

"Very well, then," says Manuel. "I suspect a wilful paradox and a forced cynicism in much of what you have said, but I shall consult with King Helmas about human life and about the figure I have to make in the world."

So they bid each other farewell, and the Zhar-Ptitza picked up his nest of cassia and sprigs of incense, and flew away with it: and as he rose in the air the Zhar-Ptitza cried, "Fine feathers make fine birds."

"But that is not the true proverb, sir," Manuel called up toward the resplendent creature, "and such perversions too, they tell me, are a mark of would-be cleverness."

"So it may seem to you now, my lad, but time is a very transforming fairy. Therefore do you wait until you are older," the bird replied, from on high, "and then you will know better than to doubt my cry or to repeat it."

XII

Ice and Iron
❖❖❖❖❖❖❖❖❖❖❖❖❖❖

THEN CAME from oversea the Bishops of Ely and Lincoln, the prior of Hurle, and the Master of the Temple, asking that King Raymond send one of his daughters, with a suitable dowry, to be the King of England's wife. "Very willingly," says Raymond Bérenger; and told them they could have his third daughter Sancha, with a thousand marks.

"But, Father," said Alianora, "Sancha is nothing but a child. A fine queen she would make!"

"Still, my dear," replied King Raymond, "you are already bespoke."

"I was not thinking about myself. I was thinking about Sancha's true welfare."

"Of course you were, my dear, and everybody knows the sisterly love you have for her."

"The pert little mess is spoilt enough as it is, Heaven knows. And if things came to the pass that I had to stand up whenever Sancha came into the room, and to sit on a footstool while she lolled back in a chair the way Meregrett does, it would be the child's ruin."

Raymond Bérenger said: "Now certainly it will be hard on you to have two sisters that are queens, and with perhaps little Beatrice also marrying some king or another when her time comes, and you staying only a countess, who are the best-looking of the lot."

"My father, I see what you would be at!" cried Alianora, aghast. "You think it is my duty to overcome my private inclinations, and to marry the King of England for ruthless and urgent political reasons!"

"I only said, my darling—"

"—For you have seen at once that I owe this great sacrifice to the future welfare of our beloved Provence. You have noted, with that keenness which nothing escapes, that with the aid of your wisdom and advice I would know very well how to manage this high King that is the master of no pocket handkerchief place like Provence but of England and of Ireland too."

"Also, by rights, of Aquitaine and Anjou and Normandy, my precious. Still, I merely observed—"

"Oh, but believe me, I am not arguing with you, my dear father, for I know that you are much wiser than I," says Alianora, bravely wiping away big tears from her lovely eyes.

"Have it your own way, then," replied Raymond Bérenger, with outspread hands. "But what is to be done about you and Count Manuel here?"

The King looked toward the tapestry of Jephthah's sacrifice, beside which Manuel sat, just then re-altering the figure of the young man with the loving look of Alianora that Manuel had made because of the urgency of his geas, and could not seem to get exactly right.

"I am sure, Father, that Manuel also will be self-sacrificing and magnanimous and sensible about it."

"Ah, yes! but what is to happen afterward? For anyone can see that you and this squinting long-legged lad are fathoms deep in love with each other."

"I think that after I am married, Father, you or King Ferdinand or King Helmas can send Count Manuel into England on some embassy, and I am sure that he and I will always be true and dear friends without affording any handle to gossip."

"Oho!" King Raymond said, "I perceive your drift, and it is toward a harbor that is the King of England's affair, and not mine. My part is to go away now, so that you two may settle the details of that ambassadorship in which Dom Manuel is to be the vicar of so many kings."

Raymond Bérenger took up his sceptre and departed, and the Princess turned to where Manuel was pottering with the three images he had made in the likeness of Helmas and Ferdinand and Alianora. "You see, now, Manuel dearest, I am heart-broken, but for the realm's sake I must marry the King of England."

Manuel looked up from his work. "Yes, I heard. I am sorry, and I never understood politics, but I suppose it cannot be helped. So would you mind standing a little more to the left? You are in the light now, and that prevents my seeing clearly what I am doing here to this upper lip."

"And how can you be messing with that wet mud when my heart is breaking!"

"Because a geas is upon me to make these images. No, I am sure I do not know why my mother desired it. But everything which is fated must be endured, just as we must now endure the obligation that is upon you to marry the high King of England."

"My being married need not matter very much, after I am Queen, for people declare this King is a poor spindling creature, and, as I was saying, you can come presently into England."

Manuel looked at her for a moment or two. She colored. He, sitting at the feet of weeping Jephthah, smiled. "Well," said Manuel, "I will come into England when you send me a goose-feather. So the affair is arranged."

"Oh, you are all ice and iron!" she said, "and you care for nothing except your wet mud images, and I detest you!"

"My dearest," Manuel answered placidly, "the trouble is that each of us desires one particular thing over and above other things. Your desire is for power and a great name and for a king who will be at once your mouthpiece, your lackey and your lover. Now, candidly, I cannot spare the time to be any of these things, because my desire is different from your desire, but is equally strong. Also, it seems to me, as I become older, and see more of men and of men's ways, that most people have no especial desire but only preferences. In a world of such wishy-washy folk you and I cannot hope to escape being aspersed with comparisons to ice and iron, but it does not become us to be flinging these venerable similes in each other's faces."

She kept silence a while. She laughed uneasily. "I so often wonder about you, Manuel, as to whether inside the big, high-colored, squinting, solemn husk is living a very wise person or a very unmitigated fool."

"I perceive there is something else which we have in common, for I, too, often wonder about that."

"It is settled, then?"

"It is settled that, instead of ruling little Arles, you are to be Queen of England, and Lady of Ireland, and Duchess of Normandy and Aquitaine, and Countess of Anjou; that our token is to be a goose-feather; and that, I diffidently repeat, you are to get out of my

89

light and interfere no longer with the discharge of my geas."

"And what will you do?"

"I must, as always, follow after my own thinking—"

"If you complete the sentence I shall undoubtedly scream."

Manuel laughed good-humoredly. "I suppose I do say it rather often, but then it is true, and the great trouble between us, Alianora, is that you do not perceive its truth."

She said, "And I suppose you will now be stalking off to some woman or another for consolation?"

"No, the consolation I desire is not to be found in petticoats. No, first of all, I shall go to King Helmas. For my images stay obstinately lifeless, and there is something lacking to each of them, and none is the figure I desire to make in this world. Now I do not know what can be done about it, but the Zhar-Ptitza informs me that King Helmas, since all doubt of himself has been put out of mind, can aid me if any man can."

"Then we must say good-bye, though not for a long while, I hope."

"Yes," Manuel said, "this is good-bye, and to a part of my living it is an eternal good-bye."

Dom Manuel left his images where the old Hebrew captain appeared to regard them with violent dumb anguish, and Manuel took both of the girl's lovely little hands, and he stood thus for a while looking down at the Princess.

Said Manuel, very sadly:

"I cry the elegy of such notions as are possible to boys alone. 'Surely,' I said, 'the informing and all-perfect soul shines through and is revealed in this beautiful body.' So my worship began for you, whose violet eyes retain at all times their chill brittle shining, and do not soften, but have been to me always as those eyes which, they say, a goddess turns toward ruined lovers who cry the elegy of hope and contentment, with lips burned bloodless by the searing of passions which she, immortal, may neither feel nor comprehend. Even so do you, dear Alianora, who are not divine, look toward me, quite unmoved by anything except incurious wonder, the while that I cry my elegy.

"I, for love, and for the glamour of bright beguiling dreams that hover and delude and allure all lovers, could never until to-day behold clearly what person I was pestering with my notions. I, being blind, could not perceive your blindness which blindly strove to understand me, and which hungered for understanding, as I for love. Thus our kisses veiled, at most, the foiled endeavorings of flesh that willingly would enter into the soul's high places, but is not able. Now, the game being over, what is the issue and end of it time must attest. At least we should each sorrow a little for what we have lost in this gaming,—you for a lover, and I for love.

"No, but it is not love which lies here expiring, now we part friendlily at the deathbed of that emotion which yesterday we shared. This emotion also was not divine; and so might not outlive the gainless months wherein, like one fishing for pearls in a millpond, I have toiled to evoke from your heart more than Heaven placed in this heart, wherein lies no love. Now the crying is stilled that was the crying of loneliness to its unfound mate: already dust is gathering light and gray upon the unmoving lips. Therefore let us bury our dead, and having placed the body in the tomb, let us honestly inscribe above this fragile, flower-like perished emotion, 'Here lieth lust, not love.'"

Now Alianora pouted. "You use such very ugly words, sweetheart: and you are talking unreasonably, too, for I am sure I am just as sorry about it as you are—"

Manuel gave her that slow sleepy smile which was Manuel. "Just," he said,—"and it is that which humiliates. Yes, you and I are second-rate persons, Alianora, and we have found each other out. It is a pity. But we will always keep our secret from the rest of the world, and our secret will always be a bond between us."

He kissed the Princess, very tenderly, and so left her.

Then Manuel of the high head departed from Arles, with his lackeys and his images, riding in full estate, and displaying to the spring sunlight the rearing silver stallion upon his shield and the motto *Mundus vult decipi*. Alianora, watching from the castle window, wept copiously, because the poor Princess had the misfortune to be really in love with Dom Manuel. But there was no doing anything with his obstinacy and his incomprehensible notions, Alianora had found, and so she set about disposing of herself and of the future through more plastic means. Her methods were altered perforce, but her aim remained unchanged: and she still intended to get everything she desired (which included Manuel) as soon as she and the King of England had settled down to some sensible way of living.

It worried this young pretty girl to consult her mirror, and to foreknow that the King of England would probably be in love with her for months and months: but then, as she philosophically reflected, all women have to submit to being annoyed by the romanticism of men. So she dried her big bright eyes, and sent for dressmakers.

She ordered two robes each of five ells, the one to be of green and lined with either cendal or sarcenet, and the other to be of brunet stuff. She selected the cloth for a pair of purple sandals, and for four pairs of boots, to be embroidered in circles around the ankles, and she selected also nine very becoming chaplets made of gold filigree and clusters of precious stones. And so she managed to get through the morning, and to put Manuel out of mind, for that while, but not for long.

XIII

What Helmas Directed

❖❖❖❖❖❖❖❖❖❖❖❖

Now THE Count of Poictesme departs from Provence, with his lackeys carrying his images, and early in April he comes to Helmas the Deep-Minded. The wise King was then playing with his small daughter Mélusine (who later dethroned and imprisoned him), but he sent the child away with a kiss, and he attentively heard Dom Manuel through.

King Helmas looked at the images, prodded them with a shriveled forefinger, and cleared his throat; and then said nothing, because, after all, Dom Manuel was Count of Poictesme.

"What is needed?" said Manuel.

"They are not true to life," replied Helmas—"particularly this one which has the look of me."

"Yes, I know that: but who can give life to my images?"

King Helmas pushed back his second best crown, wherein was set the feather from the wing of the miller's goose, and he scratched his forehead. He said, "There is a power over all figures of earth and a queen whose will is neither to loose nor to bind." Helmas turned toward a thick book, wherein was magic

"Yes, *queen* is the same as *cwen*. Therefore Queen Freydis of Audela might help you."

"Yes, for it is she that owns Schamir. But the falcons are not nesting now, and how can I go to Freydis, that woman of strange deeds?"

"Oh, people nowadays no longer use falcons; and of course nobody can go to Freydis uninvited. Still, it can be managed that Freydis will come to you when the moon is void and powerless, and when this and that has been arranged."

Thereafter Helmas the Deep-Minded told Count Manuel what was requisite. "So you will need such and such things," says King Helmas, "but, above all, do not forget the ointment."

Count Manuel went alone into Poictesme, which was his fief if only he could get it. He came secretly to Upper Morven, that place of horrible fame. Near the ten-colored stone, whereon men had sacrificed to Vel-Tyno in time's youth, he built an enclosure of peeled willow wands, and spread butter upon them, and tied them with knots of yellow ribbons, as Helmas had directed. Manuel arranged all matters within the enclosure as Helmas had directed. There Manuel waited, on the last night in April, regarding the full moon.

In a while you saw the shadowings on the moon's radiancy begin to waver and move: later they passed from the moon's face like little clouds, and the moon was naked of markings. This was a token that the Moon-Children had gone to the well from which once a month they fetch water, and that for an hour the moon would be void and powerless. With this and that ceremony Count Manuel kindled such a fire upon the old altar of Vel-Tyno as Helmas had directed.

Manuel cried aloud: "Now be propitious, infernal, terrestrial and celestial Bombo! Lady of highways, patroness of crossroads, thou who bearest the light! Thou who dost labor always in obscurity, thou enemy of the day, thou friend and companion of darkness! Thou rejoicing in the barking of dogs and in shed blood, thus do I honor thee."

Manuel did as Helmas had directed, and for an instant the screamings were pitiable, but the fire ended these speedily.

Then Manuel cried, again: "O thou who wanderest amid shadows and over tombs, and dost tether even the strong sea! O whimsical sister of the blighting sun, and fickle mistress of old death! O Gorgo, Mormo, lady of a thousand forms and qualities! now view with a propitious eye my sacrifice!"

Thus Manuel spoke, and steadily the fire upon the altar grew larger and brighter as he nourished it repugnantly.

When the fire was the height of a warrior, and queer things were happening to this side and to that side, Count Manuel spoke the ordered words: and of a sudden the flames' colors were altered, so that green shimmerings showed in the fire, as though salt were burning there. Manuel waited. This greenness shifted and writhed and increased in the heart of the fire, and out of the fire oozed a green serpent, the body of which was well-nigh as thick as a man's body.

This portent came toward Count Manuel horribly. He, who was familiar with serpents, now grasped this monster's throat, and to the touch its scales were like very cold glass.

The great snake shifted so resistlessly that Manuel was forced back toward the fire and toward a doom more dreadful than burning: and the firelight was in the snake's contemptuous wise eyes. Manuel was of stalwart person, but his strength availed him nothing until he began to recite aloud, as Helmas had directed, the multiplication tables: Freydis could not withstand mathematics.

So when Manuel had come to two times eleven the tall fire guttered as though it bended under the passing of a strong wind: then the flames burned high, and Manuel could see that he was grasping the throat of a monstrous pig. He, who was familiar with pigs, could see that this was a black pig, caked with dried curds of the Milky Way; its flesh was chill to the touch, like dead flesh; and it had long tusks, which possessed life of their own, and groped and writhed toward Manuel like fat white worms.

Then Manuel said, as Helmas had directed: "Solomon's provision for one day was thirty measures of fine flour, and threescore measures of meal, ten fat oxen, and twenty oxen out of the pastures, and a hundred sheep, beside harts, and roebucks, and fallow deer, and fatted fowl. But Elijah the Tishbite was fed by ravens that brought him bread and flesh."

Again the tall flames guttered. Now Manuel was grasping a thick heatless slab of crystal, like a mirror, wherein he could see himself quite clearly. Just as he really was, he, who was not familiar with such mirrors, could see Count Manuel, housed in a little wet dirt with old inveterate stars adrift about him everywhither; and the spectacle was enough to frighten anybody.

So Manuel said: "The elephant is the largest of all animals, and in intelligence approaches the nearest to man. Its nostril is elongated, and answers to the purpose of a hand. Its toes are undivided, and it lives two

97

hundred years. Africa breeds elephants, but India produces the largest."

The mirror now had melted into a dark warm fluid which oozed between his fingers, dripping to the ground. But Manuel held tightly to what remained between his palms, and he felt, they say, that in the fluid was struggling something small and soft and living, as though he held a tiny minnow.

Said Manuel, "A straight line is the shortest distance between two points."

Of a sudden the fire became an ordinary fire, and the witches of Amneran screamed, and Morven wss emptied of sorcery, and Count Manuel was grasping the warm soft throat of a woman. Instantly he had her within the enclosure of peeled willow wands that had been spread with butter and tied with knots of yellow ribbon, because into such an enclosure the power and the dominion of Freydis could never enter.

All these things Manuel did precisely as King Helmas had directed.

XIV

They Duel on Morven

So BY THE LIGHT of the seven candles Dom Manuel
first saw Queen Freydis in her own shape, and in the
appearance which she wore in her own country.
What Manuel thought there was never any telling:
but every other man who saw Queen Freydis in this
appearance declared that instantly all his past life became a drugged prelude to the moment wherein he
stood face to face with Freydis, the high Queen of
Audela.

Freydis showed now as the most lovely of woman-
kind. She had black plaited hair, and folds of crimson
silk were over her white flesh, and over her shoulders
was a black cloak embroidered with little gold stars
and ink-horns, and she wore sandals of gilded bronze.
But in her face was such loveliness as may not be told.

Now Freydis went from one side of the place to
the other side, and saw the magics that protected the
enclosure. "Certainly, you have me fast," the high
Queen said. "What is it you want of me?"

Manuel showed her the three images which he had
made, set there arow. "I need your aid with these."

Queen Freydis looked at them, and Freydis smiled.

"These frozen abortions are painstakingly made. What more can anybody demand?"

Dom Manuel told her that he desired to make an animated and lively figure.

Whereupon she laughed, merrily and sweetly and scornfully, and replied that never would she give such aid.

"Very well, then," said Manuel, "I have ready the means to compel you." He showed this lovely woman the instruments of her torture. His handsome young face was very grave, as though already his heart were troubled. He thrust her hand into the cruel vise which was prepared. "Now, sorceress, whom all men dread save me, you shall tell me the Tuyla incantation as the reward of my endeavors, or else a little by a little I shall destroy the hand that has wrought so many mischiefs."

Freydis in the light of the seven candles showed pale as milk. She said: "I am frail and human in this place, and have no power beyond the power of every woman, and no strength at all. Nevertheless, I will tell you nothing."

Manuel set his hand to the lever, ready to loose destruction. "To tell me what I desire you to tell me will do you no hurt—"

"No," replied Freydis: "but I am not going to take orders from you or any man breathing."

"—And for defying me you will suffer very terribly—"

"Yes," replied Freydis. "And much you will care!" she said, reproachfully.

"—Therefore I think that you are acting foolishly."

Freydis said: "You make a human woman of me, and then expect me to act upon reason. It is you who are behaving foolishly."

Count Manuel meditated, for this beyond doubt sounded sensible. From the look of his handsome young face, his heart was now exceedingly troubled. Queen Freydis breathed more freely, and began to smile, with the wisdom of women, which is not super-human, but is ruthless.

"The hand would be quite ruined, too," said Manuel, looking at it more carefully. Upon the middle finger was a copper ring, in which was set a largish black stone: this was Schamir. But Manuel looked only at the hand.

He touched it. "Your hand, Queen Freydis, whatever mischief it may have executed, is soft as velvet. It is colored like rose-petals, but it smells more sweet than they. No, certainly, my images are not worth the ruining of such a hand."

Then Manuel released her, sighing. "My geas must stay upon me, and my images must wait," says Manuel.

"Why, do you really like my hands?" asked Freydis, regarding them critically.

Manuel said: "Ah, fair sweet enemy, do not mock at me! All is in readiness to compel you to do my will. Had you preserved some ugly shape I would have conquered you. But against the shape which you now wear I cannot contend. Dragons and warlocks and chimæras and such nameless monsters as I perceive to be crowding about this enclosure of buttered willow wands I do not fear at all, but I cannot fight against the appearance which you now wear."

"Why, do you really like my natural appearance?" Freydis said, incredibly surprised. "It is a comfort, of course, to slip into it occasionally, but I had never really thought much about it one way or the other—"

She went to the great mirror which had been set

ready as Helmas directed. "I never liked my hair in these severe big plaits, either. As for those monsters yonder, they are my people, who are coming out of the fire to rescue me, in some of the forgotten shapes, as spoorns and trows and calcars, and other terrors of antiquity. But they cannot get into this enclosure of buttered willow wands, poor dears, on account of your magickings. How foolish they look—do they not?—leering and capering and gnashing their teeth, with no superstitious persons anywhere to pay attention to them."

The Queen paused: she coughed delicately. "But you were talking some nonsense or other about my natural appearance not being bad looking. Now most men prefer blondes, and, besides, you are not really listening to me, and that is not polite."

"It is so difficult to talk collectedly," said Manuel, "with your appalling servitors leering and capering and gnashing double sets of teeth all over Upper Morven—"

She saw the justice of this. She went now to that doorway through which, unless a man lifted her over the threshold, she might not pass, on account of the tonthecs and the spaks and the horseshoes.

She cried, in a high sweet voice: "A penny, a penny, twopence, a penny and a half, and a half-penny! Now do you go away, all of you, for the wisdom of Helmas is too strong for us. There is no way for you to get into, nor for me to get out of, this place of buttered willow wands, until I have deluded and circumvented this pestiferous, squinting young mortal. Go down into Bellegarde and spill the blood of Northmen, or raise a hailstorm, or amuse yourselves in one way or another way. Anyhow, do you take no thought for me, who am for the while a human woman: for my adversary is a mortal man, and in that duel never yet has the man conquered."

She turned to Manuel. She said:

"The land of Audela is my kingdom. But you embraced my penalties, you have made a human woman of me. So do I tread with wraiths, for my lost realm alone is real. Here all is but a restless contention of shadows which pass presently; here all that is visible and all the colors known to men are shadows dimming the true colors; here time and death, the darkest shadows known to men, delude you with false seemings: for all such things as men hold incontestable, because they are apparent to sight and sense, are a weariful drifting of fogs that veil the world which is no longer mine. So in this twilit world of yours do we of Audela appear to be but men and women."

"I would that such women appeared more often," said Manuel.

"The land of Audela is my kingdom, where I am Queen of all that lies behind this veil of human sight and sense. This veil may not ever be lifted; but very often the veil is pierced, and noting the broken place, men call it fire. Through these torn places men may glimpse the world that is real: and this glimpse dazzles their dimmed eyes and weakling forces, and this glimpse mocks at their lean might. Through these rent places, when the opening is made large enough, a few men here and there, not quite so witless as their fellows, know how to summon us of Audela when for an hour the moon is void and powerless: we come for an old reason: and we come as men and women."

"Ah, but you do not speak with the voices of men and women," Manuel replied, "for your voice is music."

"The land of Audela is my kingdom, and very

often, just for the sport's sake, do I and my servitors go secretly among you. As human beings we blunder about your darkened shadow world, bound by the laws of sight and sense, but keeping always in our hearts the secrets of Audela and the secret of our manner of returning thither. Sometimes, too, for the sport's sake, we imprison in earthen figures a spark of the true life of Audela: and then you little persons, that have no authentic life, but only the flickering of a vexed shadow to sustain you in brief fretfulness, say it is very pretty; and you negligently applaud us as the most trivial of men and women."

"No; we applaud you as the most beautiful," says Manuel.

"Come now, Count Manuel, and do you have done with your silly flatterings, which will never wheedle anything out of me! So you have trapped Queen Freydis in mortal flesh. Therefore I must abide in the body of a human woman, and be subject to your whims, and to your beautiful big muscles, you think, until I lend a spark of Audela's true life to your ridiculous images. But I will show you better, for I will never give in to you nor to any man breathing."

In silence Count Manuel regarded the delightful shaping and the clear burning colors of this woman's face. He said, as if in sadness: "The images no longer matter. It is better to leave them as they are."

"That is very foolish talk," Queen Freydis answered, promptly, "for they need my aid if ever any images did. Not that, however, I intend to touch them."

"Indeed, I forbid you to touch them, fair enemy. For were the images made as animated and lively as I wish them to be, I would be looking at them always, and not caring for any woman: and no woman anywhere would have the power to move me as your beauty moves me now, and I would not be valuing you the worth of an old onion."

"That is not the truth," says Freydis, angrily, "for the man who is satisfied with the figure he has made is as great a fool about women as any other man. And who are you to be forbidding me anything?"

"I would have you remember," said Manuel, very masterfully, "that they are my images, to do with as I wish. Also I would have you remember that, whatever you may pretend to be in Audela, here I am stronger than you."

Now the proud woman laughed. Defiantly she touched the nearest image, with formal ancient gestures, and you could see the black stone Schamir taking on the colors of an opal. Under her touch the clay image which had the look of Alianora shivered, and drew sobbing breath. The image rose, a living creature that was far more beautiful than human kind, and it regarded Manuel scornfully. Then it passed limping from the enclosure: and Manuel sighed.

"That is a strong magic," said Manuel: "and this is almost exactly the admirable and significant figure that I desired to make in the world. But, as I now perceive too late, I fashioned the legs of this figure unevenly, and the joy I have in its life is less than the shame that I take from its limping."

"Such magic is a trifle," Freydis replied, "although it is the only magic I can perform in an enclosure of buttered willow wands. Now, then, you see for yourself that I am not going to take orders from you. So the figure you have made, will you or nil you, must limp about in all men's sight, for not more than a few centuries, to be sure, but long enough to prove that I am not going to be dictated to."

105

"I do not greatly care, O fairest and most shrewd of enemies. A half-hour since, it seemed to me an important matter to wrest from you this secret of giving life to images. Now I have seen the miracle; I know that for the man who has your favor it is possible to become as a god, creating life, and creating lovelier living beings than any god creates, and beings which live longer, too: and even so, it is not of these things that I am really thinking, but only of your eyes."

"Why, do you like my eyes!" says Freydis,—"you, who if once you could make living images would never be caring about any woman any more?"

But Manuel told her wherein her eyes were different from the eyes of any other person, and more dangerous, and she listened, willingly enough, for Freydis was not a human woman. Thereafter it appeared that a grieving and a great trouble of mind had come upon Manuel because of the loveliness of Freydis, for he made this complaint:

"There is much loss in the world, where men war ceaselessly with sorrow, and time like a strong thief strips all men of all they prize. Yet when the emperor is beaten in battle and his broad lands are lost, he, shrugging, says, 'In the next battle I may conquer.' And when the bearded merchant's ship is lost at sea, he says, 'The next voyage, belike, will be prosperous.' Even when the life of an old beggar departs from him in a ditch, he says, 'I trust to be to-morrow a glad young seraph in paradise.' Thus hope serves as a cordial for every hurt: but for him who had beheld the loveliness of Freydis there is no hope at all.

"For, in comparison with that alien clear beauty, there is no beauty in this world. He that has beheld the loveliness of Freydis must go henceforward as a hungry person, because of troubling memories: and his fellows deride him enviously. All the world is fretted by his folly, knowing that his faith in the world's might is no longer firm-set, and that he aspires to what is beyond the world's giving. In his heart he belittles the strong stupid lords of earth; and they, being strong, plan vengeance, the while that in a corner he makes images to commemorate what is lost: and so for him who has beheld the loveliness of Freydis there is no hope at all.

"He that has willed to look upon Queen Freydis does not dread to consort with serpents nor with swine; he faces the mirror wherein a man beholds himself without self-deceiving; he views the blood that drips from his soiled hands, and knows that this, too, was needed: yet these endurings purchase but one hour. The hour passes, and therewith passes also Freydis, the high Queen. Only the memory of her hour remains, like a cruel gadfly, for which the crazed beholder of Queen Freydis must build a lodging in his images, madly endeavoring to commingle memories with wet mud: and so for him who has beheld the loveliness of Freydis there is no hope at all."

Freydis heard him through, considerately. "But I wonder to how many other women you have talked such nonsense about beauty and despair and eternity," said Freydis, "and they very probably liking to hear it, the poor fools! And I wonder how you can expect me to believe you, when you pretend to think me all these fine things, and still keep me penned in this enclosure like an old vicious cow."

"No, that is not the way it is any longer. For now the figure that I have made in the world, and all else that is in the world, and all that is anywhere without this enclosure of buttered willow wands, mean nothing to me, and there is no meaning in anything save in the loveliness of Freydis."

Dom Manuel went to the door of the enclosure, then to the windows, sweeping away the gilded tonthecs and the shining spaks, and removing from the copper nails the horseshoes that had been cast by Mohammed's mare and Hrimfaxi and Balaam's ass and Pegasus. "You were within my power. Now I destroy that power, and therewith myself. Now is the place unguarded, and all your servitors are free to enter, and all your terrors are untrammeled, to be loosed against me, who have no longer anything to dread. For I love you with such mortal love as values nothing else beside its desire, and you care nothing for me."

After a little while of looking she sighed, and said uneasily: "It is the foolish deed of a true lover. And, really, I do like you, rather. But, Manuel, I do not know what to do next! Never at any time has this thing happened before, so that all my garnered wisdom is of no use whatever. Nobody anywhere has ever dared to snap his fingers at the fell power of Freydis as you are doing, far less has anybody ever dared to be making eyes at her. Besides, I do not wish to consume you with lightnings, and to smite you with insanity appears so unnecessary."

"I love you," Manuel said, "and your heart is hard, and your beauty is beyond the thinking of man, and your will is neither to loose nor to bind. In a predicament so unexampled, how can it at all matter to me whatever you may elect to do?"

"Then certainly I shall not waste any of my fine terrors on you!" said Freydis, with a vexed tossing of her head. "Nor have I any more time to waste upon you either, for presently the Moon-Children will be coming back to their places: and before the hour is out wherein the moon stays void and powerless I must return to my own kingdom, whither you may not follow, to provoke me with any more of your nonsense. And then you will be properly sorry, I dare say, for you will be remembering me always, and there will be only human women to divert you, and they are poor creatures."

Freydis went again to the mirror, and she meditated there. "Yes, you will be remembering me with my hair in these awful plaits, and that is a pity, but still you will remember me always. And when you make images they will be images of me. No, but I cannot have you making any more outrageous parodies like astonished corpses, and people everywhere laughing at Queen Freydis!"

She took up the magical pen, laid ready as Helmas had directed, and she wrote with this gryphon's feather. "So here is the recipe for the Tuyla incantation with which to give life to your images. It may comfort you a little to perform that silly magic. It, anyhow, will prevent such good-for-nothing minxes as may have no more intelligence than to take you seriously, from putting on too many airs and graces around the images which you will make of me with my hair done so very unbecomingly."

"Nothing can ever comfort me, fair enemy, when you have gone away," said Manuel.

But he took the parchment.

XV

Bandages for the Victor

❖❖❖❖❖❖❖❖❖❖❖

THEY CAME out of the enclosure, to the old altar of
Vel-Tyno, while the moon was still void and powerless. The servitors of Freydis were thronging swiftly
toward Upper Morven, after a pleasant hour of raven-
ing and ramping about Poictesme. As spoorns and
trows and calcars and as other long forgotten shapes
they came, without any noise, so that Upper Morven
was like the disordered mind of a wretch that is dying
in fever: and to this side and to that side the witches
of Amneran sat nodding in approval of what they
saw.

Thus, one by one, the forgotten shapes came to the
fire, and cried, "A penny, a penny, twopence, a
penny and a half, and a halfpenny!" as each entered
into the fire which was the gateway to their home.

"Farewell!" said Freydis: and as she spoke she
sighed.

"Not thus must be our parting," Manuel says. "For
do you listen now, Queen Freydis! it was Helmas the
Deep-Minded who told me what was requisite.
'*Queen* is the same as *cwen*, which means *a woman*,
no more nor less,' said the wise King. 'You have but to
remember that.'"

She took his meaning. Freydis cried out, angrily: "Then all the foolishness you have been talking about my looks and your love for me was pre-arranged! And you have cheated me out of the old Tuyla mystery by putting on the appearance of loving me, and by pestering me with such nonsense as a plowman trades against the heart of a milkmaid! Now, certainly, I shall reward your candor in a fashion that will be whispered about for a long while."

With that, Queen Freydis set about a devastating magic.

"All, all was pre-arranged save one thing," said Manuel, with a yapping laugh, and not even looking at the commencing terrors. He thrust into the fire the parchment which Freydis had given him. "Yes, all was pre-arranged except that Helmas did not purge me of that which will not accept the hire of any lying to you. So the Deep-Minded's wisdom comes, at the last pinch, to naught."

Now Freydis for an instant waved back two-thirds of an appalling monster, which was as yet incompletely evoked for Dom Manuel's destruction, and Freydis cried impatiently, "But have you no sense whatever! for you are burning your hand."

And indeed the boy had already withdrawn his hand with a grimace, for in the ardor of executing his noble gesture, as Queen Freydis saw, he had not estimated how hot her fires were.

"It is but a little hurt to me who have taken a great hurt," says Manuel, sullenly. "For I had thought to lie, and in my mouth the lie turned to a truth. At least, I do not profit by my false-dealing, and I wave you farewell with empty hands burned clean of theft."

111

Then she who was a human woman said, "But you have burned your hand!"

"It does not matter: I have ointments yonder. Make haste, Queen Freydis, for the hour passes wherein the moon is void and powerless."

"There is time." She brought out water from the enclosure, and swiftly bathed Dom Manuel's hand.

From the fire now came a whispering, "Make haste, Queen Freydis! make haste, dear Fairy mistress!"

"There is time," said Freydis, "and do you stop flurrying me!" She brought from the enclosure a pot of ointment, and she dressed Manuel's hand.

"Borram, borram, Leanhaun shee!" the fire crackled. "Now the hour ends."

Then Freydis sprang from Manuel, toward the flames beyond which she was queen of ancient mysteries, and beyond which her will was neither to loose nor to bind. And she cried hastily, "A penny, a penny, twopence—"

But just for a moment she looked back at Morven, and at the man who waited upon Morven alone and hurt. In his firelit eyes she saw love out of measure and without hope. And in the breast of Freydis moved the heart of a human woman.

"I cannot help it," she said, as the hour passed. "Somebody has to bandage it, and men have no sense in these matters."

Whereon the fire roared angrily, and leaped, and fell dead, for the Moon-Children Bil and Hjuki had returned from the well which is called Byrgir, and the moon was no longer void and powerless.

"So, does that feel more comfortable?" said Freydis. She knew that within this moment age and sorrow and death had somewhere laid inevitable ambuscades from which to assail her by and by, for she was mortal after the sacred fire's extinction, and she meant to make the best of it.

For a while Count Manuel did not speak. Then he said, in a shaking voice: "O woman dear and lovely and credulous and compassionate, it is you and you alone that I must be loving eternally with such tenderness as is denied to proud and lonely queens on their tall thrones! And it is you that I must be serving always with such a love as may not be given to the figure that any man makes in this world! And though all life may be a dusty waste of endless striving, and though the ways of men may always be the ways of folly, yet are these ways our ways henceforward, and not hopeless ways, for you and I will tread them together."

"Now certainly there is in Audela no such moonstruck nonsense to be hearing, nor any such quick-footed hour of foolishness to be living through," Freydis replied, "as here to-night has robbed me of my kingdom."

"Love will repay," said Manuel, as is the easy fashion of men.

And Freydis, a human woman now in all things, laughed low and softly in the darkness. "Repay me thus, my dearest: no matter how much I may coax you in the doubtful time to come, do you not ever tell me how you happened to have the bandages and the pot of ointment set ready by the mirror. For it is bad for a human woman ever to be seeing through the devices of wise kings, and far worse for her to be seeing through the heroic antics of her husband."

Meanwhile in Arles young Alianora had arranged her own match with more circumspection. The English, who at first demanded twenty thousand marks as her jointure, had after interminable bargaining agreed to accept her with three thousand: and she was to be dowered with Plymouth and Exeter and Tiverton and Torquay and Brixham, and with the tin mines of Devonshire and Cornwall. In everything except the husband involved, she was marrying excellently, and so all Arles that night was ornamented with flags and banners and chaplets and bright hangings and flaring lamps and torches, and throughout Provence there was festivity of every sort, and the Princess had great honor and applause.

But in the darkness of Upper Morven they had happiness, no matter for how brief a while.

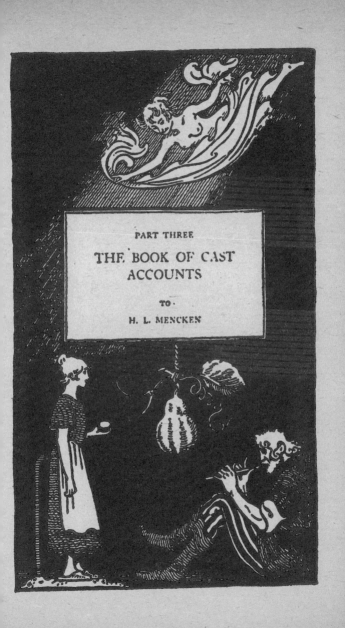

PART THREE

THE BOOK OF CAST ACCOUNTS

TO

H. L. MENCKEN

Consider, *faire Miserie*, (*quoth Manuel*) *that it lyes not in mans power to place his loue where he list, being the worke of an high Deity.* A Birde was neuer seen in Pontus, *nor true loue in a fleeting mynde: neuer shall remoue the affection of my Hearte, which in nature resembleth the stone* Abiston.

XVI

Freydis

❦❦❦❦❦❦❦❦❦❦❦❦❦

THEY OF POICTESME narrate how Queen Freydis and
Count Manuel lived together amicably upon Upper
Morven. They tell also how the iniquitous usurper,
Duke Asmund, at this time held Bellegarde close at
hand, but that his Northmen kept away from Upper
Morven, on account of the supernatural beings you
were always apt to encounter thereabouts, so that
Manuel and Freydis had, at first, no human company.

"Between now and a while," said Freydis, "you
must be capturing Bellegarde and cutting off Duke
Asmund's ugly head, because by right and by King
Ferdinand's own handwriting all Poictesme belongs to
you."

"Well, we will let that wait a bit," says Manuel,
"for I do not so heartily wish to be tied down with
parchments in a count's gilded seat as I do to travel
everywhither and see the ends of this world and judge
them. At all events, dear Freydis, I am content enough
for the present, in this little home of ours, and public
affairs can wait."

"Still, something ought to be done about it," said
Freydis. And, since Manuel displayed an obstinate
prejudice against any lethal plague, she put the puck-

erel curse upon Asmund, by which he was afflicted
with all small bodily ills that can intervene between
corns and dandruff.

On Upper Morven Freydis had reared by enchantment a modest home, that was builded of jasper and
porphyry and yellow and violet breccia. Inside, the
stone walls were everywhere covered with significant
traceries in low relief, and were incrusted at intervals
with disks and tesseræ of turquoise-colored porcelain.
The flooring, of course, was of zinc, as a defence
against the unfriendly Alfs, who are at perpetual war
with Audela, and, moreover, there was a palisade, en-
closing all, of peeled willow wands, not buttered but
oiled, and fastened with unknotted ribbons.

Everything was very simple and homelike, and here
the servitors of Freydis attended them when there was
need. The fallen Queen was not a gray witch—not in
appearance certainly, but in her endowments, which
were not limited as are the powers of black witches
and white witches. She instructed Dom Manuel in the
magic of Audela, and she and Manuel had great times
together that spring and summer, evoking ancient discrowned gods and droll monsters and instructive
ghosts to entertain them in the pauses between other
pleasures.

They heard no more, for that turn, of the clay
figure to which they had given life, save for the news
brought, by a bogglebo, that as the limping gay
young fellow went down from Morven the reputable
citizenry everywhere were horrified because he went
as he was created, stark-naked, and this was not considered respectable. So a large tumble-bug came from
the west, out of the quagmires of Philistia and followed after the animated figure, yelping and splutter-
ing, "Morals, not art!" And for that while, the figure

118

went out of Manuel's saga, thus malodorously accompanied.

"But we will make a much finer figure," says Freydis, "so it does not matter."

"Yes, by and by," says Manuel, "but we will let that wait a bit."

"You are always saying that nowadays!"

"Ah, but, my dear, it is so very pleasant to rest here doing nothing serious for a little while, now that my geas is discharged. Presently of course we must be travelling everywhither, and when we have seen the ends of this world, and have judged them, I shall have time, and greater knowledge too, to give to this image making—"

"It is not from any remote strange places, dear Manuel, but from his own land that a man must get the earth for this image making—"

"Well, be that as it may, your kisses are to me far more delicious than your magic."

"I love to hear you say that, my dearest, but still—"

"No, not at all, for you are really much nicer when you are cuddling so, than when you are running about the world pretending to be pigs and snakes and fireworks, and murdering people with your extravagant sorceries."

Saying this, he kissed her, and thus stilled her protests, for in these amiable times Queen Freydis also was at bottom less interested in magic than in kisses. Indeed, there was never any sorceress more loving and tender than Freydis, now that she had become a human woman.

If ever she was irritable it was only when Manuel confessed, in reply to jealous questionings, that he did not find her quite so beautiful nor so clever as Niafer had been: but this, as Manuel pointed out, could not be helped. For there had never been anybody like Niafer, and it would be nonsense to say otherwise.

It is possible that Dom Manuel believed this. The rather homely, not intelligent, and in no respect bedazzling servant girl may well have been—in the inexplicable way these things fell out,—the woman whom Manuel's heart had chosen, and who therefore in his eyes for the rest of time must differ from all other persons. Certainly no unastigmatic judge would have decreed this swarthy Niafer fit, as the phrase is, to hold a candle either to Freydis or Alianora: whereas Manuel did not conceal, even from these royal ladies themselves, his personal if unique evaluations.

To the other side, some say that ladies who are used to hourly admiration cannot endure the passing of a man who seems to admire not quite wholeheartedly. He who does not admire at all is obviously a fool, and not worth bothering about. But to him who admits, "You are well enough," and makes as though to pass on, there is a mystery attached: and the one way to solve it is to pursue this irritating fellow. Some (reasoning thus) assert that squinting Manuel was aware of this axiom, and that he respected it in all his dealings with Freydis and Alianora. Either way, these theorists did not ever get any verbal buttressing from Dom Manuel. Niafer dead and lost to him, he, without flaunting any unexampled ardors, fell to loving Alianora: and now that Freydis had put off immortality for his kisses, the tall boy had, again, somewhat the air of consenting to accept this woman's sacrifice, and her loveliness and all her power and wisdom, as being upon the whole the handiest available substitute for Niafer's sparse charms.

Yet others declare, more simply, that Dom Manuel was so constituted as to value more cheaply every desire after he had attained it. And these say he noted that—again in the inexplicable way these things fall out,—now Manuel possessed the unearthly Queen she had become, precisely as Alianora had become, a not extraordinary person, who in all commerce with her lover dealt as such.

"But do you really love me, O man of all men?" Freydis would say, "and, this damned Niafer apart, do you love me a little more than you love any other woman?"

"Why, are there any other women?" says Manuel, in fine surprise. "Oh, to be sure, I suppose there are, but I had forgotten about them. I have not heard or seen or thought of those petticoated creatures since my dear Freydis came."

The sorceress purred at this sort of talk, and she rested her head where there seemed a place especially made for it. "I wish I could believe your words, king of my heart. I have to strive so hard, nowadays, to goad you into saying these idiotic suitable dear things: and even when at last you do say them your voice is light and high, and makes them sound as though you were joking."

He kissed the thick coil of hair which lay fragrant against his lips. "Do you know, in spite of my joking, I do love you a great deal?"

"I would practise saying that over to myself," observed Freydis critically. "You should let your voice break a little after the first three words."

"I speak as I feel. I love you, Freydis, and I tell you so."

"Yes, but you are no longer a perpetual nuisance about it."

"Alas, my dear, you are no longer the unattainable Queen of the country on the other side of the fire,

121

and that makes a difference, certainly. It is equally certain that I love you over and above all living women."

"Ah, but, my dearest, who loves you more than any human tongue can tell?"

"A peculiarly obstinate and lovely imbecile," says Manuel; and he did that which seemed suitable.

Later Freydis sighed luxuriously. "That saves you the trouble of talking, does it not? And you talked so madly and handsomely that first night, when you wanted to get around me on account of the image, but now you do not make me any pretty speeches at all."

"Oh, heavens!" said Manuel, "but I am embracing a monomaniac. Dear Freydis, whatever I might say would be perforce the same old words that have been whispered by millions of men to many more millions of women, and my love for you is a quite unparalleled thing which ought not to be travestied by any such shopworn apparel."

"Now again you must be putting me off with solemn joking in that light high voice, and there is no faithfulness in that voice, and its talking troubles me."

"I speak as I feel. I love you, Freydis, and I tell you so, but I cannot be telling it over and over again every quarter of the hour."

"Oh, but very certainly this big squinting boy is the most unloquacious and the most stubborn brute that ever lived!"

"And would you have me otherwise?"

"No, that is the queer part of it. But it is a grief to me to wonder if you foresaw as much."

"I!" says Manuel, jovially. "But what would I be doing with any such finespun policies? My dear, until you comprehend I am the most frank and downright creature that ever lived you do not begin to appreciate me."

"I know you are, big boy. But still, I wonder," Freydis said, "and the wondering is a thin little far-off grief."

XVII

Magic of the Image-Makers
❖❖❖❖❖❖❖❖❖❖❖❖

IT WAS PRESENTLY noised abroad that Queen Freydis of Audela had become a human woman; and thereafter certain enchanters came to Upper Morven, to seek her counsel and her favor and the aid of Schamir. These were the enchanters, Manuel was told, who made images, to which they now and then contrived —nobody seemed to know quite how, and least of all did the thaumaturgists themselves,—to impart life.

Once Manuel went with Freydis into a dark place where some of these magic-workers were at labor. By the light of a charcoal fire, clay images were ruddily discernible; before these the enchanters moved unhumanly clad, and doing things which, mercifully perhaps, were veiled from Manuel by the peculiarly perfumed obscurity.

As Manuel entered the gallery one of the magic-workers was chaunting shrilly in the darkness below. "It is the unfinished Rune of the Blackbirds," says Freydis, in a whisper.

Below them the troubled wailing continued:

"—Crammed and squeezed, so entombed (on some wager I hazard), in spite of scared squawking and mutter, after the fashion that lean-faced Rajah dealt

124

with trapped heroes, once, in Calcutta. Dared you
break the crust and bullyrag 'em—hot, fierce and
angry, what wide beaks buzz plain Saxon as ever
spoke Witenagemot! Yet, singing, they sing as no
white bird does (where none rears phœnix) as near
perfection as nature gets, or, if scowls bar platitude,
notes for which there is no rejection in banks whose
coinage—oh, neat!—is gratitude."

Said, in the darkness, another enchanter:

"But far from their choiring the high King sat, in a
gold-faced vest and a gold-laced hat, counting heaped
monies, and dreaming of more francs and sequins and
Louis d'or. Meanwhile the Queen on that fateful
night, though avowing her lack of all appetite, was
still at table, where, rumor said, she was smearing her
seventh slice of bread (thus each turgescible rumor
thrives at court) with gold from the royal hives.
Through the slumberous parc, under arching trees, to
her labors went singing the maid Dénise—"

A third broke in here, saying:

"And she sang of how subtle and bitter and bright
was a beast brought forth, that was clad with the
splendor and light of the cold fair ends of the north,
like a fleshly blossom more white than augmenting
tempests that go, with thunder for weapon, to ravage
the strait waste fastness of snow. She sang how that
all men on earth said, whether its mistress at morn
went forth or waited till night,—whether she strove
through the foam and wreckage of shallow and firth,
or couched in glad fields of corn, or fled from all
human delight,—that thither it likewise would roam."

Now a fourth began:

"Thus sang Dénise, what while the siccant sheets
and coverlets that pillowed kingly dreams, with curious undergarbs of royalty, she neatly ranged: and

dreamed not of that doom which waited, yet unborn, to strike men dumb with perfect awe. As when the seventh wave poises, and sunlight cleaves it through and through with gold, as though to gild oncoming death for him that sees foredoomed—and, gasping, sees death high and splendid!—while the tall wave bears down, and its shattering makes an end of him: thus poised the sable bird while one might count one, two, and three, and four, and five, and six, but hardly seven—"

So they continued; but Manuel listened to no more. "What is the meaning of all this?" he asked, of Freydis.

"It is an experimental incantation," she replied, "in that it is a bit of unfinished magic for which the proper words have not yet been found: but between now and a while they will be stumbled on, and then this rune will live perpetually, surviving all those rhymes that are infected with thought and intelligent meanings such as are repugnant to human nature."

"Are words, then, so important and enduring?"

"Why, Manuel, I am surprised at you! In what else, pray, does man differ from the other animals except in that he is used by words?"

"Now I would have said that words are used by men."

"There is give and take, of course, but in the main man is more subservient to words than they are to him. Why, do you but think of such terrible words as religion and duty and love, and patriotism and art, and honor and common-sense, and of what these tyrannizing words do to and make of people!"

"No, that is chop-logic: for words are only transitory noises, whereas man is the child of God, and has an immortal spirit."

"Yes, yes, my dearest, I know you believe that, and I think it is delightfully quaint and sweet of you. But, as I was saying, a man has only the body of an animal to get experiences in, and the brain of an animal to think them over with, so that the thoughts and opinions of the poor dear must remain always those of a more or less intelligent animal. But his words are very often magic, as you will comprehend by and by when I have made you the greatest of image-makers."

"Well, well, but we can let that wait a bit," said Manuel.

And thereafter Manuel talked with Freydis, confessing that the appearance of these magic-workers troubled Manuel. He had thought it, he said, an admirable thing to make images that lived, until he saw and considered the appearance of these habitual makers of images. They were an ugly and rickety, short-tempered tribe, said Manuel: they were shiftless, spiteful, untruthful, and in everyday affairs not far from imbecile: they plainly despised all persons who could not make images, and they apparently detested all those who could. With Manuel they were particularly high and mighty, assuring him that he was only a prosperous and affected pseudo-magician, and that the harm done by the self-styled thaumaturgist was apt to be very great indeed. What sort of models, then, were these insane, mud-moulding solitary wasps for a tall lad to follow after? And if Manuel acquired their arts (he asked in conclusion), would he acquire their traits?

"The answer is perhaps no, and not impossibly yes," replied Freydis. "For by the ancient Tuyla mystery they extract that which is best in them to inform their images, and this is apt to leave them empty of virtue. But I would have you consider that their best

127

endures, whereas that which is best in other persons is obliterated on some battle-field or mattress or gallows. That is why I have been thinking that this afternoon—"

"No, we will let that wait a bit, for I must turn this over in my mind," said Manuel, "and my mature opinion about this matter must be expressed later."

But while his thoughts were on the affair his fingers made him droll small images of ten of the image-makers, which he set aside unquickened. Freydis smiled at these caricatures, and asked when Manuel would give them life.

"Oh, in due time," he said, "and then their antics may be diverting. But I perceive that this old Tuyla magic is practised at great price and danger, so that I am in no hurry to practise any more of it. I prefer to enjoy that which is dearer and better."

"And what can be dearer and better?"

"Youth," Manuel answered, "and you."

Queen Freydis was now a human woman in all things, so this reply delighted her hearing if not her reason. "Do these two possessions content you, king of my heart?" she asked him very fondly.

"No," Manuel said, gazing out across Morven at the cloud-dappled ridges of the Taunenfels, "nor do I look ever to be contented in this world of men."

"Indeed the run of men are poor thin-minded creatures, Manuel—"

He answered, moodily:

"But I cannot put aside the thought that these men ought to be my fellows and my intimates. Instead, I who am a famed champion go daily in distrust, almost in fear, of these incomprehensible and shatter-pated beings. To every side there is a feeble madness over-busy about long-faced nonsense from which I recoil, who must conceal this shrinking always. There is no hour in my life but I go armored in reserve and in small lies, and in my armor I am lonely. Freydis, you protest deep love for this well-armored Manuel, but what wisdom will reveal to you, or to me either, just what is Manuel? Oh, but I am puzzled by the impermanence and the loneliness and the impotence of this Manuel! Dear Freydis, do not love my body nor my manner of speaking, nor any of the ways that I have in the flesh, for all these transiencies are mortgaged to the worms. And that thought also is a grief—"

"Let us not speak of these things! Let us not think of anything that is horrid, but only of each other!"

"But I cannot put aside the thought that I, who for the while exist in this mortgaged body, cannot ever get out to you. Freydis, there is no way in which two persons may meet in this world of men: we can but exchange, from afar, despairing friendly signals, in the sure knowledge they will be misinterpreted. So do we pass, each coming out of a strange woman's womb, each parodied by the flesh of his parents, each passing futilely, with incommunicative gestures, toward the womb of a strange grave: and in this jostling we find no comradeship. No soul may travel upon a bridge of words. Indeed there is no word for my foiled huge desire to love and to be loved, just as there is no word for the big, the not quite comprehended thought which is moving in me at this moment. But that thought also is a grief—"

Manuel was still looking at the changing green and purple of the mountains and at the tall clouds trailing northward. The things that he viewed yonder were all gigantic and lovely, and they seemed not to be very greatly bothering about humankind.

Then Freydis said: "Let us not think too much,

129

dear, in our youth. It is such a waste of the glad time, and of the youth that will not ever be returning—"

"But I cannot put aside the thought that it will never be the true Manuel whom you will love or even know of, nor can I dismiss the knowledge that these human senses, through which alone we may obtain any knowledge of each other, are lying messengers. What can I ever be to you except flesh and a voice? Nor is this the root of my sorrowing, dear Freydis. For I know that my distrust of all living creatures— oh, even of you, dear Freydis, when I draw you closest,—must always be as a wall between us, a low, lasting, firm-set wall which we can never pull down. And I know that I am not really a famed champion, but only a forlorn and lonely inmate of the doubtful castle of my body; and that I, who know not truly what I am, must die in this same doubt and loneliness, behind the strong defences of posturing and bluntness and jovial laughter which I have raised for my protecting. And that thought also is a grief."

Now Manuel was as Freydis had not ever seen him. She wondered at him, she was perturbed by this fine lad's incomprehensible dreariness, with soft red willing lips so near: and her dark eyes were bent upon him with a beautiful and tender yearning which may not be told.

"I do not understand you, my dearest," said she, who was no longer the high Queen of Audela, but a mortal woman. "It is true that all the world about us is a false seeming, but you and I are real and utterly united, for we have no concealments from each other. I am sure that no two people could be happier than we are, nor better suited. And certainly such morbid notions are not like you, who, as you said yourself,

130

only the other day, are naturally so frank and down-right."

Now Manuel's thoughts came back from the clouds and the green and purple of the mountains. He looked at her very gravely for an instant or two. He laughed morosely. He said, "There!"

"But, dearest, you are strange and not yourself—"

"Yes, yes!" says Manuel, kissing her, "for the moment I had forgotten to be frank and downright, and all else which you expect of me. Now I am my old candid, jovial, blunt self again, and I shall not worry you with such silly notions any more. No, I am Manuel: I follow after my own thinking and my own desire; and if to do that begets loneliness I must endure it."

XVIII

Manuel Chooses

❦❦❦❦❦❦❦❦❦❦❦

"But I cannot understand," said Freydis, on a fine day in September, "how it is that, now the power of Schamir is in your control, and you have the secret of giving life to your images, you do not care to use either the secret or the talisman. For you make no more images, you are always saying, 'No, we will let that wait a bit,' and you do not even quicken the ten caricatures of the image-makers which you have already modeled."

"Life will be given to these in due time," said Manuel, "but that time is not yet come. Meanwhile, I avoid practise of the old Tuyla mystery for the sufficing reason that I have seen the result it has on the practitioner. A geas was upon me to make a figure in the world, and so I modeled and loaned life to such a splendid gay young champion as was to my thinking and my desire. Thus my geas, I take it, is discharged, and a thing done has an end. Heaven may now excel me by creating a larger number of living figures than I, but pre-eminence in this matter is not a question of arithmetic—"

"Ah, yes, my squinting boy has all the virtues, including that of modesty!"

"Well, but I have seen my notion embodied, seen it take breath, seen it depart from Morven in all respects, except for a little limping—which, do you know, I thought rather graceful?—in well-nigh all respects, I repeat, quite indistinguishable from the embodied notions of that master craftsman whom some call Ptha, and others Jahveh, and others Abraxas, and yet others Koshchei the Deathless. In fine, I have made a figure more admirable and significant than is the run of men, and I rest upon my laurels."

"You have created a living being somewhat above the average, that is true: but then every woman who has a fine baby does just as much—"

"The principle is not the same," said Manuel, with dignity.

"And why not, please, big boy?"

"For one thing, my image was an original and unaided production, whereas a baby, I am told, is the result of more or less hasty collaboration. Then, too, a baby is largely chance work, in that its nature cannot be exactly foreplanned and pre-determined by its makers, who, in the glow of artistic creation, must, I imagine, very often fail to follow the best æsthetic canons."

"As for that, nobody who makes new and unexampled things can make them exactly to the maker's will. Even your image limped, you remember—"

"Ah, but so gracefully!"

"—No, Manuel, it is only those necromancers who evoke the dead, and bid the dead return to the warm flesh, that can be certain as to the results of their sorcery. For these alone of magic-workers know in advance what they are making."

"Ah, this is news! So you think it is possible to evoke the dead in some more tangible form than that of an instructive ghost? You think it possible for a dead girl—or, as to that matter, for a dead boy, or a defunct archbishop, or a deceased ragpicker,—to be fetched back to live again in the warm flesh?"

"All things are possible, Manuel, at a price."

Said Manuel:

"What price would be sufficient to re-purchase the rich spoils of Death? and whence might any bribe be fetched? For all the glowing wealth and beauty of this big round world must show as a new-minted farthing beside his treasure chests, as one slight shining unimportant coin which—even this also!—belongs to earth, but has been overlooked by him as yet. Presently this hour, and whatever is strutting through this hour, is added to the heaped crypts wherein lie all that was worthiest in the old time.

"Now there is garnered such might and loveliness and wisdom as human thinking cannot conceive of. An emperor is made much of here when he has conquered some part of the world, but Death makes nothing of a world of emperors: and in Death's crowded store-rooms nobody bothers to estimate within a thousand thousand of how many emperors, and tzars and popes and pharaohs and sultans, that in their day were adored as omnipotent, are there assembled pellmell, along with all that was worthiest in the old time.

"As touches loveliness, not even Helen's beauty is distinguishable among those multitudinous millions of resplendent queens whom one finds yonder. Here are many pretty women, here above all is Freydis, so I do not complain. But yonder is deep-bosomed Semiramis, and fair-tressed Guenevere, and Magdalene that loved Christ, and Europa, the bull's laughing bride, and Lilith, whose hot kiss made Satan ardent, and a many other ladies by whose dear beauty's might were shaped the songs which cause us to remember all that was worthiest in the old time. .

"As wisdom goes, here we have prudent men of business able to add two and two together, and justice may be out of hand distinguished from injustice by an impanelment of the nearest twelve fools. Here we have many Helmases a-cackling wisely under a goose-feather. But yonder are Cato and Nestor and Merlin and Socrates, Abelard sits with Aristotle there, and the seven sages confer with the major prophets, and yonder is all that was worthiest in the old time.

"All, all, are put away in Death's heaped store-rooms, so safely put away that opulent Death may well grin scornfully at Life: for everything belongs to Death, and Life is only a mendicant scratching at his sores so long as Death permits it. No, Freydis, there can be no bribing Death! For what bribe anywhere has Life to offer which Death has not already lying disregarded in a thousand dusty coffers along with all that was worthiest in the old time?"

Freydis replied: "One thing alone. Yes, Manuel, there is one thing only which all Death's ravishings have never taken from Life, and which has not ever entered into Death's keeping. It is through weighing this fact, and through doing what else is requisite, that the very bold may bring back the dead to live again in the warm flesh."

"Well, but I have heard the histories of presumptuous men who attempted to perform such miracles, and all these persons sooner or later came to misery."

"Why, to be sure! to whom else would you have them coming?" said Freydis. And she explained the way it was.

Manuel put many questions. All that evening he was

135

thoughtful, and he was unusually tender with Freydis. And that night, when Freydis slept, Dom Manuel kissed her very lightly, then blinked his eyes, and for a moment covered them with his hand. Standing thus, the tall boy queerly moving his mouth, as though it were stiff and he were trying to make it more supple.

Then he armed himself. He took up the black shield upon which was painted a silver stallion. He crept out of their modest magic home and went down into Bellegarde, where he stole him a horse, from the stables of Duke Asmund.

And that night, and all the next day, Dom Manuel rode beyond Aigremont and Naimes, journeying away from Morven, and away from the house of jasper and porphyry and violet and yellow breccia, and away from Freydis, who had put off immortality for his kisses. He travelled northward, toward the high woods of Dun Vlechlan, where the leaves were aglow with the funereal flames of autumn: for the summer wherein Dom Manuel and Freydis had been happy together was now as dead as that estranged queer time which he had shared with Alianora.

XIX

The Head of Misery

❖❖❖❖❖❖❖❖❖❖❖❖

WHEN MANUEL had reached the outskirts of the forest he encountered there a knight in vermilion armor, with a woman's sleeve wreathed about his helmet: and, first of all, this knight demanded who was Manuel's lady love.

"I have no living love," said Manuel, "except the woman whom I am leaving without ceremony, because it seems the only way to avoiding argument."

"But that is unchivalrous, and does not look well."

"Very probably you are right, but I am not chivalrous. I am Manuel. I follow after my own thinking, and an obligation is upon me pointing toward prompt employment of the knowledge I have gained from this woman."

"You are a rascally betrayer of women, then, and an unmanly scoundrel."

"Yes, I suppose so, for I betrayed another woman, in that I permitted and indeed assisted her to die in my stead; and so brought yet another bond upon myself, and an obligation which is drawing me from a homelike place and from soft arms wherein I was content enough," says Manuel, sighing.

But the chivalrous adventurer in red armor was disgusted. "Oh, you tall squinting villain knight of the silver stallion, I wonder from whose court you can be coming, where they teach no better behavior than woman-killing, and I wonder what foul new knavery you can be planning here."

"Why, I was last in residence at Raymond Bèrenger's court," says Manuel: "and since you are bent on knowing about my private affairs, I come to this forest in search of Béda, or Kruchina, or whatever you call the Misery of earth in these parts."

"Aha, and are you one of Raymond Bérenger's friends?"

"Yes, I suppose so," says Manuel, blinking,—"yes, I suppose so, since I have prevented his being poisoned."

"This is good hearing, for I have always been one of Raymond Bérenger's enemies, and all such of his friends as I have encountered I have slain."

"Doubtless you have your reasons," said Manuel, and would have ridden by.

But the other cried furiously, "Turn, you tall fool! Turn, cowardly betrayer of women!"

He came upon Manuel like a whirlwind, and Manuel had no choice in the matter. So they fought, and presently Manuel brought the vermilion knight to the ground, and, dismounting, killed him. It was noticeable that from the death-wound came no blood, but only a flowing of very fine black sand, out of which scrambled and hastily scampered away a small vermilion-colored mouse.

Then Manuel said, "I think that this must be the peculiarly irrational part of the forest, to which I was directed, and I wonder what may have been this scarlet squabbler's grievance against King Raymond Bérenger?"

Nobody answered, so Manuel remounted, and rode on.

Count Manuel skirted the Wolflake, and came to a hut, painted gray, that stood clear of the ground, upon the bones of four great birds' feet. Upon the four corners of the hunt were carved severally the figures of a lion, a dragon, a cockatrice and an adder, to proclaim the miseries of carnal and intellectual sin, and of pride, and of death.

Here Manuel tethered his horse to a holm-oak. He raised both arms, facing the East.

"Do you now speed me!" cried Manuel, "ye thirty Barami! O all ye powers of accumulated merit, O most high masters of Almsgiving, of Morality, of Relinquishment, of Wisdom, of Fortitude, of Patience, of Truth, of Determination, of Charity, and of Equanimity! do all you aid me in my encounter with the Misery of earth!"

He piously crossed himself, and went into the hut. Inside, the walls were adorned with very old-looking frescoes that were equally innocent of perspective and reticence: the floor was of tessellated bronze. In each corner Manuel found, set upright, a many-storied umbrella of the kind used for sacred purposes in the East: each of these had a silver handle, and was worked in nine colors. But most important of all, so Manuel had been told, was the pumpkin which stood opposite to the doorway.

Manuel kindled a fire, and prepared the proper kind of soup: and at sunset he went to the window of the hut, and cried out three times that supper was ready.

One answered him, "I am coming."

Manuel waited. There was now no sound in the forest: even the few birds not yet gone south, that had been chirping of the day's adventures, were hushed on a sudden, and the breeze died in the tree-tops. Inside the hut Manuel lighted his four candles, and he disposed of one under each umbrella in the prescribed manner. His footsteps on the bronze flooring, and the rustling of his garments as he went about the hut doing what was requisite, were surprisingly sharp and distinct noises in a vast silence and in an illimitable loneliness.

Then said a thin little voice, "Manuel, open the door!"

Manuel obeyed, and you could see nobody anywhere in the forest's dusk. The twilit brown and yellow trees were still as paintings. His horse stood tethered and quite motionless, except that it was shivering.

One spoke at his feet. "Manuel, lift me over the threshold!"

Dom Manuel, recoiling, looked downward, and in the patch of candlelight between the shadows of his legs you could see a human head. He raised the head, and carried it into the hut. He could now perceive that the head was made of white clay, and could deduce that the Misery of earth, whom some call Béda, and others Kruchina, had come to him.

"Now, Manuel," says Misery, "do you give me my supper."

So Manuel set the head upon the table, and put a platter of soup before the head, and fed the soup to Misery with a gold spoon.

When the head had supped, it bade Manuel place it in the little bamboo cradle, and told Manuel to put out the lights. Many persons would not have fancied being alone in the dark with Misery, but Manuel obeyed. He knelt to begin his nightly prayer, but at once that happened which induced him to desist. So without his usual divine invocation, Dom Manuel lay down upon the bronze floor of the hut, beneath one of the tall umbrellas, and he rolled up his russet cloak for a pillow. Presently the head was snoring, and then Manuel too went to sleep. He said, later, that he dreamed of Niafer.

XX

The Month of Years
❖❖❖❖❖❖❖❖❖❖❖❖

IN THE morning, after doing the head's extraordinary bidding, Manuel went to feed his horse, and found tethered to the holm-oak the steed's skeleton picked clean. "I grieve at this," said Manuel, "but I consider it wiser to make no complaint." Indeed, there was nobody to complain to, for Misery, after having been again lifted over the threshold, had departed to put in a day's labor with the plague in the north.

Thereafter Manuel abode in this peculiarly irrational part of the forest, serving Misery for, as men in cheerier places were estimating the time, a month and a day. Of these services it is better not to speak. But the head was pleased by Manuel's services, because Misery loves company: and the two used to have long friendly talks together when Manuel's services and Misery's work for that day were over.

"And how came you, sir, to be thus housed in a trunkless head?" asked Manuel, one time.

"Why, when Jahveh created man on the morning of the sixth day, he set about fashioning me that afternoon from the clay which was left over. But he was interrupted by the coming of the Sabbath, for Jahveh was in those days, of course, a very orthodox Jew. So I was left incomplete, and must remain so always."

"I deduce that you, then, sir, are Heaven's last crowning work, and the final finishing touch to creation."

"So the pessimists tell me," the clay head assented, with a yawn. "But I have had a hard day of it, what with the pestilence in Glathion, and wars between the Emperor and the Milanese, and all those October colds, so we will talk no more philosophy."

Thus Manuel served the head of Misery, for a month of days and a day. It was a noticeable peculiarity of this part of the forest—a peculiarity well known to everybody, though not quite unanimously explained by the learned,—that each day which one spent therein passed as a year, so that Dom Manuel in appearance now aged rapidly. This was unfortunate, especially when his teeth began to fail him, because there were no dentists handy, but his interest in the other Plagues which visited this forest left Manuel little time wherein to think about private worries. For Bèda was visited by many of his kindred, such as Mitlan and Kali and Thragnar and Pwyll and Apepi and other evil principles, who were perpetually coming to the gray hut for family reunions, and to rehearse all but one of the two hundred and forty thousand spells of the Capuas. And it was at this time that Manuel got his first glimpse of Sclaug, with whom he had such famous troubles later.

So sped the month of days that passed as years. Little is known as to what happened in the gray hut, but that perhaps is a good thing. Dom Manuel never talked about it. This much is known, that all day the clay head would be roving about the world, carrying envious reports, and devouring kingdoms, and stirring

143

up patriotism and reform, and whispering malefic counsel, and bringing hurt and sorrow and despair and evil of every kind to men; and that in the evening, when at sunset Phobetor took over this lamentable work, Béda would return contentedly to Dun Vlechlan, for Manuel's services and a well-earned night's rest. On most evenings there was unspeakable company, but none of these stayed overnight. And after each night passed alone with Misery, the morning would find Manuel older looking.

"I wonder, sir, at your callousness, and at the cheery way in which you go about your dreadful business," said Manuel, once, after he had just cleansed the dripping jaws.

"Ah, but since I am all head and no heart, therefore I cannot well pity the human beings whom I pursue as a matter of allotted duty."

"That seems plausible," says Manuel, "and I perceive that if appearances are to be trusted you are not personally to blame. Still, I cannot but wonder why the world of men should thus be given over to Misery if Koshchei the Deathless, who made all things as they are, has any care for men."

"As to what goes on overhead, Manuel, you must inquire of others. There are persons in charge, I know, but they have never yet permitted Misery to enter into their high places, for I am not popular with them, and that is the truth."

"I can understand that, but nevertheless I wonder why Misery should have been created to feed upon mankind."

"Probably the cows and sheep and chickens in your barnyards, and the partridges and rabbits in your snares, and even the gasping fish upon your hook, find time to wonder in the same way about you, Dom Manuel."

"Ah, but man is the higher form of life—"

"Granting that remarkable assumption, and is any man above Misery? So you see it is logical I should feed on you."

"Still, I believe that the Misery of earth was devised as a trial and a testing to fit us for some nobler and eternal life hereafter."

"Why in this world should you think that?" the head inquired, with real interest.

"Because I have an immortal spirit, sir, and—"

"Dear me, but all this is very remarkable. Where is it, Manuel?"

"It is inside me somewhere, sir."

"Come, then, let us have it out, for I am curious to see it."

"No, it cannot get out exactly, sir, until I am dead."

"But what use will it be to you then?" said Misery: "and how can you, who have not ever been dead, be certain as to what happens when one is dead?"

"Well, I have always heard so, sir."

The head shook itself dubiously. "Now from whom of the Léshy, I wonder, can you have been hearing such fantastic stories? I am afraid somebody has been making fun of you, Manuel."

"Oh, no, sir, this is a tenet held by the wisest and most admirable of men."

"I see: it was some other man who told you all these drolleries about the eternal importance of mankind," the head observed, with an unaccountable slackening of interest. "I see: and again, you may notice that the cows and the sheep and the chickens, also, resent extinction strenuously."

"But these are creatures of the earth, sir, whereas

there is about at any rate some persons a whiff of divinity. Come now, do you not find it so?"

The head looked graver. "Yes, Manuel, most young people have in them a spark which is divine, but it is living that snuffs this out of all of you, by and large, without bothering Grandfather Death to unpeel spirits like bananas. No, the most of you go with very little spirit, if any, into the grave, and assuredly with not enough spirit to last you forever. No, Manuel, no, I never quarrel with religion, because it is almost the strongest ally I have, but these religious notions rather disgust me sometimes, for if men were immortal then Misery would be immortal, and I could never survive that."

"Now you are talking nonsense, sir," said Manuel, stoutly, "and of all sorts of nonsense cynical nonsense is the worst."

"By no means," replied the head, "since, plainly, it is far worse nonsense to assert that omnipotence would insanely elect to pass eternity with you humans. No, Manuel, I am afraid that your queer theory, about your being stuffed inside with permanent material and so on, does not very plausibly account for either your existence or mine, and that we both stay riddles without answers."

"Still, sir," said Manuel, "inasmuch as there is one thing only which all death's ravishings have never taken from life, and that thing is the Misery of earth—"

"Your premiss is indisputable, but what do you deduce from this?"

Manuel smiled slowly and sleepily. "I deduce, sir, that you, also, who have not ever been dead, cannot possibly be certain as to what happens when one is dead. And so I shall stick to my own opinion about the life to come."

"But your opinion is absurd, on the face of it."

"That may very well be, sir, but it is much more comfortable to live with than is your opinion, and living is my occupation just now. Dying I shall attend to in its due turn, and, of the two, my opinion is the more pleasant to die with. Thereafter, if your opinion be right, I shall never even know that my opinion was wrong: so that I have everything to gain, in the way of pleasurable anticipations anyhow, and I have nothing whatever to lose, by clinging to the foolish fond old faith which my fathers had before me," said Manuel, as sturdily as ever.

"Yes, but how in this world—?"

"Ah, sir," says Manuel, still smiling, "in this world men are nourished by their beliefs; and it well may be that, yonder also, their sustenance is the same."

But at this moment came Reeri (a little crimson naked man, having the head of a monkey) with his cock in one hand and his gnarled club in the other. Necessarily the Blood Demon's arrival put an end to their talking, for that turn.

XXI

Touching Repayment
❖❖❖❖❖❖❖❖❖❖❖

So Count Manuel's youth went out of him as he became more and more intimate with Misery, and an attachment sprang up between them, and the two took counsel as to all Manuel's affairs. They often talked of the royal ladies whom Manuel had loved and loved no longer.

"For at one time," Manuel admitted, "I certainly fancied myself in love with the Princess Alianora, and at another time I was in love with Queen Freydis. And even now I like them well enough, but neither of these royal ladies could make me forget the slave girl Niafer whom I loved on Vraidex. Besides, the Princess and the Queen were fond of having their own way about everything, and they were bent on hampering me with power and wealth and lofty station and such other obstacles to the following of my own thinking and my own desires. I could not endure the eternal arguing this led to, which was always reminding me, by contrast, of the quiet dear ways of Niafer and of the delight I had in the ways of Niafer. So it seemed best for everyone concerned for me to break off with Freydis and Alianora."

"As for these women," the head estimated, "you

may be for some reasons well rid of them. Yet this Alianora has fine eyes and certain powers."

"She is a princess of the Apsarasas," Manuel replied, "and therefore she has power over the butterflies and the birds and the bats, and over all creatures of the air. I know, because she has disclosed to me some of the secrets of the Apsarasas. But over her own tongue and temper the Princess Alianora has no power and no control whatever, and if I had married her she would have eventually pestered me into being a king, and giving my life over to politics and the dominion of men."

"This Freydis, too, has beautiful black hair—and certain powers—"

"She was once Queen of Audela, and therefore she retains power over all figures of earth. I know, because she has disclosed to me some of the secrets of Audela. But the worst enemy of Freydis also goes in red, and is housed by the little white teeth of Freydis, for it was this enemy that betrayed her: and if I had married her she would have coaxed me, by and by, into becoming a great maker of images, and giving my life over to such arts."

Misery said: "You have had love from these women, you have gained power and knowledge from these women. Therefore you leave them, to run after some other woman who can give you no power and knowledge, but only a vast deal of trouble. It is not heroic, Manuel, but it is human, and your reasoning is well fitted to your time of life."

"It is true that I am young as yet, sir—"

"No, not so very young, for my society is maturing you, and already you are foreplanning and talking the follies of a man in middle life."

"No matter what my age may come to be, sir, I shall always remember that when I first set up as a

149

champion, and was newly come from living modestly in attendance upon the miller's pigs, I loved the slave girl Niafer. She died. I did not die. Instead, I relinquished Niafer to Grandfather Death, and at that price I preserved my own life and procured a recipe through which I have prospered unbelievably, so that I am today a nobleman with fine clothes and lackeys, and with meadow-lands and castles of my own, if only I could obtain them. So I no longer go ragged at the elbows, and royal ladies look upon me favorably, and I find them well enough. But the joy I took in Niafer is not to be found in any of these things."

"That too is an old human story," the head said, "and yours is a delusion that comes to most men in middle life. However, for a month of years you have served me faithfully, except for twice having failed to put enough venom in my soup, and for having forgotten to fetch in any ice that evening the Old Black One was here. Still, nobody is perfect; your time of service is out; and I must repay you as need is. Will you have happiness, then, and an eternal severance between you and me?"

'I have seen but one happy person," Manuel replied. "He sat in a dry ditch, displaying vacant glittering eyes, and straws were tangled in his hair, but Tom o' Bedlam was quite happy. No, it is not happiness I desire."

The head repeated: "You have served me. I repay, as need is, with the payment you demand. What is it you demand?"

Dom Manuel said, "I demand that Niafer who was a slave girl, and is now a ghost in her pagan paradise."

"Do you think, then, that to recall the dead is possible?"

"You are cunning, sir, but I remember what Frey-

150

dis told me. Will you swear that Misery cannot bring back the dead?"

"Very willingly I will swear to it, upon all the most authentic relics in Christendom."

"Ah, yes, but will you rest one of your cold hard pointed ears against"—here Manuel whispered what he did not care to name aloud,—"the while that you swear to it."

"Of course not," Misery answered, sullenly: "since every troubled ghost that ever gibbered and clanked chains would rise confronting me if I made such an oath. Yes, Manuel, I am able to bring back the dead, but prudence forces me to lie about my power, because to exercise that power to the full would be well-nigh as ruinous as the breaking of that pumpkin. For there is only one way to bring back the dead in flesh, and if I follow that way I shall lose my head as all the others have done."

"What is that to a lover?" says Manuel.

The head sighed, and bit at its white lips. "An oath is an oath to the Léshy. Therefore do you, who are human, now make profitable use of the knowledge and of the power you get from those other women by breaking oaths! And as you have served me, so will I serve you."

Manuel called black eagles to him, in the manner the Princess Alianora had taught, and he sent them into all parts of the world for every sort of white earth. They obeyed the magic of the Apsarasas, and from Britain they brought Dom Manuel the earth called leucargillon, and they brought glisomarga from Enisgarth, and eglecopala from the Gallic provinces, and argentaria from Lacre Kai, and white earth of every description from all parts of the world.

Manuel made from this earth, as Queen Freydis had

taught him how to do, the body of a woman. He fashioned the body peculiarly, in accordance with the old Tuyla mystery, and the body was as perfect as Manuel could make it, in all ways save that it had no head.

Then Manuel sent a gold-crested wren into Provence: it entered through an upper window of the King's marmoreal palace, and went into the Princess Alianora's chamber, and fetched hence a handkerchief figured with yellow mulberries and wet with the tears which Alianora had shed in her grieving for Manuel. And Dom Manuel sent also a falcon, which returned to him with Queen Freydis' handkerchief. That was figured with white fleurs-de-lis, and that too was drenched with tears.

Whereupon, all being in readiness, Misery smiled craftily, and said:

"In the time that is passed I have overthrown high kings and prophets, and sorcerers also, as when Misery half carelessly made sport of Mithridates and of Merlin and of Moses, in ways that ballad-singers still delight to tell of. But with you, Dom Manuel, I shall deal otherwise, and I shall disconcert you by and by in a more quiet fashion. Hoh, I must grapple carefully with your love for Niafer, as with an antagonist who is not scrupulous, nor very sensible, but who is exceedingly strong. For observe: you obstinately desire this perished heathen woman, who in life, it well may be, was nothing remarkable. Therefore you have sought Misery, you have dwelt for a month of years with terror, you have surrendered youth, you are planning to defy death, you are intent to rob the deep grave and to despoil paradise. Truly your love is great."

Manuel said only, "An obligation is upon me, for the life of Niafer was given to preserve my life."

152

"Now I, whom some call Béda, and others Kruchina, and whom for the present your love has conquered—I it is, alone, who can obtain for you this woman, because in the long run I overcome all things and persons. Life is my province, and the birth cry of every infant is an oath of allegiance to me. Thus I am overlord where all serve willy-nilly except you, who have served of your own will. And as you have served me, so must I serve you."

Manuel said, "That is well."

"It is not so well as you think, for when you have this Niafer I shall return to you in the appearance of a light formless cloud, and I shall rise about you, not suddenly but a little by a little. So shall you see through me the woman for love of whom your living was once made high-hearted and fearless, and for whose sake death was derided, and paradise was ransacked: and you will ask forlornly, 'Was it for this?' Throughout the orderly, busied, unimportant hours that stretch between your dressing for the day and your undressing for the night, you will be asking this question secretly in your heart, while I pass everywhither with you in the appearance of a light formless cloud, and whisper to you secretly."

"And what will you whisper to me?"

"Not anything which you will care to repeat to anybody anywhere. Oh, you will be able to endure it, and you will be content, as human contentment goes, and my triumph will not be public. But, none the less, I shall have overthrown my present conqueror, and I shall have brought low the love which terror and death did not affright, and which the laws of earth could not control; and I, whom some call Béda, and others Kruchina, will very terribly attest that the ghost of outlived and conquered misery is common-sense."

153

"That is to-morrow's affair," replied Dom Manuel. "To-day there is an obligation upon me, and my dealings are with to-day."

Then Manuel bound the clay head of Misery in the two handkerchiefs which were wet with the tears of Alianora and of Freydis. When the cock had crowed three times, Dom Manuel unbound the head, and it was only a shapeless mass of white clay, because of the tears of Freydis and Alianora.

Manuel modeled in this clay, to the best of his ability, the head of Niafer, as he remembered her when they had loved each other upon Vraidex: and after the white head was finished he fitted it to the body which he had made from the other kinds of white earth. Dom Manuel robed this body in brown drugget such as Niafer had been used to wear in and about the kitchen at Arnaye, and he did the other things that were requisite, for this was the day of All Saints when nothing sacred ought to be neglected.

XXII

Return of Niafer

❖❖❖❖❖❖❖❖❖❖❖

Now THE TALE tells how Dom Manuel sat at the feet
of the image and played upon a flageolet. There was
wizardry in the music, Dom Manuel said afterward,
for he declared that it evoked in him a vision and a
restless dreaming that followed after Misery.

So this dreaming showed that when Misery was dis-
possessed of the earth he entered (because Misery is
unchristian) into the paradise of the pagans, where
Niafer, dead now for something over a year, went
restlessly in bliss: and Misery came shortly afterward
to Niafer, and talked with her in a thin little voice.
She listened willingly to this talk of Manuel and of
the adventures which Niafer had shared with Manuel: and now that she remembered Manuel, and his
clear young face and bright unequal eyes and his
strong arms, she could no longer be even moderately
content in the paradise of the pagans.

Thereafter Misery went about the heathens' paradise in the appearance of a light formless cloud. And
the fields of this paradise seemed less green, the air became less pure and balmy, and the sky less radiant,
and the waters of the paradisal river Eridanus grew
muddy. The poets became tired of hearing one an-

other recite, the heroes lost delight in their wrestling and chariot racing and in their exercises with the spear and the bow. "How can anybody expect us to waste eternity with recreations which are only fitted to waste time?" they demanded.

And the lovely ladies began to find the handsome lovers with whom they wandered hand in hand through never-fading groves of myrtle, and with whom they were forever reunited, rather tedious companions.

"I love you," said the lovers.

"You have been telling me that for twelve centuries," replied the ladies, yawning, "and too much of anything is enough."

"Upon my body, I think so too," declared the lovers. "I said it only out of politeness and force of habit, and I can assure you I am as tired of this lackadaisical idiocy as you are."

So everything was at sixes and sevens in this paradise: and when the mischief-maker was detected, the blessed held a meeting, for it was now the day of All Souls, on which the dead have privilege.

"We must preserve appearances," said these dead pagans, "and can have only happy-looking persons hereabouts, for otherwise our paradise will get a poor name, and the religion of our fathers will fall into disrepute."

Then they thrust Misery, and Niafer also, out of the pagan paradise, because Misery clung to Niafer in the appearance of a light formless cloud, and there was no separating the two.

These two turned earthward together, and came to the river of sweat called Rigjon. Niafer said to the fiery angel Sandalfon that guards the bridge there, "The Misery of earth is with me."

Sandalfon saw that this was so, and answered, "My fires cannot consume the Misery of earth."

They came to Hadarniel, the noisy angel whose whispering is the thunder. Niafer said, "The Misery of earth is with me."

Hadarniel replied, "Before the Misery of earth I am silent."

They came to Kemuel and his twelve thousand angels of destruction that guard the outermost gateway. Niafer said, "The Misery of earth is with me."

Kemuel answered, "I ruin and make an end of all things else, but for the Misery of earth I have contrived no ending."

So Misery and Niafer passed all the warders of this paradise: and in a dim country on the world's rim the blended spirit of Misery and the ghost of Niafer rose through a hole in the ground, like an imponderable vapor. They dissevered each from the other in a gray place overgrown with poplars, and Misery cried farewell to Niafer.

"And very heartily do I thank you for your kindness, now that we part, and now that, it may be, I shall not ever see you again," said Niafer, politely.

Misery replied:

"Take no fear for not seeing me again, now that you are about once more to become human. Certainly, Niafer, I must leave you for a little while, but certainly I shall return. There will first be for you much kissing and soft laughter, and the quiet happy ordering of your home, and the heart-shaking wonder of the child who is neither you nor Manuel, but both of you, and whose life was not ever seen before on earth: and life will burgeon with white miracles, and every blossom you will take to be eternal. Laughing, you will say of sorrow, 'What is it?' And I, whom

157

some call Béda, and others call Kruchina, shall be monstrously amused by this.

"Then your seeing will have my help, and you will observe that Manuel is very much like other persons. He will be used to having you about, and you him, and that will be the sorry bond between you. The children that have reft their flesh from your flesh ruthlessly, and that have derived their living from your glad anguish, each day will be appearing a little less intimately yours, until these children find their mates. Thereafter you will be a tolerated intruder into these children's daily living, and nobody anywhere will do more than condone your coming: you will weep secretly: and I, whom some call Béda, and others call Kruchina, shall be monstrously amused by this.

"Then I shall certainly return to you, when your tears are dried, and when you no longer believe what young Niafer once believed; and when, remembering young Niafer's desires and her intentions as to the disposal of her life, you will shrug withered shoulders. To go on living will remain desirable. The dilapidations of life will no longer move you deeply. Shrugging, you will say of sorrow, 'What is it?' for you will know grief also to be impermanent. And your inability to be quite miserable any more will assure you that your goings are attended by the ghost of outlived and conquered misery: and I, whom some call Béda, and others call Kruchina, shall be monstrously amused by this."

Said Niafer, impatiently, "Do you intend to keep me here forever under these dark twinkling trees, with your thin little talking, while Manuel stays unhappy through his want of me?"

And Misery answered nothing as he departed from Niafer, for a season.

Such were the happenings in the vision witnessed by Dom Manuel (as Dom Manuel afterward declared) while he sat playing upon the flageolet.

XXIII

Manuel Gets His Desire
❈❈❈❈❈❈❈❈❈❈❈❈

Now THE TALE tells that all this while, near the gray hut in Dun Vlechlan, the earthen image of Niafer lay drying out in the November sun; and that gray Dom Manuel—no longer the florid boy who had come into Dun Vlechlan,—sat at the feet of the image, and played upon a flageolet the air which Suskind had taught him, and with which he had been used to call young Suskind from her twilit places when Manuel was a peasant tending swine. Now Manuel was an aging nobleman, and Niafer was now a homeless ghost, but the tune had power over them, none the less, for its burden was young love and the high-hearted time of youth; so that the melody which once had summoned Suskind from her low red-pillared palace in the doubtful twilight, now summoned Niafer resistlessly from paradise, as Manuel thriftily made use of the odds and ends which he had learned from three women to win him a fourth woman.

The spirit of Niafer entered at the mouth of the image. Instantly the head sneezed, and said, "I am unhappy." But Manuel kept on playing. The spirit descended further, bringing life to the lungs and the belly, so that the image then cried, "I am hungry."

But Manuel kept on playing. So the soul was drawn further and further, until Manuel saw that the white image had taken on the colors of flesh, and was moving its toes in time to his playing; and so knew that the entire body was informed with life.

He cast down the flageolet, and touched the breast of the image with the ancient formal gestures of the old Tuyla mystery, and he sealed the mouth of the image with a kiss, so that the spirit of Niafer was imprisoned in the image which Manuel had made. Under his lips the lips which had been Misery's cried, "I love." And Niafer rose, a living girl just such as Manuel had remembered for more than a whole year: but with that kiss all memories of paradise and all the traits of angelhood departed from her.

"Well, well, dear snip," said Manuel, the first thing of all, "now it is certainly a comfort to have you back again."

Niafer, even in the rapture of her happiness, found this an unimpassioned greeting from one who had gone to unusual lengths to recover her companionship. Staring, she saw that Manuel had all the marks of a man in middle life, and spoke as became appearances. For it was at the price of his youth that Manuel had recovered the woman whom his youth desired: and Misery had subtly evened matters by awarding an aging man the woman for whose sake a lad had fearlessly served Misery. There was no longer any such lad, for the conquered had destroyed the conqueror.

Then, after a moment's consideration of this tall gray stranger, Niafer also looked graver and older. Niafer asked for a mirror: and Manuel had none.

"Now but certainly I must know at once just how faithfully you have remembered me," says Niafer.

He led the way into the naked and desolate Novem-

161

ber forest, and they came to the steel-colored Wolflake hard by the gray hut: and Niafer found she was
limping, for Manuel had not got her legs quite right,
so that for the rest of her second life she was lame.
Then Niafer gazed for a minute, or it might be for
two minutes, at her reflection in the deep cold waters
of the Wolflake.

"Is this as near as you have come to remembering
me, my dearest!" she said, dejectedly, as she looked
down at Manuel's notion of her face. For the appearance which Niafer now wore she found to be very little like that which Niafer remembered as having been
hers, in days wherein she had been tolerably familiar
with the Lady Gisèle's mirrors; and it was a grief to
Niafer to see how utterly the dearest dead go out of
mind in no long while.

"I have forgotten not one line or curve of your features," says Manuel, stoutly, "in all these months, nor
in any of these last days that have passed as years. And
when my love spurred me to make your image, Niafer, my love loaned me unwonted cunning. Even by
ordinary, they tell me, I have some skill at making images: and while not for a moment would I seem to
boast of that skill, and not for worlds would I annoy
you by repeating any of the complimentary things
which have been said about my images,—by persons
somewhat more appreciative, my dear, of the toil and
care that goes to work of this sort,—I certainly think
that in this instance nobody has fair reason to complain."

She looked at his face now: and she noted what the
month of living with Béda, with whom a day is as a
year, had done to the boy's face which she remembered. Count Manuel's face was of remodeled stuff:
youth had gone out of it, and the month of years had

etched wrinkles in it, success had hardened and caution had pinched and self-complacency had kissed it. And Niafer sighed again, as they sat reunited under leafless trees by the steel-colored Wolflake.

"There is no circumventing time and death, then, after all," said Niafer, "for neither of us is now the person that ascended Vraidex. No matter: I love you, Manuel, and I am content with what remains of you: and if the body you have given me is to your will it is to my will."

But now three rascally tall ragged fellows, each blind in one eye, and each having a thin peaked beard, came into the opening before the gray hut, trampling the dead leaves there as they shouted for Mimir. "Come out!" they cried: "come out, you miserable Mirmir, and face those three whom you have wronged!"

Dom Manuel rose from the bank of the Wolflake, and went toward the shouters. "There is no Mimir," he told them, "in Dun Vlechlan, or not at least in this peculiarly irrational part of the forest."

"You lie," they said, "for even though you have hitched a body to your head we recognize you." They looked at Niafer, and all three laughed cruelly. "Was it for this hunched, draggled, mud-faced wench that you left us, you squinting old villain? And have you so soon forgotten the vintner's parlor at Neogréant, and what you did with the gold plates?"

"No, I have not forgotten these things, for I never knew anything about them," said Manuel.

Said one of the knaves, twirling fiercely his moustachios: "Hah, shameless Mimir, do you look at me, who have known you and your blind son Oriander, too, to be unblushing knaves for these nine centuries!

163

Now, I suppose, you will be denying the affair of the squirrel also?"

"Oh, be off with your nonsense!" says Manuel, "for I have not yet had twenty-two years of living, and I never saw you before, and I hope never to see you again."

But they all set upon him with cutlasses, so there was nothing remaining save to have out his sword and fight. And when each of these one-eyed persons had vanished curiously under his death-wound, Manuel told Niafer it was a comfort to find that the month of years had left him a fair swordsman for all that his youth was gone; and that he thought they had better be leaving this part of the high woods of Dun Vlechlan, wherein unaccountable things took place, and all persons behaved unreasonably.

"Were these wood-spirits unreasonable," asks Niafer, "in saying that the countenance and the body you have given me are ugly?"

"My dear," replied Manuel, "it was their saying that which made me try to avoid the conflict, because it does not look well, not even in dealing with demons, to injure the insane."

"Manuel, and can it be you who are considering appearances?"

Dom Manuel said gravely: "My dealings with Misery and with Misery's kindred have taught me many things which I shall never forget nor very willingly talk about. One of these teachings, though, is that in most affairs there is a middle road on which there is little traffic and comparatively easy going. I must tell you that the company I have been in required a great deal of humoring, for of course it is not safe to trifle with any evil principle. No, no, one need not absolutely and openly defy convention, I perceive, in order to follow after one's own thinking," says Manuel, shrewdly, and waggling a gray beard.

"I am so glad you have learned that at last! At least, I suppose, I am glad," said Niafer, a little wistfully, as she recalled young Manuel of the high head.

"But, as I was saying, I now estimate that these tattered persons who would have prevented my leaving, as well as the red fellow that would have hindered my entering, this peculiarly irrational part of the forest, were spiritual intruders into Misery's domain whom Misery had driven out of their wits. No, Niafer, I voice no criticism, because with us two this Misery of earth, whom some call Béda, and others Kruchina, has dealt very handsomely. It troubles me to suspect that he was also called Mimir; but of this we need not speak, because a thing done has an end, even a killed grandfather. Nevertheless, I think that Dun Vlechlan is unwholesome, and I am of the opinion that you and I will be more comfortable elsewhere."

"But must we go back to looking after pigs, dear Manuel, or are you now too old for that?"

Dom Manuel smiled, and you saw that he retained at least his former lordliness. "No, now that every obligation is lifted, and we are reunited, dear snip, I can at last go traveling everywhither, so that I may see the ends of this world and judge them. And we will do whatever else we choose, for, as I must tell you, I am now a nobleman with lackeys and meadowlands and castles of my own, if only I could obtain possession of them."

"This is excellent hearing," said Niafer, "and much better than pig-stealing, and I am glad that the world has had sense enough to appreciate you, Manuel, and you it. And we will have rubies in my coronet, because I always fancied them. Now do you tell me how it all happened, and what I am to be called countess of. And we will talk about that traveling later, for I have already traveled a great distance to-day, but we must certainly have rubies."

XXIV

Three Women

❖❖❖❖❖❖❖❖❖❖❖❖❖

So MANUEL PUT on his armor, and with Manuel telling as much as he thought wise of the adventures
which he had encountered while Niafer was dead,
they left this peculiarly irrational part of the forest,
and fared out of the ruined November woods; and
presently, in those barren fields that descend toward
the sand dunes of Quentavic, came face to face with
Queen Freydis and the Princess Alianora, where these
two royal ladies and many other fine people rode toward the coast.

Alianora went magnificently this morning, on a
white horse, and wearing a kirtle of changeable green
like the sea's green in sunlight: her golden hair was
bound with a gold frontlet wherein were emeralds.
Freydis, dark and stately, was in crimson embroidered
with small gold stars and ink-horns: a hooded falcon
sat on her gloved wrist.

Now Freydis and Alianora stared at the swarthy,
flat-faced, limping peasant girl in brown drugget that
was with Count Manuel. Then Alianora stared at
Freydis.

"Is it for this dingy cripple," says Alianora, with
her proud fine face all wonder, "that Dom Manuel

has forsaken us and has put off his youth? Why, the girl is out and out ugly!"

"Our case is none the better for that," replied Freydis, the wise Queen, whose gazing rested not upon Niafer but on Manuel.

"Who are those disreputable looking, bold-faced creatures that are making eyes at you?" says Niafer.

And Manuel, marveling to meet these two sorceresses together, replied, as he civilly saluted them from a little distance, "Two royal ladies, who would be well enough were it not for their fondness for having their own way."

"And I suppose you think them handsome!"

"Yes, Niafer, I find them very beautiful. But after looking at them with æsthetic pleasure, my gaze returns adoringly to the face I have created as I willed, and to the quiet love of my youth, and I have no occasion to be thinking of queens and princesses. Instead, I give thanks in my heart that I am faring contentedly toward the nearest priest with the one woman in the world who to my finding is desirable and lovely."

"It is very sweet of you to say that, Manuel, and I am sure I hope you are telling the truth, but my faith would be greater if you had not rattled it off so glibly."

Then Alianora said: "Greetings, and for the while farewell, to you, Count Manuel! For all we ride to Quentavic, and thence I am passing over into England to marry the King of that island."

"Now, but there is a lucky monarch for you!" says Manuel, politely. He looked at Freydis, who had put off immortality for his kisses, and whom he had deserted to follow after his own thinking: these reencounters are always awkward, and Don Manuel fidgeted a little. He asked her, "And do you also go into England?"

She told him very quietly, no, that she was only going to the coast, to consult with three or four of the water-demons about enchanting one of the Red Islands, and about making her home there. She had virtually decided, she told him, to put a spell upon Sargyll, as it seemed the most desirable of these islands from what she could hear, but she must first see the place. Queen Freydis looked at him with rather embarrassing intentness all the while, but she spoke quite calmly.

"Yes, yes," Dom Manuel said, cordially, "I dare say you will be very comfortable there, and I am sure I hope so. But I did not know that you two ladies were acquainted."

"Indeed, our affairs are not your affairs," says Freydis, "any longer. And what does it matter, on this November day which has a thin sunlight and no heat at all in it? No, that girl yonder has to-day. But Alianora and I had each her yesterday; and it may be the one or it may be the other of us three who will have to-morrow, and it may be also that the disposal of that to-morrow will be remarkable."

"Very certainly," declared Alianora, with that slow, lovely, tranquil smile of hers, "I shall have my portion of to-morrow. I would have made you a king, and by and by the most powerful of all kings, but you followed after your own thinking, and cared more for messing in wet mud than for a throne. Still, this nonsense of yours has converted you into a rather distinguished looking old gentleman, so when I need you I shall summon you, with the token that we know of, Dom Manuel, and then do you come posthaste!"

Freydis said: "I would have made you the greatest of image-makers; but you followed after your own thinking, and instead of creating new and god-like beings you preferred to resurrect a dead servant girl. Nevertheless, do I bid you beware of the one living image you made, for it still lives and it alone you cannot ever shut out from your barred heart, Dom Manuel: and nevertheless, do I bid you come to me, Dom Manuel, when you need me."

Manuel replied, "I shall always obey both of you." Niafer throughout this while said nothing at all. But she had her private thoughts, to the effect that neither of these high-and-mighty trollops was in reality the person whom henceforward Dom Manuel was going to obey.

So the horns sounded. The gay cavalcade rode on, toward Quentavic. And as they went young Osmund Heleigh (Lord Brudenel's son) asked for the gallant King of Navarre, "But who, sire, was that time-battered gray vagabond, with the tarnished silver stallion upon his shield and the mud-colored cripple at his side, that our Queens should be stopping for any conference with him?"

King Thibaut said it was the famous Dom Manuel of Poictesme, who had put away his youth for the sake of the girl that was with him.

"Then is the old man a fool on every count," declared Messire Heleigh, sighing, "for I have heard of his earlier antics in Provence, and no lovelier lady breathes than Dame Alianora."

"I consider Queen Freydis to be the handsomer of the two," replied Thibaut, "but certainly there is no comparing either of these inestimable ladies with Dom Manuel's swarthy drab."

"She is perhaps some witch whose magic is more

terrible than their magic, and has besotted this ruined champion?"

"It is either enchantment or idiocy, unless indeed it be something far higher than either." King Thibaut looked grave, then shrugged. "Oy Dieus! even so, Queen Freydis is the more to my taste."

Thus speaking, the young King spurred his bay horse toward Queen Freydis (from whom he got his ruin a little later), and all Alianora's retinue went westward, very royally, while Manuel and Niafer trudged east. Much color and much laughter went one way, but the other way went contentment, for that while.

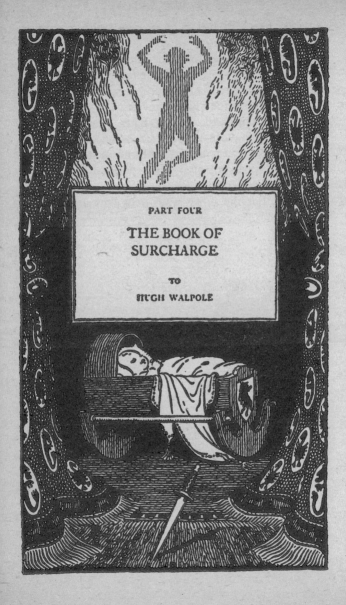

PART FOUR

THE BOOK OF
SURCHARGE

TO

HUGH WALPOLE

Soe *Manuel* *made* *all* *the* *Goddes* *that* *we* *call* mamettes *and* ydolles, *that were sett ouer the Subiection of his lyfe tyme: and euery of the goddes that Manuel wolde carue toilesomelie hadde in hys Bodie a Blemmishe; and in the mydle of the godes made he one god of the Philistines.*

XXV

Affairs in Poictesme

❖❖❖❖❖❖❖❖❖❖❖❖

THEY OF Poictesme narrate how Manuel and Niafer traveled east a little way and then turned toward the warm South; and how they found a priest to marry them, and how Manuel confiscated two horses. They tell also how Manuel victoriously encountered a rather terrible dragon at La Flèche, and near Orthez had trouble with a Groach, whom he conquered and imprisoned in a leather bottle, but they say that otherwise the journey was uneventful.

"And now that every obligation is lifted, and we are reunited, my dear Niafer," says Manuel, as they sat resting after his fight with the dragon, "we will, I repeat, be traveling everywhither, so that we may see the ends of this world and may judge them."

"Dearest," replied Niafer, "I have been thinking about that, and I am sure it would be delightful, if only people were not so perfectly horrid."

"What do you mean, dear snip?"

"You see, Manuel, now that you have fetched me back from paradise, people will be saying you ought to give me, in exchange for the abodes of bliss from which I have been summoned, at least a fairly comfortable and permanent terrestrial residence. Yes, dearest, you know what people are, and the evil-minded will be only too delighted to be saying everywhere that you are neglecting an obvious duty if you go wandering off to see and judge the ends of this world, with which, after all, you have really no especial concern."

"Oh, well, and if they do?" says Manuel, shrugging lordily. "There is no hurt in talking."

"Yes, Manuel, but such shiftless wandering, into uncomfortable places that nobody ever heard of, would have that appearance. Now there is nothing I would more thoroughly enjoy then to go traveling about at adventure with you, and to be a countess means nothing whatever to me. I am sure I do not in the least care to live in a palace of my own, and be bothered with fine clothes and the responsibility of looking after my rubies, and with servants and parties every day. But you see, darling, I simply could not bear to have people thinking ill of my dear husband, and so, rather than have that happen, I am willing to put up with these things."

"Oh, oh!" says Manuel, and he began pulling vexedly at his little gray beard, "and does one obligation beget another as fast as this! Now whatever would you have me do?"

"Obviously, you must get troops from King Ferdinand, and drive that awful Asmund out of Poictesme."

"Dear me!" says Manuel, "but what a simple matter you make of it! Shall I attend to it this afternoon?"

"Now, Manuel, you speak without thinking, for you could not possibly re-conquer all Poictesme this afternoon—"

"Oh!" says Manuel.

"No, not single-handed, my darling. You would

176

first have to get troops to help you, both horse and foot."

"My dearest, I only meant—"

"—Even then, it will probably take quite a while to kill off all the Northmen."

"Niafer, will you let me explain—"

"—Besides, you are miles away from Poictesme. You could not even manage to get there this afternoon."

Manuel put his hand over her mouth. "Niafer, when I spoke of subjugating Poictesme this afternoon I was attempting a mild joke. I will never any more attempt light irony in your presence, for I perceive that you do not appreciate my humor. Meanwhile I repeat to you, No, no, a thousand times, no! To be called Count of Poictesme sounds well, it strokes the hearing: but I will not be set to root and vegetate in a few hundred spadefuls of dirt. No, for I have but one lifetime here, and in that lifetime I mean to see this world and all the ends of this world, that I may judge them. And I," he concluded, decisively, "am Manuel, who follow after my own thinking and my own desire."

Niafer began to weep. "I simply cannot bear to think of what people will say of you."

"Come, come, my dear," says Manuel, "this is preposterous."

Niafer wept.

"You will only end by making yourself ill!" says Manuel.

Niafer continued to weep.

"My mind is quite made up," says Manuel, "so what, in God's name, is the good of this?"

Niafer now wept more and more broken-heartedly. And the big champion sat looking at her, and his broad shoulders relaxed. He viciously kicked at the heavy glistening green head of the dragon, still bleeding uglily there at his feet, but that did no good whatever. The dragon-queller was beaten. He could do nothing against such moisture, his resolution was dampened and his independence was washed away by this salt flood. And they say too that, now his youth was gone, Dom Manuel began to think of quietness and of soft living more resignedly than he acknowledged.

"Very well, then," Manuel says, by and by, "let us cross the Loir, and ride south to look for our infernal coronet with the rubies in it, and for your servants, and for some of your palaces."

So in the Christmas holidays they bring a tall burly squinting gray-haired warrior to King Ferdinand, in a lemon grove behind the royal palace. Here the sainted King, duly equipped with his halo and his goose-feather, was used to perform the lesser miracles on Wednesdays and Saturdays.

The King was delighted by the change in Manuel's looks, and said that experience and maturity were fine things to be suggested by the appearance of a nobleman in Manuel's position. But, a pest! as for giving him any troops with which to conquer Poictesme, that was quite another matter. The King needed his own soldiers for his own ends, which necessitated the immediate capture of Cordova. Meanwhile here were the Prince de Gâtinais and the Marquess di Paz, who also had come with this insane request, the one for soldiers to help him against the Philistines, and the other against the Catalans.

"Everybody to whom I ever granted a fief seems to need troops nowadays," the King grumbled, "and if any one of you had any judgment whatever you would have retained your lands once they were given you."

"Our deficiencies, sire," says the young Prince de Gâtinais, with considerable spirit, "have not been altogether in judgment, but rather in the support afforded us by our liege-lord."

This was perfectly true; but inasmuch as such blunt truths are not usually flung at a king and a saint, now Ferdinand's thin brows went up.

"Do you think so?" said the King. "We must see about it. What is that, for example?"

He pointed to the pool by which the lemon-trees were watered, and the Prince glanced at the yellow object afloat in this pool. "Sire," said de Gâtinais, "it is a lemon which has fallen from one of the trees."

"So you judge it to be a lemon. And what do you make of it, di Paz?" the King inquired.

The Marquess was a statesman who took few chances. He walked to the edge of the pool, and looked at the thing before committing himself: and he came back smiling. "Ah, sire, you have indeed contrived a cunning sermon against hasty judgment, for, while the tree is a lemon-tree, the thing that floats beneath it is an orange."

"So you, Marquess, judge it to be an orange. And what do you make of it, Count of Poictesme?" the King asks now.

If di Paz took few chances, Manuel took none at all. He waded into the pool, and fetched out the thing which floated there. "King," says big Dom Manuel, sagely blinking his bright pale eyes, "it is the half of an orange."

Said the King: "Here is a man who is not lightly deceived by the vain shows of this world, and who values truth more than dry shoes. Count Manuel, you shall have your troops, and you others must wait until you have acquired Count Manuel's powers of judgment, which, let me tell you, are more valuable than any fief I have to give."

So when the spring had opened, Manuel went into Poictesme at the head of a very creditable army, and Dom Manuel summoned Duke Asmund to surrender all that country. Asmund, who was habitually peevish under the puckerel curse, refused with opprobrious epithets, and the fighting began.

Manuel had, of course, no knowledge of generalship, but King Ferdinand sent the Conde de Tohil Vaca as Manuel's lieutenant. Manuel now figured imposingly in jeweled armor, and the sight of his shield bearing the rampant stallion and the motto *Mundus vult decipi* became in battle a signal for the more prudent among his adversaries to distinguish themselves in some other part of the conflict. It was whispered by backbiters that in counsel and in public discourse Dom Manuel sonorously repeated the orders and opinions provided by Tohil Vaca: either way, the official utterances of the Count of Poictesme roused everywhere the kindly feeling which one reserves for old friends, so that no harm was done.

To the contrary, Dom Manuel now developed an invaluable gift for public speaking, and in every place which he conquered and occupied he made powerful addresses to the surviving inhabitants before he had them hanged, exhorting all right-thinking persons to crush the military autocracy of Asmund. Besides, as Manuel pointed out, this was a struggle such as the world had never known, in that it was a war to end war forever, and to ensure eternal peace for everybody's children. Never, as he put it forcefully, had men fought for a more glorious cause. And so on and

180

so on, said he, and these uplifting thoughts had a fine effect upon everyone.

"How wonderfully you speak!" Dame Niafer would say admiringly.

And Manuel would look at her queerly, and reply: "I am earning your home, my dear, and your servants' wages, and some day these verbal jewels will be perpetuated in a real coronet. For I perceive that a former acquaintance of mine was right in pointing out the difference between men and the other animals."

"Ah, yes, indeed! " said Niafer, very gravely, and not attaching any particular meaning to it, but generally gathering that she and Manuel were talking about something edifying and pious. For Niafer was now a devout Christian, as became a Countess of Poictesme, and nobody anywhere entertained a more sincere reverence for solemn noises.

"For instance," Dame Niafer continued, "they tell me that these lovely speeches of yours have produced such an effect upon the Philistines yonder that their Queen Stultitia has proffered an alliance, and has promised to send you light cavalry and battering-rams."

"It is true she has promised to send them, but she has not done so."

"None the less, Manuel, you will find that the moral effect of her approbation will be invaluable; and, as I so often think, that is the main thing after all—"

"Yes, yes," says Manuel, impatiently, "we have plenty of moral approbation and fine speaking here, and in the South we have a saint to work miracles for us, but it is Asmund who has that army of splendid reprobates, and they do not value morality and rhetoric the worth of an old finger-nail."

181

So the fighting continued throughout that spring, and in Poictesme it all seemed very important and unexampled, just as wars usually appear to the people that are engaged in them. Thousands of men were slain, to the regret of their mothers and sweethearts, and very often of their wives. And there was the ordinary amount of unparalleled military atrocities and perfidies and ravishments and burnings and so on, and the endurers took their agonies so seriously that it is droll to think of how unimportant it all was in the outcome.

For this especial carnage was of supreme and world-wide significance so long ago that it is now not worth the pains involved to rephrase for inattentive hearing the combat of the knights at Perdigon—out of which came alive only Guivric and Coth and Anavalt and Gonfal,—or to speak of the once famous battle of the tinkers, or to retell how the inflexible syndics of Montors were imprisoned in a cage and slain by mistake. It no longer really matters to any living person how the Northmen burned the bridge of boats at Manneville; nor how Asmund trod upon a burnedthrough beam at the disastrous siege of Évre, and so fell thirty feet into the midst of his enemies and broke his leg, but dealt so valorously that he got safe away; nor how at Lisuarte unarmored peasants beat off Manuel's followers with scythes and pitchforks and clubs.

Time has washed out the significance of these old heroisms as the color is washed from flimsy cloths; so that chroniclers act wisely when they wave aside, with undipped pens, the episode of the brave Siennese and their green poison at Bellegarde, and the doings of the Anti-Pope there, and grudge the paper needful to record the remarkable method by which gaunt

Tohil Vaca levied a tax of a livre on every chimney in Poictesme.

It is not even possible, nowadays, to put warm interest in those once notable pots of blazing sulphur and fat and quicklime that were emptied over the walls of Storisende, to the discomfort of Manuel's men. For although this was a very heroic war, with a parade of every sort of high moral principle, and with the most sonorous language employed upon both sides, it somehow failed to bring about either the reformation or the ruin of humankind: and after the conclusion of the murdering and general breakage, the world went on pretty much as it has done after all other wars, with a vague notion that a deal of time and effort had been unprofitably invested, and a conviction that it would be inglorious to say so.

Therefore it suffices to report that there was much killing and misery everywhere, and that in June, upon Corpus Christi day, the Conde de Tohil Vaca was taken, and murdered, with rather horrible jocosity which used unusually a heated poker, and Manuel's forces were defeated and scattered.

XXVI

Deals with the Stork

❖❖❖❖❖❖❖❖❖❖❖❖❖

Now MANUEL, driven out of Poictesme, went with his wife to Novogath, which had been for some seven years the capital of Philistia. Queen Stultitia, the sixtieth of that name to rule, received them friendlily. She talked alone with Manuel for a lengthy while, in a room that was walled with glazed tiles of faience and had its ceiling incrusted with moral axioms, everywhere affixed thereto in a light lettering of tin, so as to permit of these axioms being readily changed. Stultitia sat at a bronze reading-desk: she wore rose-colored spectacles, and at her feet dozed, for the while, her favorite plaything, a blind, small, very fat white bitch called Luck.

The Queen still thought that an alliance could be arranged against Duke Asmund as soon as public sentiment could be fomented in Philistia, but this would take time. "Have patience, my friend!" she said, and that was easy saying for a prosperous great lady sitting comfortably crowned and spectacled in her own palace, under her own chimneys and skylights and campaniles and domes and towers and battlements.

But in the mean while Manuel and Niafer had not so much as a cowshed wherein to exercise this recommended virtue. So Manuel made inquiries, and learned that Queen Freydis had taken up her abode on Sargyll, most remote of the Red Islands.

"We will go to Freydis," he told Niafer.

"But, surely, not after the way that minx probably believes you treated her?" said Niafer.

Manuel smiled the sleepy smile that was Manuel. "I know Freydis better than you know her, my dear."

"Yes, but can you depend upon her? "

"I can depend upon myself, and that is more important."

"But, Manuel, you have another dear friend in England; and in England, although the Lord knows I never want to lay eyes on her, we might at least be comfortable—"

Manuel shook his head: "I am very fond of Alianora, because she resembles me as closely as it is possible for a woman to resemble a man. That makes two excellent reasons—one for each of us, snip,—why we had better not go into England."

So, in their homeless condition, they resolved to set out for Sargyll,—"to visit that other dear friend of yours," as Niafer put it, in tones more eloquent than Manuel seemed quite to relish.

Dame Niafer, though, now began to complain that Manuel was neglecting her for all this statecraft and fighting and speech-making and private conference with fine ladies; and she began to talk again about what a pity it was that she and Manuel would probably never have any children to be company for Niafer. Niafer complained rather often nowadays, about details which are here irrelevant: and she was used to lament with every appearance of sincerity that, in making the clay figure for Niafer to live in, Manuel should have been so largely guided by the elsewhere estimable qualities of innocence and imagination. It frequently put her, she said, to great inconvenience.

Now Manuel had been inquiring about this and that and the other since his arrival in Novogath, and so Manuel to-day replied with lordly assurance. "Yes, yes, a baby or two!" says Manuel. "I think myself that would be an excellent idea, while we are waiting for Queen Stultitia to make up her subjects' minds, and have nothing else in particular to do—"

"But, Manuel, you know perfectly well—"

"—And I am sufficiently versed in the magic of the Apsarasas to be able to summon the stork, who by rare good luck is already indebted to me—"

"What has the stork to do with this?"

"Why, it is he who must bring the babies to be company for you."

"But, Manuel," said Niafer, dubiously, "I do not believe that the people of Rathgor, or of Poictesme either, get their babies from the stork."

"Doubtless, like every country, they have their quaint local customs. We have no concern, however with these provincialities just now, for we are in Philistia. Besides, as you cannot well have forgotten, our main dependence is upon the half-promised alliance with Queen Stultitia, who is, as far as I can foresee, my darling, the only monarch anywhere likely to support us."

"But what has Queen Sutltitia to do with my having a baby?"

"Everything, dear snip. You must surely understand it is most important for one in my position to avoid in any way offending the sensibilities of the Philistines."

"Still, Manuel, the Philistines themselves have babies, and I do not see how they could have conceivably objected to my having at any rate a very small one if only you had made me right—"

"Not at all! nobody objects to the baby in itself, now that you are a married woman. The point is that the babies of the Philistines are brought to them by the stork; and that even an allusion to the possibility of misguided persons obtaining a baby in any other way these Philistines consider to be offensive and lewd and lascivious and obscene."

"Why, how droll of them! But are you sure of that, Manuel!"

"All their best-thought-of and most popular writers, my dear, are unanimous upon the point; and their Seranim have passed any number of laws, their oil-merchants have founded a guild, especially to prosecute such references. No, there is, to be sure, a dwindling sect which favors putting up with what babies you may find in the cabbage patch, but all really self-respecting people when in need of offspring arrange to be visited by the stork."

"It is certainly a remarkable custom, but it sounds convenient if you can manage it," said Niafer. "What I want is the baby, though, and of course we must try to get the baby in the manner of the Philistines, if you know that manner, for I am sure I have no wish to offend anybody."

So Manuel prepared to get a baby in the manner preferred by the Philistines. He performed the suitable incantation, putting this and that together in the manner formerly employed by the Thessalian witches and sorcerers, and he cried aloud a very ancient if indecent charm from the old Latin, saying, as Queen Stultitia had told him to say, without any mock-modest mincing of words:

Dictum est antiqua sandalio mulier habitavit,
Quæ multos pueros habuit tum ut potuit nullum
Quod faciundum erat cognoscere. Sic Domina Anser.

Then Manuel took from his breast-pocket a piece of
blue chalk and five curious objects something like
small black stars. With the chalk he drew upon the
floor two parallel straight lines. Manuel walked on
one of these chalk lines very carefully, then beckoned
Niafer to him. Standing there, he put his arms about
her and kissed her. Then he placed the five black stars
in a row,—

* * * * *

—and went over to the next line.

The stork having been thus properly summoned,
Manuel recalled to the bird the three wishes which
had been promised when Manuel saved the stork's
life: and Manuel said that for each wish he would
take a son fetched to him by the stork in the manner
of the Philistines.

The stork thought it could be arranged. "Not this
morning, though, as you suggest, for, indebted as I
am to you, Dom Manuel, I am also a very busy bird.
No, I have any number of orders that were put in
months before yours, and I must follow system in my
business, for you have no notion what elaborate and
exact accounts are frequently required by the married
men that receive invoices from me."

"Come now," says Manuel, "do you be accommo-
dating, remembering how I once saved your life from
the eagle, and my wife and I will order all our babies
now, and spare you the trouble of keeping any accounts whatever, so far as we are concerned."

"Oh, if you care to deal with such wholesale irregularity, and have no more consideration than to keep casting old debts in my bill, I might stretch a point in order to be rid of you," the stork said, sighing.

"Now, but surely," Manuel considered, "you might be a little more cheerful about this matter."

"And why should I, of all the birds that go about the heavens, be cheerful? "

"Well, somehow one expects a reasonable gaiety in you who bring hilarity and teething-rings into so many households—"

The stork answered:

"I bring the children, stainless and dear and helpless, and therewith I, they say, bring joy. Now of the joy I bring to the mother let none speak, for miracles are not neatly to be caged in sentences, nor is truth always expedient. To the father I bring the sight of his own life, by him so insecurely held, renewed and strengthened in a tenement not yet impaired by time and folly: he is no more disposed to belittle himself here than elsewhere; and it is himself that he cuddles in this small, soft, incomprehensible and unsoiled incarnation. For, as I bring the children, they have no evil in them and no cowardice and no guile.

"I bring the children, stainless and dear and helpless, when later I return, to those that yesterday were children. And in all ways time has marred, and living has defaced, and prudence has maimed, until I grieve to entrust that which I bring to what remains of that which yesterday I brought. In the old days children were sacrificed to a brazen burning god, but time affects more subtle hecatombs: for Moloch slew outright. Yes, Moloch, being divine, killed as the dog kills, furiously, but time is that transfigured cat, an ironist. So living mars and defaces and maims, and living appears wantonly to soil and to degrade its prey before destroying it.

"I bring the children, stainless and dear and helpless, and I leave them to endure that which is fated. Daily I bring into this world the beauty and innocence and high-heartedness and faith of children: but life has no employment, or else life has no sustenance, for these fine things which I bring daily, for always I, returning, find the human usages of living have extinguished these excellences in those who yesterday were children, and that these virtues exist in no aged person. And I would that Jahveh had created me an eagle or a vulture or some other hateful bird of prey that furthers a less grievous slaying and a more intelligible wasting than I further."

To this, Dom Manuel replied, in that grave and matter-of-fact way of his: "Now certainly I can see how your vocation may seem, in a manner of speaking, a poor investment; but, after all, your business is none of my business, so I shall not presume to criticize it. Instead, let us avoid these lofty generalities, and to you tell me when I may look for those three sons of mine."

Then they talked over this matter of getting babies, Manuel walking on the chalk line all the while, and Manuel found he could have, if he preferred it so, three girls in place of one of the boys, since the demand for sons was thrice that for daughters. To Niafer it was at once apparent that to obtain five babies in place of three was a clear bargain. Manuel said he did not want any daughters, they were too much of a responsibility, and he did not intend to be bothered with them. He was very firm and lordly about it. Then Niafer spoke again, and when she had ended, Manuel wished for two boys and three girls. There-

"I am also a very busy bird"

after the stork subscribed five promissory notes, and they executed all the other requisite formalities.

The stork said that by a little management he could let them have one of the children within a day or so. "But how long have you two been married?" he asked.

"Oh, ever so long," said Manuel, with a faint sigh.

"Why, no, my dearest," said Niafer, "we have been married only seven months."

"In that event," declared the stork, "you had better wait until month after next, for it is not the fashion among my patrons to have me visiting them quite so early."

"Well," said Manuel, "we wish to do everything in conformance to the preferences of Philistia, even to the extent of following such incomprehensible fashions." So he arranged to have the promised baby delivered at Sargyll, which, he told the stork, would be their address for the remainder of the summer.

XXVII

They Come to Sargyll

✦✦✦✦✦✦✦✦✦✦✦✦

THEN MANUEL and Niafer put out to sea, and after
two days' voyaging they came to Sargyll and to the
hospitality of Queen Freydis. Freydis was much
talked about at that time on account of the way in
which King Thibaut had come to his ruin through
her, and on account of her equally fatal dealings with
the Duke of Istria and the Prince of Camwy and
three or four other lords. So the ship-captains whom
Dom Manuel first approached preferred not to ven-
ture among the Red Islands. Then the Jewish master
of a trading vessel—a lean man called Ahasuerus—
said, "Who forbids it?" and carried them uneventfully
from Novogath to Sargyll. They narrate how Oriander the Swimmer followed after the yellow ship, but
he attempted no hurt against Manuel, at least not for
that turn.

Thus Manuel came again to Freydis. He had his
first private talk with her in a room that was hung
with black and gold brocade. White mats lay upon
the ground, and placed irregularly about the room
were large brass vases filled with lotus blossoms.
Here Freydis sat on a three-legged stool, in conference with a panther. From the ceiling hung rigid blue

and orange and reddish-brown serpents, all dead and embalmed; and in the middle of the ceiling was painted a face which was not quite human, looking downward, with evil eyes half closed, and with its mouth half open in discomfortable laughter.

Freydis was clad in scarlet completely, and, as has been said, a golden panther was talking to her when Dom Manuel came in. She at once dismissed the beast, which smiled amicably at Dom Manuel, and then arched high its back in the manner of all the cat tribe, and so flattened out into a thin transparent goldness, and, flickering, vanished upward as a flame leaves a lampwick.

"Well, well, you bade me come to you, dear friend, when I had need of you," says Manuel, very cordially shaking hands, "and nobody's need could be more great than mine."

"Different people have different needs," Freydis replied, rather gravely, "but all passes in this world."

"Friendship, however, does not pass, I hope."

She answered slowly: "It is we who pass, so that the young Manuel whom I loved in a summer that is gone, is nowadays as perished as that summer's gay leaves. What, grizzled fighting-man, have you to do with that young Manuel who had comeliness and youth and courage, but no human pity and no constant love? and why should I be harboring his light-hearted mischiefs against you? Ah, no, gray Manuel, you are quite certain no woman would do that; and people say you are shrewd. So I bid you very welcome to Sargyll, where my will is the only law."

"You at least have not changed," Dom Manuel replied, with utter truth, "for you appear to-day, if anything, more fair and young than you were that first night upon Morven when I evoked you from tall flames to lend life to the image I had made. Well, that seems now a lengthy while ago, and I make no more images."

"Your wife would be considering it a waste of time," Queen Freydis estimated.

"No, that is not quite the way it is. For Niafer is the dearest and most dutiful of women, and she never crosses my wishes in anything."

Freydis now smiled a little, for she saw that Manuel believed he was speaking veraciously. "At all events," said Freydis, "it is a queer thing surely that in the month which is to come the stork will be fetching your second child to a woman resting under my roof and in my golden bed. Yes, Thurinel has just been telling me of your plan, and it is a queer thing. Yet it is a far queerer thing that your first child, whom no stork fetched nor had any say in shaping, but whom you made of clay to the will of your proud youth and in your proud youth's likeness, should be limping about the world somewhere in the appearance of a strapping tall young fellow, and that you should know nothing about his doings."

"Ah! what have you heard? and what do you know about him, Freydis?"

"I suspicion many things, gray Manuel, by virtue of my dabblings in that gray art which makes neither for good nor evil."

"Yes," said Manuel, practically, "but what do you know?"

She took his hand again. "I know that in Sargyll, where my will is the only law, you are welcome, false friend and very faithless lover."

He could get no more out of her, as they stood there under the painted face which looked down upon them with discomfortable laughter.

So Manuel and Niafer remained at Sargyll until the baby should be delivered. King Ferdinand, then in the midst of another campaign against the Moors, could do nothing for his vassal just now. But glittering messengers came from Raymond Bérenger, and from King Helmas, and from Queen Stultitia, each to discuss this and that possible alliance and aid by and by. Everybody was very friendly if rather vague. But Manuel for the present considered only Niafer and the baby that was to come, and he let statecraft bide.

Then two other ships, that were laden with Duke Asmund's men, came also, in an attempt to capture Manuel: so Freydis despatched a sending which caused these soldiers to run about the decks howling like wolves, and to fling away their swords and winged helmets, and to fight one against the other with hands and teeth until all were slain.

The month passed thus uneventfully. And Niafer and Freydis became the best and most intimate of friends, and their cordiality to each other could not but have appeared to the discerning rather ominous.

"She seems to be a very good-hearted sort of a person," Niafer conceded, in matrimonial privacy, "though certainly she is rather queer. Why, Manuel, she showed me this afternoon ten of the drollest figures to which—but, no, you would never guess it in the world,—to which she is going to give life some day, just as you did to me when you got my looks and legs and pretty much everything else all wrong."

"When does she mean to quicken them?" Dom Manuel asked: and he added, "Not that I did, dear snip, but I shall not argue about it."

"Why, that is the droll part of it, and I can quite understand your unwillingness to admit how little you had remembered about me. When the man who

196

made them has been properly rewarded, she said, with, Manuel, the most appalling expression you ever saw."

"What were these images like?" asked Dom Manuel.

Niafer described them: she described them unsympathetically, but there was no doubt they were the images which Manuel had left unquickened upon Upper Morven.

Manuel nodded, smiled, and said: "So the man who made these images is to be properly rewarded! Well, that is encouraging, for true merit should always be rewarded."

"But, Manuel, if you had seen her look! and seen what horrible misshapen creatures they were—!"

"Nonsense!" said Manuel, stoutly: "you are a dear snip, but that does not make you a competent critic of either physiognomy or sculpture."

So he laughed the matter aside; and this, as it happened, was the last that Dom Manuel heard of the ten images which he had made upon Upper Morven. But they of Poictesme declared that Queen Freydis did give life to these figures, each at a certain hour, and that her wizardry set them to live as men among mankind, with no very happy results, because these images differed from naturally begotten persons by having inside them a spark of the life of Audela.

Thus Manuel and his wife came uneventfully to August; all the while there was never a more decorous or more thoughtful hostess than Queen Freydis; and nobody would have suspected that sorcery underlay the running of her household. It was only through Dom Manuel's happening to arise very early one morning, at the call of nature, that he chanced to be passing through the hall when, at the moment of sun-

197

rise, the night-porter turned into an orange-colored rat, and crept into the wainscoting: and Manuel of course said nothing about this to anybody, because it was none of his affair.

XXVIII

How Melicent Was Welcomed

So THE MONTH passed prosperously and uneventfully, while the servitors of Queen Freydis behaved in every respect as if they were human beings: and at the end of the month the stork came.

Manuel and Niafer, it happened, were fishing on the river bank rather late that evening, when they saw the great bird approaching, high overhead, all glistening white in the sunset, except for his thin scarlet legs and the blue shadowings in the hollows of his wings. From his beak depended a largish bundle, in pale blue wrappings, so that at a glance they knew the stork was bringing a girl.

Statelily the bird lighted on the window sill, as though he were quite familiar with this way of entering Manuel's bedroom, and the bird went in, carrying the child. This was a high and happy moment for the fond parents as they watched him, and they kissed each other rather solemnly.

Then Niafer left Manuel to get together the fishing tackle, and she hastened into the house to return to the stork the first of his promissory notes in exchange for the baby. And as Manuel was winding up the lines, Queen Freydis came to him, for she too had seen the stork's approach; and was, she said, with a grave smile, well pleased that the affair was settled.

"For now the stork has come, yet others may come," says Freydis, "and we shall celebrate the happy event with a gay feast this night in honor of your child."

"That is very kind and characteristic of you," said Manuel, "but I suppose you will be wanting me to make a speech, and I am quite unprepared."

"No, we will have none of your high-minded and devastating speeches at our banquet. No, for your place is with your wife. No, Manuel, you are not bidden to this feast, for all that it is to do honor to your child. No, no, gray Manuel, you must remain upstairs this evening and throughout the night, because this feast is for them that serve me: and you do not serve me any longer, and the ways of them that serve me are not your ways."

"Ah!" says Manuel, "so there is sorcery afoot! Yes, Freydis, I have quite given over that sort of thing. And while not for a moment would I seem to be criticizing anybody, I hope before long to see you settling down, with some fine solid fellow, and forsaking these empty frivolities for the higher and real pleasures of life."

"And what are these delights, gray Manuel?"

"The joy that is in the sight of your children playing happily about your hearth, and developing into honorable men and gracious women, and bringing their children in turn to cluster about your tired old knees, as the winter evenings draw in, and in the cosy fire-light you smile across the curly heads of these children's children at the dear wrinkled white-haired face of your beloved and time-tested helpmate, and are satisfied, all in all, with your life, and know that, by and large, Heaven has been rather undeservedly kind to you," says Manuel, sighing. "Yes, Freydis, yes, you may believe me that such are the real joys of life; and that such pleasures are more profitably pursued than are the idle gaieties of sorcery and witchcraft, which indeed at our age, if you will permit me to speak thus frankly, dear friend, are hardly dignified."

Freydis shook her proud dark head. Her smiling was grim.

"Decidedly, I shall not ever understand you. Doddering patriarch, do you not comprehend you are already discoursing about a score or two of grandchildren on the ground of having a five-minute-old daughter, whom you have not yet seen? Nor is that child's future, it may be, yours to settle—But go to your wife, for this is Niafer's man who is talking, and not mine. Go up, Methuselah, and behold the new life which you have created and cannot control!"

Manuel went to Niafer, and found her sewing. "My dear, this will not do at all, for you ought to be in bed with the newborn child, as is the custom with the mothers of Philistia."

"What nonsense!" says Niafer, "when I have to be changing every one of the pink bows on Melicent's caps for blue bows."

"Still, Niafer, it is eminently necessary for us to be placating the Philistines in all respects, in this delicate matter of your having a baby."

Niafer grumbled, but obeyed. She presently lay in the golden bed of Freydis: then Manuel duly looked at the contents of the small heaving bundle at Niafer's side: and whether or no he scaled the conventional peaks of emotion was nobody's concern save Manuel's. He began, in any event, to talk in the vein which

201

fathers ordinarily feel such high occasions to demand. But Niafer, who was never romantic nowadays, merely said that, anyhow, it was a blessing it was all over, and that she hoped, now, they would soon be leaving Sargyll.

"But Freydis is so kind, my dear," said Manuel, "and so fond of you!"

"I never in my life," declared Niafer, "knew anybody to go off so terribly in their looks as that two-faced cat has done since the first time I saw her prancing on her tall horse and rolling her snake eyes at you. As for being fond of me, I trust her exactly as far as I can see her."

"Yet, Niafer, I have heard you declare, time and again—"

"But if you did, Manuel, one has to be civil."

Manuel shrugged, discreetly. "You women!" he observed, discreetly.

"—As if it were not as plain as the nose on her face —and I do not suppose that even you, Manuel, will be contending she has a really good nose,—that the woman is simply itching to make a fool of you, and to have everybody laughing at you, again! Manuel, I declare I have no patience with you when you keep arguing about such unarguable facts!"

Manuel, exercising augmented discretion, now said nothing whatever.

"—And you may talk yourself black in the face, Manuel, but nevertheless I am going to name the child Melicent, after my own mother, as soon as a priest can be fetched from the mainland to christen her. No, Manuel, it is all very well for your dear friend to call herself a gray witch, but I do not notice any priests coming to this house unless they are especially sent for, and I draw my own conclusions."

"Well, well, let us not argue about it, my dear."

"Yes, but who started all this arguing and fault-finding, I would like to know!"

"Why, to be sure I did. But I spoke without thinking. I was wrong. I admit it. So do not excite yourself, dear snip."

"—And as if I could help the child's not being a boy!"

"But I never said—"

"No, but you keep thinking it, and sulking is the one thing I cannot stand. No, Manuel, no, I do not complain, but I do think that, after all I have been through with, sleeping around in tents, and running away from Northmen, and never having a moment's comfort, after I had naturally figured on being a real countess—" Niafer whimpered sleepily.

"Yes, yes," says Manuel, stroking her soft crinkly hair.

"—And with that silky hell-cat watching me all the time,—and looking ten years younger than I do, now that you have got my face and legs all wrong,—and planning I do not know what—"

"Yes, to be sure," says Manuel, soothingly: "you are quite right, my dear."

So a silence fell, and presently Niafer slept. Manuel sat with hunched shoulders, watching the wife he had fetched back from paradise at the price of his youth. His face was grave, his lips were puckered and protruded. He smiled by and by, and he shook his head. He sighed, not as one who is grieved, but like a man perplexed and a little weary.

Now some while after Niafer was asleep, and when the night was fairly advanced, you could hear a whizzing and a snorting in the air. Manuel went to the window, and lifted the scarlet curtain figured

203

with ramping gold dragons, and he looked out, to find a vast number of tiny bluish lights skipping about confusedly and agilely in the darkness, like shining fleas. These approached the river bank, and gathered there. Then the assembled lights began to come toward the house. You could now see these lights were carried by dwarfs who had the eyes of owls and the long beaks of storks. These dwarfs were jumping and dancing about Freydis like an insane body-guard.

Freydis walked among them very remarkably attired. Upon her head shone the uræus crown, and she carried a long rod of cedar-wood topped with an apple carved in bluestone, and at her side came the appearance of a tall young man.

So they all approached the house, and the young man looked up fixedly at the unlighted window, as though he were looking at Manuel. The young man smiled: his teeth gleamed in the blue glare. Then the whole company entered the house, and from Manuel's station at the window you could see no more, but you could hear small prancing hoof-beats downstairs and the clattering of plates and much whinnying laughter. Manuel was plucking irresolutely at his grizzled short beard, for there was no doubt as to the strapping tall young fellow.

Presently you could hear music: it was the ravishing Nis air, which charms the mind into sweet confusion and oblivion, and Manuel did not make any apparent attempt to withstand its wooing. He hastily undressed, knelt for a decorous interval, and climbed vexedly into bed.

XXIX

Sesphra of the Dreams
❖❖❖❖❖❖❖❖❖❖❖❖

IN THE MORNING Dom Manuel arose early, and left
Niafer still sleeping with the baby. Manuel came
down through the lower hall, where the table was as
the revelers had left it. In the middle of the disordered
room stood a huge copper vessel half full of liquor,
and beside it was a drinking-horn of gold. Manuel
paused here, and drank of the sweet heather-wine as
though he had need to hearten himself.

He went out into the bright windy morning, and as
he crossed the fields he came up behind a red cow
who was sitting upon her haunches, intently reading a
largish book bound in green leather, but at sight of
Manuel she hastily put aside the volume, and began
eating grass. Manuel went on, without comment, toward the river bank, to meet the image which he had
made of clay, and to which through unholy arts he
had given life.

The thing came up out of the glistening ripples of
brown water, and the thing embraced Manuel and
kissed him. "I am pagan," the thing said, in a sweet
mournful voice, "and therefore I might not come to
you until your love was given to the unchristened. For
I was not ever christened, and so my true name is not

known to anybody. But in the far lands where I am worshipped as a god I am called Sesphra of the Dreams."

"I did not give you any name," said Manuel; and then he said: "Sesphra, you that have the appearance of Alianora and of my youth! Sesphra, how beautiful you are!"

"Is that why you are trembling, Manuel?"

"I tremble because the depths of my being have been shaken. Since youth went out of me, in the high woods of Dun Vlechlan, I have lived through days made up of small frettings and little pleasures and only half earnest desires, which moved about upon the surface of my being like minnows in the shoals of a still lake. But now that I have seen and heard you, Sesphra of the Dreams, and your lips have touched my lips, a passion moves in me that possesses all of me, and I am frightened."

"It is the passion which informs those who make images. It is the master you denied, poor foolish Manuel, and the master who will take no denial."

"Sesphra, what is your will with me?"

"It is my will that you and I go hence on a long journey, into the far lands where I am worshipped as a god. For I love you, my creator, who gave life to me, and you love me more than aught else, and it is not right that we be parted."

"I cannot go on any journey, just now, for I have my lands and castles to regain, and my wife and my newborn child to protect."

Sesphra began to smile adorably: you saw that his teeth were strangely white and very strong. "What are these things to me or you, or to anyone that makes images? We follow after our own thinking and our own desires."

"I lived thus once upon a time," said Manuel, sighing, "but nowadays there is a bond upon me to provide for my wife, and for my child too, and I have not much leisure left for anything else."

Then Sesphra began to speak adorably, as he walked on the river bank, with one arm about Dom Manuel. Always Sesphra limped as he walked. A stiff and obdurate wind was ruffling the broad brown shining water, and as they walked, this wind buffeted them, and tore at their clothing. Manuel clung to his hat with one hand, and with the other held to lame Sesphra of the Dreams. Sesphra talked of matters not to be recorded.

"That is a handsome ring you have there," says Sesphra, by and by.

"It is the ring my wife gave me when we were married," Manuel replied.

"Then you must give it to me, dear Manuel."

"No, no, I cannot part with it."

"But it is beautiful, and I want it," Sesphra said. So Manuel gave him the ring.

Now Sesphra began again to talk of matters not to be recorded.

"Sesphra of the Dreams," says Manuel, presently, "you are bewitching me, for when I listen to you I see that Manuel's imperilled lands make such a part of earth as one grain of sand contributes to the long narrow beach we are treading. I see my fond wife Niafer as a plain-featured and dull woman, not in any way remarkable among the millions of such women as are at this moment preparing breakfast or fretting over other small tasks. I see my newborn child as a mewing lump of flesh. And I see Sesphra whom I made so strong and strange and beautiful, and it is as if in a half daze I hear that obdurate wind commingled with

207

the sweet voice of Sesphra while you are talking of matters which it is not safe to talk about."

"Yes, that is the way it is, Manuel, and the way it should be, and the way it always will be as long as life is spared to you, now. So let us go into the house, and write droll letters to King Helmas and Raymond Bérenger and Queen Stultitia, in reply to the fine offers they have been making you."

They came back into the empty banquet-hall. This place was paved with mother of pearl and copper; six porphyry columns supported the musicians' gallery. To the other end were two alabaster urns upon green pedestals that were covered with golden writing in the old Dirgham.

Here Manuel cleared away the embossed silver plates from one corner of the table. He took pen and ink, and Sesphra told him what to write.

Sesphra sat with arms folded, and as he dictated he looked up at the ceiling. This ceiling was of mosaic work, showing four winged creatures that veiled their faces with crimson and orange-tawny wings; suspended from this ceiling by bronze chains hung ostrich eggs, bronze lamps and globes of crystal.

"But these are very insulting replies," observed Dom Manuel, when he had finished writing, "and they will make their recipients furious. These princes, Sesphra, are my good friends, and they are powerful friends, upon whose favor I am dependent."

"Yes, but how beautiful these replies are worded! See now, dear Manuel, how divertingly you have described King Helmas' hideous nose in your letter to King Helmas, and how trenchant is that paragraph about the scales of his mermaid wife—"

"I admit that passage is rather droll—"

"—And in your letter to the pious Queen Stultitia

that which you say about the absurdities of religion, here, and the fun you make of her spectacles, are masterpieces of paradox and of very exquisite prose—"

"Those bits, to be sure, are quite neatly put—"

"—So I must see to it that these replies are sent, to make people admire you everywhere."

"Yet, Sesphra, all these princes are my friends, and their goodwill is necessary to me—"

"No, Manuel. For you and I will not bother about these stupid princes any more, nor will you need any friends except me; for we will go to this and that remote strange place, and our manner of living will be such and such, and we will do so and so, and we will travel everywhither and see the ends of this world and judge them. And we will not ever be parted until you die."

"What will you do then, dear Sesphra?" Manuel asks him fondly.

"I shall survive you, as all gods outlive their creators. And I must depute the building of your monument to men of feeble minds which have been properly impaired by futile studies and senility. That is the way in which all gods are doomed to deal with their creators: but that need not trouble us as yet."

"No," Manuel said, "I cannot go with you. For in my heart is enkindling such love of you as frightens me."

"It is through love men win to happiness, poor lonely Manuel."

Now when Manuel answered Sesphra there was in Manuel's face trouble and bewilderment. And Manuel said:

"Under your dear bewitchments, Sesphra, I confess that through love men win to sick disgust and self-despising, and for that reason I will not love any more.

Now breathlessly the tall lads run to clutch at stars, above the brink of a drab quagmire, and presently time trips them— Oh, Sesphra, wicked Sesphra of the Dreams, you have laid upon me a magic so strong that, horrified, I hear the truth come babbling from long-guarded lips which no longer obey me, because of your dear bewitchments.

"Look you, adorable and all-masterful Sesphra, I have followed noble loves. I aspired to the Unattainable Princess, and thereafter to the unattainable Queen of a race that is more fine and potent than our race, and afterward I would have no less a love than an unattainable angel in paradise. Hah, I must be fit mate for that which is above me, was my crying in the old days; and such were the indomitable desires that one by one have made my living wonderful with dear bewitchments.

"The devil of it was that these proud aims did not stay unattained! Instead, I was cursed by getting my will, and always my reward was nothing marvelous and rare, but that quite ordinary figure of earth, a human woman. And always in some dripping dawn I have turned with abhorrence from myself and from the sated folly that had hankered for such prizes, which, when possessed, showed as not wonderful in anything, and which possession left likable enough, but stripped of dear bewitchments.

"No, Sesphra, no: men are so made that they must desire to mate with some woman or another, and they are furthermore so made that to mate with a woman does not content their desire. And in this gaming there is no gain, because the end of loving, for everybody except those lucky persons whose love is not requited, must always be a sick disgust and a self-despising, which the wise will conduct in silence, and not

210

talk about as I am talking now under your dear bewitchments."

Then Sesphra smiled a little, saying, "And yet, poor Manuel, there is, they tell me, no more uxorious husband anywhere."

"I am used to her," Manuel replied, forlornly, "and I suppose that if she were taken away from me again I would again be attempting to fetch her back. And I do not like to hurt the poor foolish heart of her by going against her foolish notions. Besides, I am a little afraid of her, because she is always able to make me uncomfortable. And above all, of course, the hero of a famous love-affair, such as ours has become, with those damned poets everywhere making rhymes about my fidelity and devotion, has to preserve appearances. So I get through each day, somehow, by never listening very attentively to the interminable things she tells me about. But I often wonder, as I am sure all husbands wonder, why Heaven ever made a creature so tedious and so unreasonably dull of wit and so opinionated. And when I think that for the rest of time this creature is to be my companion I usually go out and kill somebody. Then I come back, because she knows the way I like my toast."

"Instead, dear Manuel, you must go away from this woman who does not understand you—"

"Yes," Manuel said, with grave conviction, "that is exactly the trouble."

"—And you must go with me who understand you all through. And we will travel everywhither, so that we may see the ends of this world and judge them."

"You tempt me, Sesphra, with an old undying desire, and you have laid strong enchantments on me, but, no, I cannot go with you."

211

The hand of Sesphra closed upon the hand of Manuel caressingly.

Manuel said: "I will go with you. But what will become of the woman and the child whom I leave behind me unfriended?"

"That is true. There will be nobody to look out for them, and they will perish miserably. That is not important, but perhaps upon the whole it would be better for you to kill them before we depart from Sargyll."

"Very well, then," says Manuel, "I will do that, but you must come up into the room with me, for I cannot bear to lose sight of you."

Now Sesphra smiled more unrestrainedly, and his teeth gleamed. "I shall not ever leave you now until you die."

XXX

Farewell to Freydis

•❖❖❖❖❖❖❖❖❖❖❖❖❖❖•

THEY WENT upstairs together, into the room with scarlet hangings, and to the golden bed where, with seven sorts of fruit properly arranged at the bedside, Dom Manuel's wife Niafer lay asleep. Manuel drew his dagger. Niafer turned in her sleep, so that she seemed to offer her round small throat to the raised knife. You saw now that on the other side of the golden bed sat Queen Freydis, making a rich glow of color there, and in her lap was the newborn naked child.

Freydis rose, holding the child to her breast, and smiling. A devil might smile thus upon contriving some new torment for lost souls, but a fair woman's face should not be so cruel. Then this evil joy passed from the face of Freydis. She dipped her fingers into the bowl of water with which she had been bathing the child, and with her finger-tips she made upon the child's forehead the sign of a cross.

Said Freydis, "Melicent, I baptize thee in the name of the Father, and of the Son, and of the Holy Ghost."

Sesphra passed wildly toward the fireplace, crying, "A penny, a penny, twopence, a penny and a half, and a halfpenny!" At his call the fire shot forth tall flames, and Sesphra entered these flames as a man goes

213

between parted curtains, and instantly the fire collapsed and was as it had been. Already the hands of Freydis were moving deftly in the Sleep Charm, so that Niafer did not move. Freydis to-day was resplendently robed in flame-colored silk, and about her dark hair was a circlet of burnished copper.

Manuel had dropped his dagger so that the point of it pierced the floor, and the weapon stood erect and quivering. But Manuel was shaken for a moment more horribly than shook the dagger: you would have said he was convulsed with horror and self-loathing. So for an instant he waited, looking at Dame Niafer, who slept untroubled, and at fiery-colored Freydis, who was smiling rather queerly: and then the old composure came back to Manuel.

"Breaker of all oaths," says Freydis, "I must tell you that this Sesphra is pagan, and cannot thrive except among those whose love is given to the unchristened. Thus he might not come to Sargyll until the arrival of this little heathen whom I have just made Christian. Now we have only Christian terrors here; and again your fate is in my hands."

Dom Manuel looked grave. "Freydis," he said, "you have rescued me from very unbecoming conduct. A moment more and I would have slain my wife and child because of this Sesphra's resistless magic."

Says Freydis, still smiling a queer secret smile: "Indeed, there is no telling into what folly and misery Sesphra would not have led you. For you fashioned his legs unevenly, and he has not ever pardoned you his lameness."

"The thing is a devil," Manuel said. "And this is the figure I desired to make, this is the child of my long dreams and labors! This is the creature I designed to be more admirable and significant than the drab men I found in streets and lanes and palaces! Certainly, I have loosed among mankind a blighting misery which I cannot control at all."

"The thing is you as you were once, gray Manuel. You had comeliness and wit and youth and courage, and these you gave the image, shaping it boldly to your proud youth's will and in your proud youth's likeness. But human pity and any constant love you did not then have to give, either to your fellows or to the fine figure you made, nor, very certainly, to me. So you amused yourself by making Sesphra and by making me that which we are to-day."

Now again showed subtly evil thoughts in the face of this shrewd flaming woman who had so recently brought about the destruction of King Thibaut, and of the Duke of Istria, and of those other enamored lords. And Dom Manuel began to regard her more intently.

In Manuel's sandals the average person would have reflected, long before this, that Manuel and his wife and child were in this sorcerous place at the mercy of the whims and the unwholesome servitors of this not very dependable looking witch-woman. The average person would have recollected distastefully that unusual panther and that discomfortable night-porter and the madness which had smitten Duke Asmund's men, and the clattering vicious little hoofs of the shrill dwarfs; and to the average person this room would have seemed a desirable place to be many leagues away from.

But candid blunt Dom Manuel said, with jovial laughter: "You speak as if you had not grown more adorable every day, dear Freydis, and as though I would not be vastly flattered to think I had any part in the improvement. You should not fish thus unblushingly for compliments."

The sombre glitterings that were her eyes had narrowed, and she was looking at his hands. Then Freydis said: "There are pin-points of sweat upon the back of your hands, gray Manuel, and so alone do I know that you are badly frightened. Yes, you are rather wonderful, even now."

"I am not unduly frightened, but I am naturally upset by what has just happened. Anybody would be. For I do not know what I must anticipate in the future, and I wish that I had never meddled in this mischancy business of creating things I cannot manage."

Queen Freydis moved in shimmering splendor toward the fireplace. She paused there, considerately looking down at the small contention of flames. "Did you not, though, again create much misery when for your pleasure you gave life to this girl child? Certainly you must know that there will be in her life—if life indeed be long spared to her," said Freydis, reflectively,—"far less of joy than of sorrow, for that is the way it is with the life of everybody. But all this likewise is out of your hands. In Sesphra and in the child and in me you have lightly created that which you cannot control. No, it is I who control the outcome."

Now a golden panther came quite noiselessly into the room, and sat to the right of Freydis, and looked at Dom Manuel.

"Why, to be sure," says Manuel, heartily, "and I am sure, too, that nobody is better qualified to handle it. Come now, Freydis, just as you say, this is a serious situation, and something really ought to be done about this situation. Come now, dear friend, in what way can we take back the life we gave this lovely fiend?"

"And would I be wanting to kill my husband?" Queen Freydis asked, and she smiled wonderfully. "Why, but yes, this fair lame child of yours is my

216

husband to-day,—poor, frightened, fidgeting gray Manuel,—and I love him, for Sesphra is all that you were when I loved you, Manuel, and when you condescended to take your pleasure of me."

Now an orange-colored rat came into the room, and sat down upon the hearth to the left hand of Freydis, and looked at Dom Manuel. And the rat was as large as the panther.

Then Freydis said: "No, Manuel, Sesphra must live for a great while, long after you have been turned to graveyard dust: and he will limp about wherever pagans are to be found, and he will always win much love from the high-hearted pagans because of his comeliness and because of his unfading jaunty youth. And whether he will do any good anywhere is doubtful, but it is certain he will do harm, and it is equally certain that already he weighs my happiness as carelessly as you once weighed it."

Now came into the room another creature, such as no madman has ever seen or imagined, and it lay down at the feet of Freydis, and it looked at Dom Manuel. Couched thus, this creature yawned and disclosed unreassuring teeth.

"Well, Freydis," says Dom Manuel, handsomely, "but, to be sure, what you tell me puts a new complexion upon matters, and not for worlds would I be coming between husband and wife—"

Queen Freydis looked up from the flames, toward Dom Manuel, very sadly. Freydis shrugged, flinging out her hands above the heads of the accursed beasts. "And at the last I cannot do that, either. So do you two dreary, unimportant, well-mated people remain undestroyed, now that I go to seek my husband, and now I endeavor to win my pardon for not letting him torment you. Eh, I was tempted, gray Manuel, to let

217

my masterful fine husband have his pleasure of you, and of this lean ugly hobbling creature and her brat, too, as formerly you had your pleasure of me. But women are so queerly fashioned that at the last I cannot, quite, consent to harm this gray, staid, tedious fellow, nor any of his chattels. For all passes in this world save one thing only: and though the young Manuel whom I loved in a summer that is gone, be nowadays as perished as that summer's gay leaves, it is certain a woman's folly does not ever perish."

"Indeed, I did not merit that you should care for me," says Manuel, rather unhappily. "But I have always been, and always shall be sincerely fond of you, Freydis, and for that reason I rejoice to deduce that you are not, now, going to do anything violent and irreparable and such as your better nature would afterward regret."

"I loved you once," she said, "and now I am assured the core of you was always a cold and hard and colorless and very common pebble. But it does not matter now that I am a mortal woman. Either way, you have again made use of me. I have afforded you shelter when you were homeless. And now again you will be getting your desire."

Queen Freydis went to the window, and lifted the scarlet curtain figured with ramping gold dragons; but the couching beasts stayed by the hearth, and they continued to look at Dom Manuel.

"Yes, now again, gray Manuel, you will be getting your desire. That ship which shows at the river bend, with serpents and castles painted on its brown sails, is Miramon Lluagor's ship, which he has sent to fetch you from Sargyll: and the last day of your days of exile is now over. For Miramon is constrained by one who is above us all; therefore Miramon comes gladly and very potently to assist you. And I—who have served your turn!—I may now depart, to look for Sesphra, and for my pardon if I can get it."

"But whither do you go, dear Freydis?" Dom Manuel spoke as though he again felt quite fond of her.

"What does that matter," she answered, looking long and long at him, "now that Count Manuel has no further need of me?" Then Freydis looked at Niafer, lying there in a charmed sleep. "I neither love nor entirely hate you, ugly and lame and lean and fretful Niafer, but assuredly I do not envy you. You are welcome to your fidgeting gray husband. My husband is a ruthless god. My husband does not grow old and tender-hearted and subservient to me, and he never will." Thereafter Freydis bent downward, and Freydis kissed the child she had christened. "Some day you will be a woman, Melicent, and then you will be loving some man or another man. I could hope that you will then love the man who will make you happy, but that sort of man has not yet been found."

Dom Manuel came to her, not heeding the accursed beasts at all, and he took both the hands of Freydis in his hands. "My dear, and do you think I am a happy man?"

She looked up at him: when she answered, her voice trembled. "I made you happy, Manuel. I would have made you happy always."

"I wonder if you would have? Ah, well, at all events, the obligation was upon me. At no time in a man's life, I find, is there lacking some obligation or another: and we must meet each as we best can, not hoping to succeed, just aiming not to fall short too far. No, it is not a merry pursuit. And it is a ruining pursuit!"

She said, "I had not thought ever to be sorry for you— Why should I grieve for you, gray traitor?"

Harshly he answered: "Oho, I am not proud of what I have made of my life, and of your life, and of the life of that woman yonder, but do you think I will be whining about it! No, Freydis: the boy that loved and deserted you is here,"—he beat upon his breast,—"locked in, imprisoned while time lasts, dying very lonelily. Well, I am a shrewd gaoler: he shall not get out. No, even at the last, dear Freydis, there is the bond of silence."

She said, impotently, "I am sorry— Even at the last you contrive for me a new sorrow—"

For a moment they stood looking at each other, and she remembered thereafter his sad and quizzical smiling. These two had nothing more to share in speech or deed.

Then Freydis went away, and the accursed beasts and her castle too went with her, as smoke passes. Manuel was thus left standing out of doors in a reaped field, alone with his wife and child while Miramon's ship came about. Niafer slept. But now the child awoke to regard the world into which she had been summoned willy-nilly, and the child began to whimper.

Dom Manuel patted this intimidating small creature gingerly, with a strong comely hand from which his wedding ring was missing. That would require explanations.

It therefore seems not improbable that he gave over this brief period of waiting, in a reaped field, to wondering just how much about the past he might judiciously tell his wife when she awoke to question him, because in the old days that was a problem which no considerate husband failed to weigh with care.

XXXI

Statecraft

Now FROM the ship's gangway came seven trumpeters
dressed in glistening plaids: each led with a silver
chain a grayhound, and each of the seven hounds carried in his mouth an apple of gold. After these followed three harp-players and three clergymen and
three jesters, all bearing crested staves and wearing
chaplets of roses. Then Miramon Lluagor, lord of the
nine sleeps and prince of the seven madnesses, comes
ashore. An incredible company followed. But with
him came his wife Gisèle and their little child Demetrios, thus named for the old Count of Arnaye: and it
was this boy that, they say, when yet in swaddling-
bands, was appointed to be the slayer of his own father, wise Miramon Lluagor.

Dame Niafer was wakened, and the two women
went apart to compare and discuss their babies. They
put the children in one cradle. A great while afterward were these two again to lie together thus, and
from this mating was the girl to get long sorrow, and
the boy his death.

Meanwhile the snub-nosed lord of the nine sleeps
and the squinting Count of Poictesme sat down upon
the river bank to talk about more serious matters than

221

croup and teething. The sun was high by this time, so Kan and Muluc and Ix and Cauac came in haste from the corners of the world, and held up a blue canopy to shelter the conferring between their master and Don Manuel.

"What is this," said Miramon Lluagor to Dom Manuel, first of all, "that I hear of your alliance with Philistia, and of your dickerings with a people who say that my finest designs are nothing but indigestion?"

"I have lost Poictesme," says Manuel, "and the Philistines offer to support me in my pretensions."

"But that will never do! I who design all dreams can never consent to that, and no Philistine must ever enter Poictesme. Why did you not come to me for help at the beginning, instead of wasting time upon kings and queens?" demands the magician, fretfully. "And are you not ashamed to be making any alliance with Philistia, remembering how you used to follow after your own thinking and your own desire?"

"Well," Manuel replies, "I have had as yet nothing save fair words from Philistia, and no alliance is concluded."

"That is more than well. Only, let us be orderly about this. Imprimis, you desire Poictesme—"

"No, not in particular, but appearances have to be preserved, and my wife thinks it would look better for me to redeem this country from the oppression of the heathen Northmen, and so provide her with a suitable home."

"Item, then I must obtain this country for you, because there is no sense in withstanding our wives in such matters."

"I rejoice at your decision—"

"Between ourselves, Manuel, I fancy you now begin

222

to understand the reasons which prompted me to bring you the magic sword Flamberge at the beginning of our acquaintance, and have learned who it is that wears the breeches in most marriages."

"No, that is not the way it is at all, Miramon, for my wife is the dearest and most dutiful of women, and never crosses my wishes in anything."

Miramon nodded his approval. "You are quite right, for somebody might be overhearing us. So, let us get on, and do you stop interrupting me. Item, you must hold Poictesme, and your heirs forever after must hold Poictesme, not in fee but by feudal tenure. Item, you shall hold these lands, not under any saint like Ferdinand, but under a quite different sort of liege-lord."

"I can see no objection to your terms, thus far. But who is to be my overlord?"

"A person whom you may remember," replied Miramon, and he beckoned toward the rainbow throng of his followers.

One of them at this signal came forward. He was a tall lean youngster, with ruddy cheeks, wide-set brown eyes, and a smallish head covered with crisp, tightly-curling dark red hair: and Manuel recognized him at once, because Manuel had every reason to remember the queer talk he had held with this Horvendile just after Niafer had ridden away with Miramon's dreadful half-brother.

"But do you not think that this Horvendile is insane?" Dom Manuel asked the magician, privately.

"I confess he very often has that appearance."

"Then why do you make him my overlord?"

"I have my reasons, you may depend upon it, and if I do not talk about them you may be sure that for this reticence also I have my reasons."

"But is this Horvendile, then, one of the Léshy? Is he the Horvendile whose great-toe is the morning star?"

"I may tell you that it was he who summoned me to help you in distress, of which I had not heard upon Vraidex, but why should I tell you any more, Dom Manuel? Come, is it not enough that am offering you a province and comparatively tranquil terms of living with your wife, that you must have all my old secrets to boot?"

"You are right," says Manuel, "and prospective benefactors must be humored." So he rested content with his ignorance, nor did he ever find out about Horvendile, though later Manuel must have had horrible suspicions.

Meanwhile, Dom Manuel affably shook hands with the red-headed boy, and spoke of their first meeting. "And I believe you were not talking utter foolishness after all, my lad;" says Manuel, laughing, "for I have learned that the strange and dangerous thing which you told me is very often true."

"Why, how should I know," quiet Horvendile replied, "when I am talking foolishness and when not?"

Manuel said: "Still, I can understand your talking only in part. Well, but it is not right for us to understand our overlords, and, madman or not, I prefer you to Queen Stultitia and her preposterous rose-colored spectacles. So let us proceed in due form, and draw up the articles of our agreement."

This was done, and they formally subscribed the terms under which Dom Manuel and the descendants of Dom Manuel were to hold Poictesme perpetually in fief to Horvendile. It was the most secret sort of compact, and to divulge its ten stipulations would even now be most disastrous. So the terms of this compact were not ever made public. Thus all men stayed at no larger liberty to criticize its provisos than his circumstances had granted to Dom Manuel, upon whom marrying had put the obligation to provide, in one way or another way, for his wife and child.

MUNDUS VULT DECIPI

XXXII

The Redemption of Poictesme
❖❖❖❖❖❖❖❖❖❖❖❖❖

WHEN THESE MATTERS were concluded, and the future of Poictesme had been arranged in every detail, then Miramon Lluagor's wife told him that long words and ink-bottles and red seals were well enough for men to play with, but that it was high time something sensible was done in this matter, unless they expected Niafer to bring up the baby in a ditch.

The magician said, "Yes, my darling, you are quite right, and I will see to it the first thing after dinner."

He then said to Dom Manuel, "Now Horvendile informs me that you were duly born in a cave at about the time of the winter solstice, of a virgin mother and of a father who was not human."

Manuel replied, "Certainly that is true. But why do you now stir up these awkward old stories?"

"You have duly wandered from place to place, bringing wisdom and holiness to men—"

"That also is generally known."

"You have duly performed miracles, such as reviving dead persons and so on—"

"That too is undeniable."

"You have duly sojourned with evil in a desert

place, and have there been tempted to despair and blaspheme and to commit other iniquities."

"Yes, something of the sort did occur in Dun Vlechlan."

"And, as I well know, you have by your conduct of affairs upon Vraidex duly disconcerted me, who am the power of darkness—"

"Ah! ah! you, Miramon, are then the power of darkness!"

"I control all dreams and madnesses, Dom Manuel; and these are the main powers of darkness."

Manuel seemed dubious, but he only said: "Well, let us get on! It is true that all these things have happened to me, somehow."

The magician looked at the tall warrior for a while, and in the dark soft eyes of Miramon Lluagor was a queer sort of compassion. Miramon said, "Yes, Manuel, these portents have marked your living thus far, just as they formerly distinguished the beginnings of Mithras and of Huitzilopochtli and of Tammouz and of Heracles—"

"Yes, but what does it matter if these accidents did happen to me, Miramon?"

"—As they happened to Gautama and to Dionysos and to Krishna and to all other reputable Redeemers," Miramon continued.

"Well, well, all this is granted. But what, pray, am I to deduce from all this?"

Miramon told him.

Dom Manuel, at the end of Miramon's speaking, looked peculiarly solemn, and Manuel said: "I had thought the transformation surprising enough when King Ferdinand was turned into a saint, but this tops all! Either way, Miramon, you point out an obligation so tremendous that the less said about it, the wiser;

227

and the sooner this obligation is discharged and the ritual fulfilled, the more comfortable it will be for everybody."

So Manuel went away with Miramon Lluagor into a secret place, and there Dom Manuel submitted to that which was requisite, and what happened is not certainly known. But this much is known, that Manuel suffered, and afterward passed three days in an underground place, and came forth on the third day.

Then Miramon said: "All this being duly performed and well rid of, we do not now violate any messianic etiquette if we forthwith set about the redemption of Poictesme. Now then, would you prefer to redeem with the forces of good or with the forces of evil?"

"Not with the forces of evil," said Manuel, "for I saw many of these in the high woods of Dun Vlechlan, and I do not fancy them as allies. But are good and evil all one to you of the Léshy?"

"Why should we tell you, Manuel?" says the magician.

"That, Miramon, is a musty reply."

"It is not a reply, it is a question. And the question has become musty because it has been handled so often, and no man has ever been able to dispose of it."

Manuel gave it up, and shrugged. "Well, let us conquer as we may, so that God be on our side."

Miramon replied: "Never fear! He shall be, in every shape and attribute."

So Miramon did what was requisite, and from the garrets and dustheaps of Vraidex came strong allies. For, to begin with, Miramon dealt unusually with a little fish, and as a result of these dealings came to them, during the afternoon of the last Thursday in September, as they stood on the seashore north of

Manneville, a darkly colored champion clad in yellow. He had four hands, in which he carried a club, a shell, a lotus and a discus; and he rode upon a stallion whose hide glittered like new silver.

Manuel said, "This is a good omen, that the stallion of Poictesme should have aid brought to it by yet another silver stallion."

"Let us not speak of this bright stallion," Miramon hastily replied, "for until this Yuga is over he has no name. But when the minds of all men are made clear as crystal then a christening will be appointed for this stallion, and his name will be Kalki, and by the rider upon this stallion Antan will be redeemed."

"Well," Manuel said, "that seems fair enough. Meanwhile, with this dusky gentleman's assistance, I gather, we are to redeem Poictesme."

"Oh, no, Dom Manuel, he is but the first of our Redeemers, for there is nothing like the decimal system, and you will remember it was in our treaty that in Poictesme all things are to go by tens forever."

Thereafter Miramon did what was requisite with some acorns, and the splutterings were answered by low thunder. So came a second champion to aid them. This was a pleasant looking young fellow with an astonishingly red beard: he had a basket slung over his shoulder, and he carried a bright hammer. He rode in a chariot drawn by four goats.

"Come, this is certainly a fine stalwart fighting-man," says Manuel, "and to-day is a lucky day for me, and for this ruddy gentleman also, I hope."

"To-day is always his day," Miramon replied, "and do you stop interrupting me in my incantations, and hand me that flute."

So Manuel stayed as silent as that brace of monstrous allies while Miramon did yet another curious

229

thing with a flute and a palm-branch. Thereafter came an amber-colored champion clad in dark green, and carrying a club and a noose for the souls of the dead. He rode upon a buffalo, and with him came an owl and a pigeon.

"I think—" said Manuel.

"You do not!" said Miramon. "You only talk and fidget, because you are upset by the appearance of your allies; and such talking and fidgeting is very disturbing to an artist who is striving to reanimate the past."

Thus speaking, Miramon turned indignantly to another evocation. It summoned a champion in a luminous chariot drawn by scarlet mares. He was golden-haired, with ruddy limbs, and was armed with a bow and arrows: he too was silent, but he laughed, and you saw that he had several tongues. After him came a young shining man who rode on a boar with golden bristles and bloodied hoofs: this warrior carried a naked sword, and on his back, folded up like a cloth, was a ship to contain the gods and all living creatures. And the sixth Redeemer was a tall shadow-colored person with two long gray plumes affixed to his shaven head: he carried a sceptre and a thing which, Miramon said, was called an ankh, and the beast he rode on was surprising to observe, for it had the body of a beetle, with human arms, and the head of a ram, and the four feet of a lion.

"Come," Manuel said, "but I have never seen just such a steed as that."

"No," Miramon replied, "nor has anybody else, for this is the Hidden One. But do you stop your eternal talking, and pass me the salt and that young crocodile."

With these two articles Miramon dealt so as to

evoke a seventh ally. Serpents were about the throat and arms of this champion, and he wore a necklace of human skulls: his long black hair was plaited remarkably; his throat was blue, his body all a livid white except where it was smeared with ashes. He rode upon the back of a beautiful white bull. Next, riding on a dappled stag, came one appareled in vivid stripes of yellow and red and blue and green: his face was dark as a raincloud, he had one large round eye, white tusks protruded from his lips, and he carried a gaily painted urn. His unspeakable attendants leaped like frogs. The jolliest looking of all the warriors came thereafter, with a dwarfish body and very short legs; he had a huge black-bearded head, a flat nose, and his tongue hung from his mouth and waggled as he moved. He wore a belt and a necklace, and nothing else whatever except the plumes of the hawk arranged as a head-dress: and he rode upon a great sleek tortoise-shell cat.

Now when these unusual appearing allies stood silently aligned before them on the seashore, Dom Manuel said, with a polite bow toward this appalling host, that he hardly thought Duke Asmund would be able to withstand such Redeemers. But Miramon repeated that there was nothing like the decimal system.

"That half-brother of mine, who is lord of the tenth kind of sleeping, would nicely round off this dizain," says Miramon, scratching his chin, "if only he had not such a commonplace, black-and-white appearance, apart from being one of those dreadful Realists, without a scrap of æsthetic feeling— No, I like color, and we will levy now upon the West!"

So Miramon dealt next with a little ball of bright feathers. Then a last helper came to them, riding on a jaguar, and carrying a large drum and a flute from

231

which his music issued in the shape of flames. This champion was quite black, but he was striped with blue paint, and golden feathers grew all over his left leg. He wore a red coronet in the shape of a rose, a short skirt of green paper, and white sandals; and he carried a red shield that had in its centre a white flower with the four petals placed crosswise. Such was he who made up the tenth.

Now when this terrible dizain was completed the lord of the seven madnesses laid fire to a wisp of straw, and he cast it to the winds, saying that thus should the anger of Miramon Lluagor pass over the land. Then he turned to these dreadful ten whom he had revivified from the dustheaps and garrets of Vraidex, and it became apparent that Miramon was deeply moved.

Said Miramon:

"You, whom I made for man's worship when earth was younger and fairer, hearken, and learn why I breathe new life into husks from my scrap-heaps! Gods of old days, discrowned, disjected, and treated as rubbish, hark to the latest way of the folk whose fathers you succored! They have discarded you utterly. Such as remember deride you, saying:

"'The brawling old lords that our grandfathers honored have perished, if they indeed were ever more than some curious notions bred of our grandfathers' questing, that looked to find God in each rainstorm coming to nourish their barley, and God in the heat-bringing sun, and God in the earth which gave life. Even so was each hour of their living touched with odd notions of God and with lunacies as to God's kindness. We are more sensible people, for we understand all about the freaks of the wind and the weather, and find them in no way astounding. As for whatever gods may exist, they are civil, in that they let us alone in our lifetime; and so we return their politeness, knowing that what we are doing on earth is important enough to need undivided attention.'

"Such are the folk that deride you, such are the folk that ignore the gods whom Miramon fashioned, such are the folk whom to-day I permit you freely to deal with after the manner of gods. Do you now make the most of your chance, and devastate all Poictesme in time for an earlyish supper!"

The faces of these ten became angry, and they shouted, "Blaerde Shay Alphenio Kasbue Gorfons Albuifrio!"

All ten went up together from the sea, traveling more swiftly than men travel, and what afterward happened in Poictesme was for a long while a story very fearful to hear and heard everywhere.

Manuel did not witness any of the tale's making as he waited alone on the seashore. But the land was sick, and its nausea heaved under Manuel's wounded feet, and he saw that the pale, gurgling, glistening sea appeared to crawl away from Poictesme slimily. And at Bellegarde and Naimes and Storisende and Lisuarte, and in all the strongly fortified inland places, Asmund's tall fighting-men beheld one or another of the angry faces which came up from the sea, and many died swiftly, as must always happen when anybody revives discarded dreams, nor did any of the Northmen die in a shape recognizable as human.

When the news was brought to Dom Manuel that his redemption of Poictesme was completed, then Dom Manuel unarmed, and made himself presentable in a tunic of white damask and a girdle adorned with garnets and sapphires. He slipped over his left shoulder a baldric set with diamonds and emeralds, to sus-

233

tain the unbloodied sword with which he had conquered here as upon Vraidex. Over all he put on a crimson mantle. Then the former swineherd concealed his hands, not yet quite healed, with white gloves, of which the one was adorned with a ruby, and the other was a sapphire; and, sighing, Manuel the Redeemer (as he was called thereafter) entered into his kingdom, and they of Poictesme received him far more gladly than he them.

Thus did Dom Manuel enter into the imprisonment of his own castle and into the bonds of high estate, from which he might not easily get free to go a-traveling everywhither, and see the ends of this world and judge them. And they say that in her low red-pillared palace Suskind smiled contentedly and made ready for the future.

MUNDUS · VULT · DECIPI ·

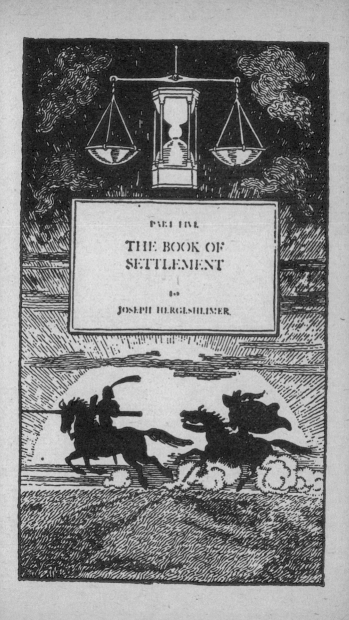

PART FIVE

THE BOOK OF SETTLEMENT

JOSEPH HERGESHEIMER

Thus *Manuel reigned in vertue and honoure with that noble Ladye his wyfe: and he was beloued and dradde of high and lowe degree, for he dyde ryghte and iustice* according to the auncient Manner, *kepynge hys land in dignitie and goode Appearance, and hauynge the highest place in hys tyme.*

XXXIII

Now Manuel Prospers

❖❖❖❖❖❖❖❖❖❖❖

THEY OF POICTESME narrate fine tales as to the deeds that Manuel the Redeemer performed and incited in the days of his reign. They tell also many things that seem improbable, and therefore are not included in this book: for the old songs and tales incline to make of Count Manuel's heydey a rare golden age.

So many glorious exploits are, indeed, accredited to Manuel and to the warriors whom he gathered round him in his famous Fellowship of the Silver Stallion,—and among whom, Holden and courteous Anavalt and Coth the Alderman and Gonfal and Donander had the pre-eminence, where all were hardy,—that it is very difficult to understand how so brief a while could have continued so many doings. But the tale-tellers of Poictesme have been long used to say of a fine action, —not falsely, but misleadingly,—"Thus it was in Count Manuel's time," and the tribute by and by has been accepted as a dating. So has chronology been hacked to make loftier his fame, and the glory of Dom Manuel has been a magnet that has drawn to itself the magnanimities of other days and years.

But there is no need here to speak of these legends, about the deeds which were performed by the Fel-

lowship of the Silver Stallion, because these stories are
recorded elsewhere. Some may be true, the others are
certainly not true; but it is indisputable that Count
Manuel grew steadily in power and wealth and proud
repute. Miramon Lluagor still served him, half-a-
musedly, as Dom Manuel's seneschal; kings now were
Manuel's co-partners; and the former swineherd had
somehow become the fair and trusty cousin of emperors. And Madame Niafer, the great Count's wife, was
everywhere stated, without any contradiction from
her, to be daughter to the late Soldan of Barbary.

Guivric the Sage illuminated the tree which showed
the glorious descent of Dame Niafer from Kaiumarth,
the first of all kings, and the first to teach men to
build houses: and this tree hung in the main hall of
Storisende. "For even if some errors may have crept in
here and there," said Dame Niafer, "it looks very
well."

"But, my dear," said Manuel, "your father was not
the Soldan of Barbary: instead, he was the second
groom at Arnaye, and all this lineage is a preposterous
fabrication."

"I said just now that some errors may have crept in
here and there," assented Dame Niafer, composedly,
"but the point is, that the thing really looks very well,
and I do not suppose that even you deny that."

"No, I do not deny that this glowing mendacity
adds to the hall's appearance."

"So now, you see for yourself!" said Niafer, trium-
phantly. And after that her new ancestry was never
questioned.

And in the meanwhile Dom Manuel had sent messengers over land and sea to his half-sister Math at
Rathgor, bidding her sell the mill for what it would
fetch. She obeyed, and brought to Manuel's court her

husband and their two boys, the younger of whom rose later to be Pope of Rome. Manuel gave the miller the vacant fief of Montors; and thereafter you could nowhere have found a statelier fine lady than the Countess Matthiette de Montors. She was still used to speak continually of what was becoming to people of our station in life, but it was with a large difference; and she got on with Niafer as well as could be expected, but no better.

And early in the summer of the first year of Manuel's reign (just after Dom Manuel fetched to Storisende the Sigel of Scoteia, as the spoils of his famous fight with Oriander the Swimmer), the stork brought to Niafer the first of the promised boys. For the looks of the thing, this child was named, not after the father whom Manuel had just killed, but after the Emmerick who was Manuel's nominal father: and it was this Emmerick that afterward reigned long and notably in Poictesme.

So matters went prosperously with Dom Manuel, and there was nothing to trouble his peace of mind, unless it were some feeling of responsibility for the cult of Sesphra, whose worship was now increasing everywhere among the nations. In Philistia, in particular, Sesphra was now worshipped openly in the legislative halls and churches, and all other religion, and all decency, was smothered under the rituals of Sesphra. Everywhere to the west and north his followers were delivering windy discourses and performing mad antics, and great hurt came of it all by and by. But if this secretly troubled Dom Manuel, the Count, here as elsewhere, exercised to good effect his invaluable gift for holding his tongue.

Nor did he ever speak of Freydis either, though it is recorded that when news came of the end which she

239

had made in Teamhair under the oppression of the Druids and the satirists, Dom Manuel went silently into the Room of Ageus, and was not seen any more that day. That in such solitude he wept is improbable, for his hard vivid eyes had forgotten this way of exercise, but it is highly probable that he remembered many things, and found not all of them to his credit.

So matters went prosperously with gray Manuel; he had lofty palaces and fair woods and pastures and ease and content, and whensoever he went into battle attended by his nine lords of the Silver Stallion, his adversaries perished; he was esteemed everywhere the most lucky and the least scrupulous rogue alive: to crown all which the stork brought by and by to Storisende the second girl, whom they named Dorothy, for Manuel's mother. And about this time too, came a young poet from England (Ribaut they called him, and he met an evil end at Coventry not long thereafter), bringing to Dom Manuel, where the high Count sat at supper, a goose-feather.

The Count smiled, and he twirled the thing between his fingers, and he meditated. He shrugged, and said: "Needs must. But for her ready wit, my head would have been set to dry on a silver pike. I cannot well ignore that obligation, if she, as it now seems, does not intend to ignore it."

Then he told Niafer he must go into England.

Niafer looked up from the marmalade with which she was finishing off her supper, to ask placidly, "And what does that dear yellow-haired friend of yours want with you now?"

"My dear, if I knew the answer to that question it would not be necessary for me to travel oversea."

"It is easy enough to guess, though," Dame Niafer said darkly, although, in point of fact, she too was wondering why Alianora should have sent for Manuel; "and I can quite understand how in your sandals you prefer not to have people know about such doings, and laughing at you everywhere, again."

Dom Manuel did not reply; but he sighed.

"—And if any importance whatever were attached to my opinion in this house I might be saying a few things; but, as it is, it is much more agreeable, all around, to let you go your own hard-headed way and find out by experience that what I say is true. So now, Manuel, if you do not mind, I think we had better be talking about something else a little more pleasant."

Dom Manuel still did not say anything. The time, as has been noted, was just after supper, and as the high Count and his wife sat over the remnants of this meal, a minstrel was making music for them.

"You are not very cheerful company, I must say," Niafer observed, in a while, "although I do not for a moment doubt your yellow-haired friend will find you gay enough—"

"No, Niafer, I am not happy to-night."

"Yes, and whose fault is it? I told you not to take two helpings of that beef."

"No, no, dear snip, it is not indigestion, but rather it is that music, which is plaguing me."

"Now, Manuel, how can music bother anybody! I am sure the boy plays his violin very nicely indeed, especially when you consider his age."

Said Manuel:

"Yes, but the long low sobbing of the violin, troubling as the vague thoughts begotten by that season wherein summer is not yet perished from the earth, but lingers wanly in the tattered shrines of summer, speaks of what was and of what might have been. A

241

blind desire, the same which on warm moonlit nights was used to shake like fever in the veins of a boy whom I remember, is futilely plaguing a gray fellow with the gray wraiths of innumerable old griefs and with small stinging memories of long-dead delights. Such thirsting breeds no good for staid and aging men, but my lips are athirst for lips whose loveliness no longer exists in flesh, and I thirst for a dead time and its dead fervors to be reviving, so that young Manuel may love again.

"To-night now surely somewhere, while this music sets uncertain and probing fingers to healed wounds, an aging woman, in everything a stranger to me, is troubled just thus futilely, and she too remembers what she half forgets. 'We that of old were one, and shuddered heart to heart, with our young lips and our souls too made indivisible,'—thus she is thinking, as I think—'has life dealt candidly in leaving us to potter with half measures and to make nothing of severed lives that shrivel far apart?' Yes, she to-night is sad as I, it well may be; but I cannot rest certain of this, because there is in young love a glory so bedazzling as to prevent the lover from seeing clearly his co-worshipper, and therefore in that dear time when we served love together I learned no more of her than she of me.

"Of all my failures this is bitterest to bear, that out of so much grieving and aspiring I have gained no assured knowledge of the woman herself, but must perforce become lachrymose over such perished tinsels as her quivering red lips and shining hair! Of youth and love is there no more, then, to be won than virginal breasts and a small white belly yielded to the will of the lover, and brief drunkenness, and afterward such puzzled yearning as now dies into acquiescence, very much as the long low sobbing of that violin yonder dies into stillness now the song is done?"

So it was that gray Manuel talked in a half voice, sitting there resplendently robed in gold and crimson, and twiddling between his fingers a goose-feather.

"Yes," Niafer said, presently, "but, for my part, I think he plays very nicely indeed."

Manuel gave an abrupt slight jerking of the head. Dom Manuel laughed. "Dear snip," said he, "come, honestly now, what have you been meditating about while I talked nonsense?"

"Why, I was thinking I must remember to look over your flannels the first thing to-morrow, Manuel, for everybody knows what that damp English climate is in autumn—"

"My dearest," Manuel said, with grave conviction, "you are the archetype and flawless model of all wives."

XXXIV

Farewell to Alianora

❖❖❖❖❖❖❖❖❖❖❖❖

Now Dom Manuel takes ship and goes into England:
and for what happened there we have no authority
save the account which Dom Manuel rendered on his
return to his wife.

Thus said Dom Manuel:

He went straight to Woodstock, where the King
and Queen then were. At Woodstock Dom Manuel
was handsomely received, and there he passed the
month of September—

(*"Why need you stay so long, though?"* Dame
Niafer inquired.

*"Well," Manuel explained, "one thing led to an-
other, as it were."*

"H'm!" Niafer remarked.)

He had presently a private talk with the Queen.
How was she dressed? As near as Manuel recalled, she
wore a green mantle fastened in front with a square
fermoir of gems and wrought gold; under it, a close
fitting gown of gold-diapered brocade, with tight
sleeves so long that they half covered her hands, something like mitts. Her crown was of floriated trefoils
surmounting a band of rubies. Of course, though,
they might have been only garnets—

244

("*And where was it that she dressed up in all this finery to talk with you in private?*"

"*Why, at Woodstock, naturally.*"

"*I know it was at Woodstock, but whereabouts at Woodstock?*"

"*It was by a window, my dear, by a window with panes of white glass and wooden lattices and a pent covered with lead.*"

"*Your account is very circumstantial, but where was the window?*"

"*Oh, now I understand you! It was in a room.*"

"*What sort of room?*"

"*Well, the walls were covered with gay frescoes from Saxon history; the fireplace was covered with very handsomely carved stone dragons; and the floor was covered with new rushes. Indeed, the Queen has one of the neatest bedrooms I have ever seen.*"

"*Ah, yes,*" said Niafer: "*and what did you talk about during the time that you spent in your dear friend's bedroom?*")

Well, he found all going well with Queen Alianora (Dom Manuel continued) except that she had not yet provided an heir for the English throne, and it was this alone which was troubling her. It was on account of this that she had sent for Count Manuel.

"It is considered not to look at all well, after three years of marriage," the Queen told him, "and people are beginning to say a number of unkind things."

"It is the common fate of queens," Dom Manuel replies, "to be exposed to the criticism of envious persons."

"No, do not be brilliant and aphoristic, Manuel, for I want you to help me more practically in this matter."

245

"Very willingly will I help you if I can. But how can I?"

"Why, you must assist me in getting a baby,—a boy baby, of course."

"I am willing to do all that I can, because certainly it does not look well for you to have no son to be King of England. But how can I, of all persons, help you in this affair?"

"Now, Manuel, after getting three children you surely ought to know what is necessary!"

Dom Manuel shook a gray head. "My children came from a source which is exhausted."

"That would be deplorable news if I believed it, but I am sure that if you will let me take matters in hand I can convince you to the contrary—"

"Well, I am open to conviction."

"—Although I scarcely know how to begin, because I know that you will think this hard on you—"

He took her hand. Dom Manuel admitted to Niafer without reserve that here he took the Queen's hand, saying: "Do not play with me any longer, Alianora, for you must see plainly that I am now eager to serve you. So do not be embarrassed, but come to the point, and I will do what I can."

"Why, Manuel, both you and I know perfectly well that, even with your Dorothy ordered, you still hold the stork's note for another girl and another boy, to be supplied upon demand, after the manner of the Philistines."

"No, not upon demand, for the first note has nine months to run, and the other falls due even later. But what has that to do with it?"

"Now, Manuel, truly I hate to ask this of you, but my need is desperate, with all this criticizing and gossip. So for old time's sake, and for the sake of the life

I gave you as a Christmas present, through telling my dear father an out-and-out story, you must let me have that first promissory note, and you must direct the stork to bring the boy baby to me in England, and not to your wife in Poictesme."

So that was what Dame Alianora had wanted.

(*"I knew that all along," observed Dame Niafer, —untruthfully, but adhering to her general theory that it was better to appear omniscient in dealing with one's husband.*)

Well, Dom Manuel was grieved by the notion of being parted from his child prior to its birth, but he was moved alike by his former fondness for Alianora, and by his indebtedness to her, and by the obligation that was on him to provide as handsomely as possible for his son. Nobody could dispute that as King of England the boy's station in life would be immeasurably above the rank of the Count of Poictesme's younger brother. So Manuel made a complaint as to his grief and as to Niafer's grief at thus prematurely losing their loved son—

(*"Shall I repeat what I said, my dear?"*)

"No, Manuel, I never understand you when you are trying to be highflown and impressive.")

Well, then, Dom Manuel made a very beautiful complaint, but in the outcome Dom Manuel consented to this sacrifice.

He would not consent, though, to remain in England, as Alianora wanted him to do.

"No," he said, nobly, "it would not look at all well for you to be taking me as your lover, and breaking your marriage-vows to love nobody but the King. No, Alianora, I will help you to get the baby you need, inasmuch as I am indebted to you for my life and have two babies to spare, but I am not willing to have anything to do with the breaking of your marriage-vows, because it is a crime which is forbidden by the Holy Scriptures, and of which Niafer would certainly hear sooner or later."

(*"Oh, Manuel, you did not say that!"*

"My dear, those were my exact words. And why not?"

"That was putting it sensibly of course, but it would have sounded much better if you had expressed yourself entirely upon moral grounds. It is most important, Manuel, as I am sure I have told you over and over again, for people in our position to show a proper respect for morality and religion and things of that sort whenever they come up in the conversation; but there is no teaching you anything except by bitter experience, which I sincerely hope may be spared you, and one might as well be arguing with a brick wall, and so you may go on.")

Well, the Queen wept and coaxed, but Manuel was firm. So Manuel spent that night in the Queen's room, performing the needful incantations, and arranging matters with the stork, and then Dom Manuel returned home. And that—well, really that was all.

Such was the account which Dom Manuel rendered his wife. "And upon the whole, Niafer, I consider it a very creditable stroke of business, for as King of England the child will enjoy advantages which we could never have afforded him."

"Yes," said Niafer, "and what does that dear friend of yours look like nowadays?"

"—Besides, should the boy turn out badly our grief will be considerably lessened by the circumstance that, through never seeing this son of ours, our affection for him will never be inconveniently great."

"There is something in that, for already I can see

that Emmerick inherits his father's obstinacy, and it naturally worries me, but what does the woman look like nowadays?"

"—Then, even more important than these considerations—"

"Nothing is more important, Manuel, in this very curious sounding affair, than the way that woman looks nowadays."

"Ah, my dear," says Manuel, diplomatically, "I did not like to speak of that, I confess, for you know these blondes go off in their appearance so quickly—"

"Of course they do, but still—"

"—And it not being her fault, after all, I did not like to tell you about Dame Alianora's looking so many years older than you do, since your being a brunette gives you an unfair advantage to begin with."

"Ah, it is not that," said Niafer, still rather grim-visaged, but obviously mollified. "It is the life she is leading, with her witchcraft and her familiar spirits and that continual entertaining and excitement, and everybody tells me she has already taken to dyeing her hair."

"Oh, it had plainly had something done to it," says Manuel, lightly. "But it is a queen's duty to preserve such remnants of good looks as she possesses."

"So there, you see!" said Niafer, quite comfortable again in her mind when she noted the careless way in which Dom Manuel spoke of the Queen.

A year or two earlier Dame Niafer would perhaps have been moved to jealousy: now her only concern was that Manuel might possibly be led to make a fool of himself and to upset their manner of living. With every contented wife her husband's general foolishness is an axiom, and prudent philosophers do not distinguish here between cause and effect.

As for Alianora's wanting to take Manuel as a lover, Dame Niafer found the idea mildly amusing, and very nicely indicative of those washed-out, yellow-haired women's intelligence. To be harboring romantic notions about Manuel seemed to Manuel's wife so fantastically out of reason that she half wished the poor creature could without scandal be afforded a chance to find out for herself all about Manuel's thousand and one finicky ways and what he was in general to live with.

That being impossible, Niafer put the crazy woman out of mind, and began to tell Manuel about what had happened, and not for the first time either, while he was away, and about just how much more she was going to stand from Sister Math, and about the advantages of a perfectly plain understanding for everybody concerned. And with Niafer that was the end of Count Manuel's discharging of his obligation to Alianora.

Of course there were gossips who said this, that and the other. Some asserted that Manuel's tale in itself contained elements of improbability: others declared that Queen Alianora, who was far deeplier versed in the magic of the Apsarasas than was Dom Manuel, could just as well have summoned the stork without his assistance. It was true the stork was under no especial obligations to Alianora: even so, said these gossips, it would have looked far better, and a queen could not be too particular, and it simply showed you about these foreign Southern women; and although they of course wished to misjudge no one, there was no sense in pretending to ignore what everybody practically knew to be a fact, and was talking about everywhere, and some day you would see for yourself.

But after all, Dom Manuel and the Queen were the

only persons qualified to speak of these matters with authority, and this was Dom Manuel's account of them. For the rest, he was sustained against tittle-tattle by the knowledge that he had performed a charitable deed in England, for the Queen's popularity was enhanced, and all the English, but particularly their King, were delighted, by the fine son which the stork duly brought to Alianora the following June.

Manuel never saw this boy, who afterward ruled over England and was a highly thought-of warrior, nor did Dom Manuel ever see Queen Alianora any more. So Alianora goes out of the story, to bring long years of misery and ruining wars upon the English, and to Dom Manuel no more beguilements. For they say Dom Manuel could never resist her, because of that underlying poverty in the correct emotions which, as some say, Dom Manuel shared with her, and which they hid from all the world except each other.

XXXV

The Troubling Window
❖❖❖❖❖❖❖❖❖❖❖❖

IT SEEMED, in a word, that trouble had forgotten Count Manuel. None the less, Dom Manuel opened a window, at his fine home at Storisende, on a fine, sunlit, warmish morning (for this was the last day of April) to confront an outlook more perturbing than his hard vivid eyes had yet lighted on.

So he regarded it for a while. Considerately Dom Manuel now made experiments with three windows in this Room of Ageus, and found how, in so far as one's senses could be trusted, the matter stood. Thereafter, as became an intelligent person, he went back to his writing-table, and set about signing the requisitions and warrants and other papers which Ruric the clerk had left there.

Yet all the while Dom Manuel's gaze kept lifting to the windows. There were three of them, set side by side, each facing south. They were of thick clear glass, of a sort whose manufacture is a lost art, for these windows had been among the spoils brought back by Duke Asmund from nefarious raidings of Philistia, in which country these windows had once been a part of the temple of Ageus, an immemorial god of the Philistines. For this reason the room was called the Room of Ageus.

Through these windows Count Manuel could see familiar fields, the long avenue of poplars and the rising hills beyond. All was as it had been yesterday, and as all had been since, nearly three years ago, Count Manuel first entered Storisende. All was precisely as it had been, except, to be sure, that until yesterday Dom Manuel's table had stood by the farthest window. He could not remember that until to-day this window had ever been opened, because since his youth had gone out of him Count Manuel was becoming more and more susceptible to draughts.

"It is certainly very curious," Dom Manuel said, aloud, when he had finished with his papers.

He was again approaching the very curious window when his daughter Melicent, now nearly three years old, came noisily, and in an appallingly soiled condition, to molest him. She had bright beauty later, but at three she was one of those children whom human powers cannot keep clean for longer than three minutes.

Dom Manuel kept for her especial delectation a small flat paddle on his writing-table, and this he now caught up.

"Out of the room with you, little pest!" he blustered, "for I am busy."

So the child, as was her custom, ran back into the hallway, and stood there, no longer in the room, but with one small foot thrust beyond the doorsill, while she laughed up at her big father, and derisively stuck out a tiny curved red tongue at the famed overlord of Poictesme. Then Dom Manuel, as was his custom, got down upon the floor to slap with his paddle at the intruding foot, and Melicent squealed with delight, and pulled back her foot in time to dodge the paddle, and thrust out her other foot beyond the sill, and tried to withdraw that too before it was spanked.

So it was they gave over a quarter of an hour to rioting, and so it was that grave young Ruric found them. Count Manuel rather sheepishly arose from the floor, and dusted himself, and sent Melicent into the buttery for some sugar cakes. He told Ruric what were the most favorable terms he could offer the burgesses of Narenta, and he gave Ruric the signed requisitions.

Presently, when Ruric had gone, Dom Manuel went again to the farthest window, opened it, and looked out once more. He shook his head, as one who gives up a riddle. He armed himself, and rode over to Perdigon, whither sainted King Ferdinand had come to consult with Manuel about contriving the assassination of the Moorish general, Al-Mota-wakkil. This matter Dom Manuel deputed to Guivric the Sage; and so was rid of it.

In addition, Count Manuel had on hand that afternoon an appeal to the judgment of God, over some rather valuable farming lands; but it was remarked by the spectators that he botched the unhorsing and severe wounding of Earl Ladinas, and conducted it rather as though Dom Manuel's heart were not in the day's business. Indeed, he had reason, for while supernal mysteries were well enough if one were still a hare-brained lad, or even if one set out in due form to seek them, to find such mysteries obtruding themselves unsought into the home-life of a well-thought-of nobleman was discomposing, and to have the windows of his own house playing tricks on him seemed hardly respectable.

All that month, too, some memory appeared to trouble Dom Manuel, in the back of his mind, while the lords of the Silver Stallion were busied in the pursuit of Othmar and Othmar's brigands in the Taunen-fels: and as soon as Dom Manuel had captured and hanged the last squad of these knaves, Dom Manuel rode home and looked out of the window, to find matters unchanged.

Dom Manuel meditated. He sounded the gong for Ruric. Dom Manuel talked with the clerk about this and that. Presently Dom Manuel said: "But one stifles here. Open that window."

The clerk obeyed. Manuel at the writing-table watched him intently. But in opening the window the clerk had of necessity stood with his back toward Count Manuel, and when Ruric turned, the dark young face of Ruric was impassive.

Dom Manuel, playing with the jeweled chain of office about his neck, considered Ruric's face. Then Manuel said: "That is all. You may go."

But Count Manuel's face was troubled, and for the rest of this day he kept an eye on Ruric the young clerk. In the afternoon it was noticeable that this Ruric went often, on one pretext and another, into the Room of Ageus when nobody else was there. The next afternoon, in broad daylight, Manuel detected Ruric carrying into the Room of Ageus, of all things, a lantern. The Count waited a while, then went into the room through its one door. The room was empty. Count Manuel sat down and drummed with his fingers upon the top of his writing-table.

After a while the third window was opened. Ruric the clerk climbed over the sill. He blew out his lantern.

"You are braver than I," Count Manuel said, "it may be. It is certain you are younger. Once, Ruric, I would not have lured any dark and prim-voiced young fellow into attempting this adventure, but would have essayed it myself post-haste. Well, but I have other duties now, and appearances to keep up: and people would talk if they saw a well-thought-of nobleman well settled in life climbing out of his own windows, and there is simply no telling what my wife would think of it."

The clerk had turned, startled, dropping his lantern with a small crash. His hands went jerkily to his smooth chin, clutching it. His face was white as a leper's face, and his eyes now were wild and glittering, and his head was drawn low between his black-clad shoulders, so that he seemed a hunchback as he confronted his master. Another queer thing Manuel could notice, and it was that a great lock had been sheared away from the left side of Ruric's black hair.

"What have you learned," says Manuel, "out yonder?"

"I cannot tell you," replied Ruric, laughing sillily, "but in place of it, I will tell you a tale. Yes, yes, Count Manuel, I will tell you a merry story of how a great while ago our common grandmother Eve was washing her children one day near Eden when God called to her. She hid away the children that she had not finished washing: and when the good God asked her if all her children were there, with their meek little heads against His knees, to say their prayers to Him, she answered, Yes. So God told her that what she had tried to hide from God should be hidden from men: and He took away the unwashed children, and made a place for them where everything stays young, and where there is neither good nor evil, because these children are unstained by human sin and unredeemed by Christ's dear blood."

The Count said, forwning: "What drunken nonsense are you talking at broad noon? It is not any foolish tatter of legend that I am requiring of you, my boy, but civil information as to what is to be encountered out yonder."

"All freedom and all delight," young Ruric told him wildly, "and all horror and all rebellion."

Then he talked for a while. When Ruric had ended this talking, Count Manuel laughed scornfully, and spoke as became a well-thought-of nobleman.

Ruric whipped out a knife, and attacked his master, crying, "I follow after my own thinking and my own desires, you old, smug, squinting hypocrite!"

So Count Manuel caught Ruric by the throat, and with naked hands Dom Manuel strangled the young clerk.

"Now I have ridded the world of much poison, I think," Dom Manuel said, aloud, when Ruric lay dead at Manuel's feet. "In any event, I cannot have that sort of talking about my house. Yet I wish I had not trapped the boy into attempting this adventure, which by rights was my adventure. I did not always avoid adventures."

He summoned two to take away the body, and then Manuel went to his bedroom, and was clothed by his lackeys in a tunic of purple silk, and a coronet was placed on his gray head, and the trumpets sounded as Count Manuel sat down to supper. Pages in ermine served him, bringing Manuel's food upon gold dishes, and pouring red wine and white from golden beakers into Manuel's gold cup. Skilled music-men played upon viols and harps and flutes while the high Count of Poictesme ate richly seasoned food and talked sedately with his wife.

They had not fared thus when Manuel had just come from herding swine, and Niafer was a servant trudging on her mistress' errands, and when these two had eaten very gratefully the Portune's bread and cheese. They had not any need to be heartened with rare wines when they endured so many perils upon Vraidex and in Dun Vlechlan because of their love for each other. For these two had once loved marvelously. Now minstrels everywhere made songs about their all-conquering love, which had derided death; and nobody denied that, even now, these two got on together amicably.

But to-night Dame Niafer was fretted, because the pastry-cook was young Ruric's cousin, and was, she feared, as likely as not to fling off in a huff on account of Dom Manuel's having strangled the clerk.

"Well, then do you raise the fellow's wages," said Count Manuel.

"That is easily said, and is exactly like a man. Why, Manuel, you surely know that then the meat-cook, and the butler, too, would be demanding more, and that there would be no end to it."

"But, my dear, the boy was talking mad blasphemy, and was for cutting my throat with a great horn-handled knife."

"Of course that was very wrong of him," said Dame Niafer, comfortably, "and not for an instant, Manuel, am I defending his conduct, as I trust you quite understand. But even so, if you had stopped for a moment to think how hard it is to replace a servant nowadays, and how unreliable is the best of them, I believe you would have seen how completely we are at their mercy."

Then she told him all about her second waiting-woman, while Manuel said, "Yes," and "I never heard the like," and "You were perfectly right, my dear," and so on, and all the while appeared to be thinking about something else in the back of his mind.

XXXVI

Excursions from Content
✦✦✦✦✦✦✦✦✦✦✦✦✦

THEREAFTER COUNT MANUEL could not long remain away from the window through which Ruric had climbed with a lantern, and through which Ruric had returned insanely blaspheming against law and order.

The outlook from this window was somewhat curious. Through the two other windows of Ageus, set side by side with this one, and in appearance similar to it in all respects, the view remained always unchanged, and just such as it was from the third window so long as you looked through the thick clear glass. But when the third window of Ageus was opened, all the sunlit summer world that you had seen through the thick clear glass was gone quite away, and you looked out into a limitless gray twilight wherein not anything was certainly discernible, and the air smelt of spring. It was a curious experience for Count Manuel, thus to regard through the clear glass his prospering domains and all the rewards of his famous endeavors, and then find them vanished as soon as the third window was opened. It was curious, and very interesting; but such occurrences make people dubious about things in which, as everybody knows, it is wisdom's part to believe implicitly.

Now the second day after Ruric had died, the season now being June, Count Manuel stood at the three windows, and saw in the avenue of poplars his wife, Dame Niafer, walking hand in hand with little Melicent. Niafer, despite her lameness, was a fine figure of a woman, so long as he viewed Niafer through the closed window of Ageus. Dom Manuel looked contentedly enough upon the wife who was the reward of his toil and suffering in Dun Vlechlan, and the child who was the reward of his amiability and shrewdness in dealing with the stork, all seemed well so long as he regarded them through the closed third window.

His hand trembled somewhat as he now opened this window, to face gray sweetly-scented nothingness. But in the window glass, you saw, the appearance of his flourishing gardens remained unchanged: and in the half of the window to the right hand were quivering poplars, and Niafer and little Melicent were smiling at him, and the child was kissing her hand to him. All about this swinging half of the window was nothingness; he, leaning out, and partly closing this half of the window, could see that behind the amiable picture was nothingness: it was only in the old glass of Ageus that his wife and child appeared to live and move.

Dom Manuel laughed, shortly. "Hah, then," says he, "that tedious dear nagging woman and that priceless snub-nosed brat may not be real. They may be merely happy and prosaic imaginings, hiding the night which alone is real. To consider this possibility is troubling. It makes for even greater loneliness. None the less, I know that I am real, and certainly the grayness before me is real. Well, no matter what befell Ruric yonder, it must be that in this grayness there is some other being who is real and dissatisfied. I must go to seek this being, for here I become as a drugged person among sedate and comfortable dreams which are made doubly weariful by my old master's whispering of that knowledge which was my father's father's."

Then in the gray dusk was revealed a face that was not human, and the round toothless mouth of it spoke feebly, saying, "I am Lubrican, and I come to guide you if you dare follow."

"I have always thought that 'dare' was a quaint word," says Manuel, with the lordly swagger which he kept for company.

So he climbed out of the third window of Ageus. When later he climbed back, a lock had been sheared from the side of his gray head.

Now the tale tells that thereafter Dom Manuel was changed, and his attendants gossiped about it. Dame Niafer also was moved to mild wonderment over the change in him, but did not think it very important, because there is never any accounting for what a husband will do. Besides, there were other matters to consider, for at this time Easterlings came up from Piaja (which they had sacked) into the territories of King Theodoret, and besieged Megaris, and the harried King had sent messengers to Dom Manuel.

"But this is none of my affair," said Manuel, "and I begin to tire of warfare, and of catching cold by sleeping on hard-won battle-fields."

"You would not take cold, as I have told you any number of times," declared Niafer, "if you would eat more green vegetables instead of stuffing yourself with meat, and did not insist on overheating yourself at the fighting. Still, you had better go."

"My dear, I shall do nothing of the sort."

261

"Yes, you had better go, for these Easterlings are notorious pagans—"

"Now other persons have been pagans once upon a time, dear snip—"

"A great many things are much worse, Manuel," says Niafer, with that dark implication before which Dom Manuel always fidgeted, because there was no telling what it might mean. "Yes, these Easterlings are quite notorious pagans, and King Theodoret has at least the grace to call himself a Christian, and, besides, it will give me a chance to get your rooms turned out and thoroughly cleaned."

So Manuel, as was his custom, did what Niafer thought best. Manuel summoned his vassals, and brought together his nine lords of the Fellowship of the Silver Stallion, and, without making any stir with horns and clarions, came so swiftly and secretly under cover of night upon the heathen Easterlings that never was seen such slaughter and sorrow and destruction as Dom Manuel wrought upon those tall pagans before he sat down to breakfast.

He attacked from Sannazaro. The survivors therefore fled, having no choice, through the fields east of Megaris. Manuel followed, and slew them in the open.

The realm was thus rescued from dire peril, and Manuel was detained for a while in Megaris, by the ensuing banquets and religious services and the executions of the prisoners and the nonsense of the King's sister. For this romantic and very pretty girl had set King Theodoret to pestering Manuel with magniloquent offers of what Theodoret would do and give if only the rescuer of Megaris would put aside his ugly crippled wife and marry the King's lovely sister.

Manuel laughed at him. Some say that Manuel and the King's sister dispensed with marriage: others accuse Dom Manuel of exhibiting a continence not very well suited to his exalted estate. It is certain, in any event, that he by and by returned into Poictesme, with a cold in his head to be sure, but with fresh glory and much plunder and two new fiefs to his credit: and at Storisende Dom Manuel found that his rooms had been thoroughly cleaned and set in such perfect order that he could lay hands upon none of his belongings, and that the pastry-cook had left.

"It simply shows you!" says Dame Niafer, "and all I have to say is that now I hope you are satisfied."

Manuel laughed without merriment. "Everything is in a conspiracy to satisfy me in these sleek times, and it is that which chiefly plagues me."

He chucked Niafer under the chin, and told her she should be thinking of what a famous husband she had nowadays, instead of bothering about pastry-cooks. Then he fell to asking little Melicent about how much she had missed Father while Father was away, and he dutifully kissed the two other children, and he duly admired the additions to Emmerick's vocabulary during Father's absence. And afterward he went alone into the Room of Ageus.

Thereafter he was used to spend more and more hours in the Room of Ageus, and the change in Count Manuel was more and more talked about. And the summer passed: and whether or no Count Manuel had, as some declared, contracted unholy alliances, there was no denying that all prospered with Count Manuel, and he was everywhere esteemed the most lucky and the least scrupulous rogue alive. But, very certainly, he was changed.

XXXVII

Opinions of Hinzelmann
❖❖❖❖❖❖❖❖❖❖❖❖❖

Now THE TALE tells that on Michaelmas morning little
Melicent, being in a quiet mood that time, sat with
her doll in the tall chair by the third window of
Ageus while her father wrote at his big table. He was
pausing between phrases to think and to bite at his
thumb-nail, and he was so intent upon this letter to
Pope Innocent that he did not notice the slow opening of the third window: and Melicent had been in
conference with the queer small boy for some while
before Dom Manuel looked up abstractedly toward
them. Then Manuel seemed perturbed, and he called
Melicent to him, and she obediently scrambled into
her father's lap.

There was silence in the Room of Ageus. The
queer small boy sat leaning back in the chair which
little Melicent had just left. He sat with his legs
crossed, and with his gloved hands clasping his right
knee, as he looked appraisingly at Melicent. He displayed a beautiful sad face, with curled yellow hair
hanging about his shoulders, and he was dressed in a
vermilion silk coat: at his left side, worn like a sword,
was a vast pair of shears. He wore also a pointed hat

of four interblended colors, and his leather gloves were figured with pearls.

"She will be a woman by and by," the strange boy said, with a soft and delicate voice, "and then she too will be coming to us, and we will provide fine sorrows for her."

"No, Hinzelmann," Count Manuel replied, as he stroked the round straw-colored head of little Melicent. "This is the child of Niafer. She comes of a race that has no time to be peering out of dubious windows."

"It is your child too, Count Manuel. Therefore she too, between now and her burial, will be wanting to be made free of my sister Suskind's kingdom, as you have been made free of it, at a price. Oh, very certainly you have paid little as yet save the one lock of your gray hair, but in time you will pay the other price which Suskind demands. I know, for it is I who collect my sister Suskind's revenues, and when the proper hour arrives, believe me, Count Manuel, I shall not be asking your leave, nor is there any price which you, I think, will not be paying willingly."

"That is probable. For Suskind is wise and strange, and the grave beauty of her youth is the fulfilment of an old hope. Life had become a tedious matter of much money and much bloodshed, but she has restored to me the gold and crimson of dawn."

"So, do you very greatly love my sister Suskind?" says Hinzelmann, smiling rather sadly.

"She is my heart's delight, and the desire of my desire. It was she for whom, unwittingly, I had been longing always, since I first went away from Suskind, to climb upon the gray heights of Vraidex in my long pursuit of much wealth and fame. I had seen my wishes fulfilled, and my dreams accomplished; all the

265

godlike discontents which ennobled my youth had died painlessly in cushioned places. And living had come to be a habit of doing what little persons expected, and youth was gone out of me, and I, that used to follow with a high head after my own thinking and my own desires, could not any longer very greatly care for anything. Now I am changed: for Suskind has made me free once more of the Country of the Young and of the ageless self-tormenting youth of the gray depths which maddened Ruric, but did not madden me."

"Look you, Count Manuel, but that penniless young nobody, Ruric the clerk, was not trapped as you are trapped. For from the faith of others there is no escape upon this side of the window. World-famous Manuel the Redeemer has in this place his luck and prosperity to maintain until the orderings of unimaginative gods have quite destroyed the Manuel that once followed after his own thinking. For even the high gods here note with approval that you have become the sort of person in whom the gods put confidence, and so they favor you unscrupulously. Here all is pre-arranged for you by the thinking of others. Here there is no escape for you from acquiring a little more wealth to-day, a little more meadowland to-morrow, with daily a little more applause and honor and envy from your fellows, along with always slowly increasing wrinkles and dulling wits and an augmenting paunch, and with the smug approval of everybody upon earth and in heaven. That is the reward of those persons whom you humorously call successful persons."

Dom Manuel answered very slowly, and to little Melicent it seemed that Father's voice was sad.

Said Manuel: "Certainly, I think there is no escape

for me upon this side of the window of Ageus. A bond was put upon me to make a figure in this world, and I discharged that obligation. Then came another and yet another obligation to be discharged. And now has come upon me a geas which is not to be lifted either by toils or by miracles. It is the geas which is laid on every person, and the life of every man is as my life, with no moment free from some bond or another. Heh, youth vaunts windily, but in the end nobody can follow after his own thinking and his own desire. At every turn he is confronted by that which is expected, and obligation follows obligation, and in the long run no champion can be stronger than everybody. So we succumb to this world's terrible unreason, willy-nilly, and Helmas has been made wise, and Ferdinand has been made saintly, and I have been made successful, by that which was expected of us, and by that which none of us had ever any real chance to resist in a world wherein all men are nourished by their beliefs."

"And does not success content you?"

"Ah, but," asked Manuel slowly, just as he had once asked Horvendile in Manuel's lost youth, "what is success? They tell me I have succeeded marvelously in all things, rising from low beginnings, to become the most lucky and the least scrupulous rogue alive: yet, hearing men's applause, I sometimes wonder, for I know that a smaller-hearted creature and a creature poorer in spirit is posturing in Count Manuel's high cushioned places than used to go afield with the miller's pigs."

"Why, yes, Count Manuel, you have made endurable terms with this world by succumbing to its foolishness: but do you take comfort, for that is the one way open to anybody who has not rightly seen and judged the ends of this world. At worst, you have had all your desires, and you have made a very notable figure in Count Manuel's envied station."

"But I starve there, Hinzelmann, I dry away into stone, and this envied living is reshaping me into a complacent idol for fools to honor, and the approval of fools is converting the heart and wits of me into the stony heart and wits of an idol. And I look back upon my breathless old endeavors, and I wonder drearily, 'Was it for this?' "

"Yes," Hinzelmann said: and he shrugged, without ever putting off that sad smile of his. "Yes, yes, all this is only another way of saying that Béda has kept his word. But no man gets rid of Misery, Count Manuel, except at a price."

They stayed silent for a while. Count Manuel stroked the round straw-colored head of little Melicent. Hinzelmann played with the small cross which hung at Hinzelmann's neck. This cross appeared to be woven of plaited strings, but when Hinzelmann shook the cross it jingled like a bell.

"Yet, none the less," says Hinzelmann, "here you remain. No, certainly, I cannot understand you, Count Manuel. As a drunkard goes back to the destroying cask, so do you continue to return to your fine home at Storisende and to the incessant whispering of your father's father, for all that you have but to remain in Suskind's low red-pillared palace to be forever rid of that whisper and of this dreary satiating of human desires."

"I shall of course make my permanent quarters there by and by," Count Manuel said, "but not just yet. It would not be quite fair to my wife for me to be leaving Storisende just now, when we are getting in the crops, and when everything is more or less upset already—"

"I perceive you are still inventing excuses, Count Manuel, to put off yielding entire allegiance to my sister."

"No, it is not that, not that at all! It is only the upset condition of things, just now, and, besides, Hinzelmann, the stork is to bring us the last girl child the latter part of next week. We are to call her Ettarre, and I would like to have a sight of her, of course— In fact, I am compelled to stay through mere civility, inasmuch as the Queen of Philistia is sending the very famous St. Holmendis especially to christen this baby. And it would be, Hinzelmann, the height of rudeness for me to be leaving home, just now, as though I wanted to avoid his visit—"

Hinzelmann still smiled rather sadly. "Last month you could not come to us because your wife was just then outworn with standing in the hot kitchen and stewing jams and marmalades. Dom Manuel, will you come when the baby is delivered and this Saint has been attended to and all the crops are in?"

"Well, but Hinzelmann, within a week or two we shall be brewing this year's ale, and I have always more or less seen to that—"

Still Hinzelmann smiled sadly. He pointed with his small gloved hand toward Melicent. "And what about your other enslavement, to this child here?"

"Why, certainly, Hinzelmann, the brat does need a father to look out for her, so long as she is the merest baby. And naturally, I have been thinking about that of late, rather seriously—"

Hinzelmann spoke with deliberation. "She is very nearly the most stupid and the most unattractive child

269

I have ever seen. And I, you must remember, am blood brother to Cain and Seth as well as to Suskind."

But Dom Manuel was not provoked. "As if I did not know the child is in no way remarkable! No, my good Hinzelmann, you that serve Suskind have shown me strange dear things, but nothing more strange and dear than a thing which I discovered for myself. For I am that Manuel whom men call the Redeemer of Poictesme, and my deeds will be the themes of harpers whose grandparents are not yet born; I have known love and war and all manner of adventure: but all the sighings and hushed laughter of yesterday, and all the trumpet-blowing and shouting, and all that I have witnessed of the unreticent fond human ways of great persons who for the while have put aside their state, and all the good that in my day I may have done, and all the evil that I have certainly destroyed, —all this seems trivial as set against the producing of this tousled brat. No, to be sure, she is backward as compared with Emmerick, or even Dorothy, and she is not, as you say, an at all remarkable child, though very often, I can assure you, she does things that would astonish you. Now, for instance—"

"Spare me!" said Hinzelmann.

"Well, but it really was very clever of her," Dom Manuel stipulated, with disappointment. "However, I was going to say that I, who have harried pagandom, and capped jests with kings, and am now setting terms for the Holy Father, have come to regard the doings of this ill-bred, selfish, ugly, little imp as more important than my doings. And I cannot resolve to leave her, just yet. So, Hinzelmann, my friend, I think I will not thoroughly commit myself, just yet. But after Christmas we will see about it."

"And I will tell you the two reasons of this shilly-shallying, Count Manuel. One reason is that you are human, and the other reason is that in your head there are gray hairs."

"What, can it be," said the big warrior, forlornly, "that I who have not yet had twenty-six years of living am past my prime, and that already life is going out of me?"

"You must remember the price you paid to win back Dame Niafer from paradise. As truth, and not the almanac, must estimate these things you are now nearer fifty-six."

"Well," Manuel said, stoutly, "I do not regret it, and for Niafer's sake I am willing to become a hundred and six. But certainly it is hard to think of myself as an old fellow on the brink of the scrap-pile."

"Oho, you are not yet so old, Count Manuel, but that Suskind's power is greater than the power of the child: and besides, there is a way to break the power of the child. Death has merely scratched small wrinkles, very lightly, with one talon, to mark you as his by and by. That is all as yet: and so the power of my high sister Suskind endures over you, who were once used to follow after your own thinking and your own desire, for there remains in you a leaven even to-day. Yes, yes, though you deny her to-day, you will be entreating her to-morrow, and then it may be she will punish you. Either way, I must be going now, since you are obstinate, for it is at this time I run about the September world collecting my sister's revenues, and her debtors are very numerous."

And with that the boy, still smiling gravely, slipped out of the third window into the gray sweet-smelling dusk, and little Melicent said, "But, Father, why did that queer sad boy want me to be climbing out of the window with him?"

"So that he might be kind to you, my dear, as he estimates kindness."

"But why did the sad boy want a piece of my hair?" asked Melicent; "and why did he cut it off with his big shiny shears, while you were writing, and he was playing with me?"

"It was to pay a price," says Manuel.

He knew now that the Alf charm was laid on his loved child, and that this was the price of his junketings. He knew also that Suskind would never remit this price.

Then Melicent demanded, "And what makes your face so white?"

"It must be pale with hunger, child: so I think that you and I had better be getting to our dinner."

XXXVIII

Farewell to Suskind

BUT AFTER dinner Dom Manuel came alone into the Room of Ageus, and equipped himself as the need was, and he climbed out of the charmed window for the last time. His final visit to the depths was horrible, they say, and they relate that of all the deeds of Dom Manuel's crowded lifetime the thing that he did on this day was the most grim. But he won through all, by virtue of his equipment and his fixed heart. So when Dom Manuel returned he clasped in his left hand a lock of fine straw-colored hair, and on both his hands was blood let from no human veins.

He looked back for the last time into the gray depths. A crowned girl rose beside him noiselessly, all white and red, and she clasped her bloodied lovely arms about him, and she drew him to her hacked young breasts, and she kissed him for the last time. Then her arms were loosed from about Dom Manuel, and she fell away from him, and was swallowed by the gray sweet-scented depths.

"And so farewell to you, Queen Suskind," says Count Manuel. "You who were not human, but knew only the truth of things, could never understand our foolish human notions. Otherwise you would never have demanded the one price I may not pay."

"Weep, weep for Suskind!" then said Lubrican, wailing feebly in the gray and April-scented dusk; "for it was she alone who knew the secret of preserving that dissatisfaction which is divine where all else falls away with age into the acquiescence of beasts."

"Why, yes, but unhappiness is not the true desire of man," says Manuel. "I know, for I have had both happiness and unhappiness, and neither contented me."

"Weep, weep for Suskind!" then cried the soft and delicate voice of Hinzelmann: "for it was she that would have loved you, Manuel, with that love of which youth dreams, and which exists nowhere upon your side of the window, where all kissed women turn to stupid figures of warm earth, and all love falls away with age into the acquiescence of beasts."

"Oh, it is very true," sais Manuel, "that all my life henceforward will be a wearying business because of long desires for Suskind's love and Suskind's lips and the grave beauty of her youth, and for all the high-hearted dissatisfactions of youth. But the Alf charm is lifted from the head of my child, and Melicent will live as Niafer lives, and it will be better for all of us, and I am content."

From below came many voices wailing confusedly. "We weep for Suskind. Suskind is slain with the one weapon that might slay her: and all we weep for Suskind, who was the fairest and the wisest and the most unreasonable of queens. Let all the Hidden Children weep for Suskind, whose heart and life was April, and who plotted courageously against the orderings of unimaginative gods, and who has been butchered to preserve the hair of a quite ordinary child."

Then said the Count of Poictesme: "And that young Manuel who was in his day a wilful champion, and who fretted under ordered wrongs, and who went everywhither with a high head a-boasting that he followed after his own thinking and his own desire,—why, that young fellow also is now silenced and dead. For the well-thought-of Count of Poictesme must be as the will and the faith and as the need of others may dictate: and there is no help for it, and no escape, and our old appearances must be preserved upon this side of the window in order that we may all stay sane."

"We weep, and with long weeping raise the dirge for Suskind—!"

"But I, who do not weep,—I raise the dirge for Manuel. For I must henceforward be reasonable in all things, and I shall never be quite discontented any more: and I must feed and sleep as the beasts do, and it may be that I shall even fall to thinking complacently about my death and glorious resurrection. Yes, yes, all this is certain, and I may not ever go a-traveling everywhither to see the ends of this world and judge them: and the desire to do so no longer moves in me, for there is a cloud about my goings, and there is a whispering which follows me, and I too fall away into the acquiescence of beasts. Meanwhile no hair of the child's head has been injured, and I am content."

"Let all the Hidden Children, and all else that lives except the tall gray son of Oriander, whose blood is harsh sea-water, weep for Suskind! Suskind is dead, that was unstained by human sin and unredeemed by Christ's dear blood, and youth has perished from the world. Oh, let us weep, for all the world grows chill and gray as Oriander's son."

"And Oriander too is dead, as I well know that

slew him in my hour. Now my hour passes; and I pass
with it, to make way for the needs of my children, as
he perforce made way for me. And in time these children, and their children after them, pass thus, and always age must be in one mode or another slain by
youth. Now why this should be so, I cannot guess,
nor do I see that much good comes of it, nor do I find
that in myself which warrants any confidences from
the most high controlling gods. But I am certain that
no hair of the child's head has been injured; and I am
certain that I am content."

Thus speaking, the old fellow closed the window.

And within the moment little Melicent came to
molest him, and she was unusually dirty and dishev-
eled, for she had been rolling on the terrace pavement,
and had broken half the fastenings from her clothing:
and Dom Manuel wiped her nose rather forlornly. Of
a sudden he laughed and kissed her. And Count Manuel said he must send for masons to wall up the third
window of Ageus, so that it might not ever be opened
any more in Count Manuel's day for him to breathe
through it the dim sweet-scented air of spring.

XXXIX

The Passing of Manuel

❖❖❖❖❖❖❖❖❖❖❖❖

THEN AS Dom Manuel turned from the window of Ageus, it seemed that young Horvendile had opened the door yonder, and after an instant's pensive staring at Dom Manuel, had gone away. This happened, if it happened at all, so furtively and quickly that Count Manuel could not be sure of it: but he could entertain no doubt as to the other person who was confronting him. There was not any telling how this lean stranger had come into the private apartments of the Count of Poictesme, nor was there any need for Manuel to wonder over the management of this intrusion, for the new arrival was not, after all, an entire stranger to Dom Manuel.

So Manuel said nothing, as he stood there stroking the round straw-colored head of little Melicent. The stranger waited, equally silent. There was no noise at all in the room until afar off a dog began to howl.

"Yes, certainly," Dom Manuel said, "I might have known that my life was bound up with the life of Suskind, since my desire of her is the one desire which I have put aside unsatisfied. O rider of the white horse, you are very welcome."

The other replied: "Why should you think that I

277

know anything about this Suskind or that we of the Léshy keep any account of your doings? No matter what you may elect to think, however, it was decreed that the first person I found here should ride hence on my black horse. But you and the child stand abreast. So you must choose again, Dom Manuel, whether it be you or another who rides on my black horse."

Then Manuel bent down, and he kissed little Melicent. "Go to your mother, dear, and tell her—" He paused here. He queerly moved his mouth, as though it were stiff and he were trying to make it more supple.

Says Melicent, "But what am I to tell her, Father?"

"Oh, a very funny thing, my darling. You are to tell Mother that Father has always loved her over and above all else, and that she is always to remember that and—why, that in consequence she is to give you some ginger cakes," says Manuel, smiling.

So the child ran happily away, without once looking back, and Manuel closed the door behind her, and he was now quite alone with his lean visitor.

"Come," says the stranger, "so you have plucked up some heart after all! Yet it is of no avail to posture with me, who know you to be spurred to this by vanity rather than by devotion. Oh, very probably you are as fond of the child as is requisite, and of your other children too, but you must admit that after you have played with any one of them for a quarter of an hour you become most heartily tired of the small squirming pest."

Manuel intently regarded him, and squinting Manuel smiled sleepily. "No; I love all my children with the customary paternal infatuation."

"Also you must have your gesture by sending at the last a lying message to your wife, to comfort the poor

soul against to-morrow and the day after. You are
—magnanimously, you like to think,—according her
this parting falsehood, half in contemptuous kindness
and half in relief, because at last you are now getting
rid of a complacent and muddle-headed fool of
whom, also, you are most heartily tired."

"No, no," says Manuel, still smiling; "to my partial
eyes dear Niafer remains the most clever and beautiful
of women, and my delight in her has not ever wav-
ered. But wherever do you get these curious
notions? "

"Ah, I have been with so many husbands at the last,
Count Manuel."

And Manuel shrugged. "What fearful indiscretions
you suggest! No, friend, that sort of thing has an ill
sound, and they should have remembered that even at
the last there is the bond of silence."

"Come, come, Count Manuel, you are a queer cool
fellow, and you have worn these masks and attitudes
with tolerable success, as your world goes. But you
are now bound for a diversely ordered world, a world
in which your handsome wrappings are not to the
purpose."

"Well, I do not know how that may be," replies
Count Manuel, "but at all events there is a decency in
these things and an indecency, and I shall never of my
own free will expose the naked soul of Manuel to
anybody. No, it would be no pleasant spectacle, I
think: certainly, I have never looked at it, nor did I
mean to. Perhaps, as you assert, some power which is
stronger than I may some day tear all masks aside:
but this will not be my fault, and I shall even then reserve the right to consider that stripping as a rather
vulgar bit of tyranny. Meanwhile I must, of necessity,
adhere to my own sense of decorum, and not to that

279

of anybody else, not even to the wide experience of one"—Count Manuel bowed,—"who is, in a manner of speaking, my guest."

"Oh, as always, you posture very tolerably, and men in general will acclaim you as successful in your life. But do you look back! For the hour has come, Count Manuel, for you to confess, as all persons confess at my arrival, that you have faltered between one desire and another, not ever knowing truly what you desired, and not ever being content with any desire when it was accomplished."

"Softly, friend! For I am forced to gather from your wild way of talking that you of the Léshy indeed do not keep any record of our human doings."

The stranger raised what he had of eyebrows. "But how can we," he inquired, "when we have so many matters of real importance to look after?"

Candid blunt Dom Manuel answered without any anger, speaking even jovially, but in all maintaining the dignity of a high prince assured of his own worth.

"That excuses, then, your nonsensical remarks. I must make bold to inform you that everybody tells me I have very positive achievements to look back upon. I do not care to boast, you understand, and to be forced into self-praise is abhorrent to me. Yet truthfulness is all important at this solemn hour, and anyone hereabouts can tell you it was I who climbed gray Vraidex, and dealt so hardily with the serpents and other horrific protectors of Miramon Lluagor that I destroyed most of them and put the others to flight. Thereafter men narrate how I made my own terms with the terrified magician, according him his forfeited life in exchange for a promise to live henceforward more respectfully and to serve under me in the war which I was already planning against the

Northmen. Yes, and men praise me, too, because I managed to accomplish all these things while I was hampered by having to look out for and protect a woman."

"I know," said the lean stranger, "I know you somehow got the better of that romantic visionary half-brother of mine, and made a warrior out of him: and I admit this was rather remarkable. But what does it matter now?"

"Then they will tell you it was I that wisely reasoned with King Helmas until I turned him from folly, and I that with holy arguments converted King Ferdinand from his wickedness. I restored the magic to the robe of the Apsarasas when but for me its magic would have been lost irrevocably. I conquered Freydis, that woman of strange deeds, and single-handed I fought against her spoorns and calcars and other terrors of antiquity, slaying, to be accurate, seven hundred and eighty-two of them. I also conquered the Misery of earth, whom some called Béda, and others Kruchina, and yet others Mimir, after a very notable battle which we fought with enchanted swords for a whole month without ever pausing for rest. I went intrepidly into the paradise of the heathen, and routed all its terrific warders, and so fetched hence the woman whom I desired. Thus, friend, did I repurchase that heroic and unchanging love which exists between my wife and me."

"Yes," said the stranger, "Why, that too is very remarkable. But what does it matter now?"

"—For it is of common report among men that nothing has ever been able to withstand Dom Manuel. Thus it was natural enough, men say, that, when the lewd and evil god whom nowadays so many adore as Sesphra of the Dreams was for establishing his power by making an alliance with me, I should have driven him howling and terrified into the heart of a great fire. For myself, I say nothing; but when the very gods run away from a champion there is some adequate reason: and of this exploit, and of all these exploits, and of many other exploits, equally incredible and equally well vouched for, all person hereabouts will tell you. As to the prodigies of valor which I performed in redeeming Poictesme from the oppression of the Northmen, you will find documentary evidence in those three epic poems, just to your left there, which commemorate my feats in this campaign—"

"Nobody disputes this campaign also may have been remarkable, and certainly I do not dispute it: for I cannot see that these doings matter a button's worth in my business with you, and, besides, I never argue."

"And no more do I! because I abhor vainglory, and I know these affairs are now a part of established history. No, friend, you cannot destroy my credit in this world, whereas in the world for which I am bound, you tell me, they make no account of our doings. So, whether or not I did these things, I shall always retain, in this world and in the next, the credit for them, without any need to resort to distasteful boasting. And that, as I was going on to explain, is precisely why I do not find it necessary to tell you about these matters, or even to allude to them."

"Oh, doubtless, it is something to have excelled all your fellows in so many ways," the stranger conceded, with a sort of grudging respect: "but, I repeat, what does it matter now?"

"And, if you will pardon my habitual frankness, friend, that query with so constant repetition becomes a trifle monotonous. No, it does not dishearten me, I am past that. No, I once opened a window, the more clearly to appraise the most dear rewards of my endeavors— That moment was my life, that single quiet moment summed up all my living, and"—here Manuel smiled gravely,—"still without boasting, friend, I must tell you that in this moment all doubt as to my attested worth went out of me, who had redeemed a kingdom, and begotten a king, and created a god. So you waste time, my friend, in trying to convince me of all human life's failure and unimportance, for I am not in sympathy with this modern morbid pessimistic way of talking. It has a very ill sound, and nothing whatever is to be gained by it."

The other answered shrewdly: "Yes, you speak well, and you posture handsomely, in every respect save one. For you call me 'friend.' Hah, Manuel, from behind the squinting mask a sick and satiated and disappointed being spoke there, howsoever resolutely you keep up appearances."

"There spoke mere courtesy, Grandfather Death," says Manuel, now openly laughing, "and for the rest, if you again will pardon frankness, it is less with the contents of my heart than with its continued motion that you have any proper concern."

"Truly it is no affair of mine, Count Manuel, nor do any of your doings matter to me. Therefore let us be going now, unless—O most unusual man, who at the last assert your life to have been a successful and important business,—unless you now desire some time wherein to bid farewell to your loved wife and worshipped children and to all your other fine works."

Dom Manuel shrugged broad shoulders. "And to what end? No, I am Manuel. I have lived in the loneliness which is common to all men, but the difference is that I have known it. Now it is necessary for me, as it is necessary for all men, to die in this same loneliness, and I know that there is no help for it."

"Once, Manuel, you feared to travel with me, and you bid Niafer mount in your stead on my black horse, saying, 'Better she than I.' "

"Yes, yes, what curious things we do when we are boys! Well, I am wiser now, for since then I have achieved all that I desired, save only to see the ends of this world and to judge them, and I would have achieved that too, perhaps, if only I had desired it a little more heartily. Yes, yes, I tell you frankly, I have grown so used to getting my desire that I believe, even now, if I desired you to go hence alone you also would obey me."

Grandfather Death smiled thinly. "I reserve my own opinion. But take it what you say is true,—and do you desire me to go hence alone?"

"No," says Manuel, very quietly.

Thereupon Dom Manuel passed to the western window, and he stood there, looking out over broad rolling uplands. He viewed a noble country, good to live in, rich with grain and metal, embowered with tall forests, and watered by pleasant streams. Walled cities it had, and castles crowned its eminences. Very far beneath Dom Manuel the leaded roofs of his fortresses glittered in the sunset, for Storisende guarded the loftiest part of all inhabited Poictesme. He overlooked, directly, the turrets or Ranec and of Asch; to the south was Nérac; northward showed Perdigon: and the prince of no country owned any finer castles than were these four, in which lived Manuel's servants.

"It is strange," says Dom Manuel, "to think that everything I am seeing was mine a moment since, and it is queer too to think of what a famous fellow was this Manuel the Redeemer, and of the fine things he did, and it is appalling to wonder if all the other applauded heroes of mankind are like him. Oh, certainly, Count Manuel's achievements were notable and such as were not known anywhere before, and men will talk of them for a long while. Yet, looking back,—now that this famed Count of Poictesme means less to me,— why, I seem to see only the strivings of an ape reft of his tail, and grown rusty at climbing, who has reeled blunderingly from mystery to mystery, with pathetic makeshifts, not understanding anything, greedy in all desires, and always honeycombed with poltroonery. So in a secret place his youth was put away in exchange for a prize that was hardly worth the having; and the fine geas which his mother laid upon him was exchanged for the common geas of what seems expected."

"Such notions," replied Grandfather Death, "are entertained by many of you humans in the light-headed time of youth. Then common-sense arises like a light formless cloud about your goings, and you half forget these notions. Then I bring darkness."

"In that quiet dark, my friend, it may be I shall again become the Manuel whom I remember, and I may get back again my own undemonstrable ideas, in place of the ideas of other persons, to entertain me in that darkness. So let us be going thither."

"Very willingly," said Grandfather Death; and he started toward the door.

"Now, pardon me," says Manuel, "but in Poictesme the Count of Poictesme goes first in any company. It may seem to you an affair of no importance, but nowadays I concede the strength as well as the foolishness of my accustomed habits, and all my life long I have gone first. So do you ride a little way behind me, friend, and carry this shroud and napkin, till I have need of them."

Then the Count armed and departed from Storisende, riding on the black horse, in jeweled armor, and carrying before him his black shield upon which was emblazoned the silver stallion of Poictesme and the motto *Mundus vult decipi.* Behind him was Grandfather Death on the white horse, carrying the Count's grave-clothes in a neat bundle. They rode toward the sunset, and against the yellow sunset each figure showed jet black.

And thereafter Count Manuel was seen no more in Poictesme, nor did anyone ever know certainly whither he journeyed. There was a lad called Jurgen, the son of Coth of the Rocks, who came to Storisende in a frenzy of terror, very early the next morning, with a horrific tale of incredible events witnessed upon Upper Morven: but the child's tale was not heeded, because everybody knew that Count Manuel was unconquerable, and—having everything which men desire,—would never be leaving all these amenities of his own will, and certainly would never be taking part in any such dubious doings. Therefore little Jurgen was spanked, alike for staying out all night and for his wild lying: and they of Poictesme awaited the return of their great Dom Manuel; and not for a long while did they suspect that Manuel had departed homeward, after having succeeded in everything. Nor for a long while was the whole of little Jurgen's story made public.

XL

Colophon: Da Capo

❖❖❖❖❖❖❖❖❖❖❖❖❖

Now SOME of Poictesme—but not all they of Poictesme, because the pious deny this portion of the tale, and speak of an ascension,—some narrate that after the appalling eucharist which young Jurgen witnessed upon Upper Morven, the Redeemer of Poictesme rode on a far and troubling journey with Grandfather Death, until the two had passed the sunset, and had come to the dark stream of Lethe.

"Now we must ford these shadowy waters," said Grandfather Death, "in part because your destiny is on the other side, and in part because by the contact of these waters all your memories will be washed away from you. And that is requisite to your destiny."

"But what is my destiny?"

"It is that of all loving creatures, Count Manuel. If you have been yourself you cannot reasonably be punished, but if you have been somebody else you will find that this is not permitted."

"That is a dark saying, only too well suited to this doubtful place, and I do not understand you."

"No," replied Grandfather Death, "but that does not matter."

Then the black horse and the white horse entered the water: and they passed over, and the swine of Eubouleus were waiting for them, but these were not yet untethered.

So in the moment which remained Dom Manuel looked backward and downward, and he saw that Grandfather Death had spoken truly. For all the memories of Manuel's life had been washed away from him, so that these memories were left adrift and submerged in the shadowy waters of Lethe. Drowned there was the wise countenance of Helmas, and the face of St. Ferdinand with a tarnished halo about it, and the puzzled features of Horvendile; and glowing birds and glistening images and the shimmering designs of Miramon thronged there confusedly, and among them went with moving jaws a head of sleek white clay. The golden loveliness of Alianora, and the dark splendor of Freydis and, derisively, the immortal young smile of Sesphra, showed each for a moment, and was gone. Then Niafer's eyes displayed their mildly wondering disapproval for the last time, and the small faces of children that in the end were hers and not Manuel's passed with her: and the shine of armor, and a tossing heave of jaunty banners, and gleaming castle turrets, and all the brilliancies and colors that Manuel had known and loved anywhere, save only the clear red and white of Suskind's face, seemed to be passing incoherently through the still waters, like bright broken wreckage which an undercurrent was sweeping away.

And Manuel sighed, almost as if in relief. "So this," he said, "this is the preposterous end of him who was everywhere esteemed the most lucky and the least scrupulous rogue of his day!"

"Yes, yes," replied Grandfather Death, as slowly he

untethered one by one the swine of Eubouleus. "Yes, it is indeed the end, since all your life is passing away there, to be beheld by your old eyes alone, for the last time. Thus I see nothing there but ordinary water, and I wonder what it is you find in that dark pool to keep you staring so."

"I do not very certainly know," said Manuel, "but, a little more and more mistily now, I seem to see drowned there all the loves and the desires and the adventures I had when I wore another body than this dilapidated gray body I now wear. And yet it is a deceiving water, for there, where it should reflect the remnants of the old fellow that is I, it shows, instead, the face of a young boy who is used to following after his own thinking and his own desires."

"Certainly it is queer you should be saying that; for that, as everybody knows, was the favorite by-word of your namesake the famous Count Manuel who is so newly dead in Poictesme yonder. . . . But what is that thing?"

Manuel raised from looking at the water just the handsome and florid young face which Manuel had seen reflected in the water. As his memories vanished, the tall boy incuriously wondered who might be the snub-nosed stranger that was waiting there with the miller's pigs, and was pointing, as if in mild surprise, toward the two stones overgrown with moss and supporting a cross of old worm-eaten wood. For the stranger pointed at the unfinished, unsatisfying image which stood beside the pool of Haranton, wherein, they say, strange dreams engender. . . .

"What is that thing?" the stranger was asking, yet again. . . .

"It is the figure of a man," said Manuel, "which I have modeled and remodeled, and cannot get exactly to my liking. So it is necessary that I keep laboring at it, until the figure is to my thinking and my desire."

Thus it was in the old days.

EXPLICIT